KURSK DOWN

ROSS SMITH

HEMBURY
BOOKS

HEMBURY
—BOOKS—

First published by Hembury Books in 2026
hemburybooks.com.au
info@hemburybooks.com

Paperback ISBN 9781923517615
Ebook ISBN 9781923517608

A catalogue record for this book is available from the National Library of Australia

ABOUT THE AUTHOR

In his debut novel, Ross Smith writes a high-stakes military and submarine thriller in the tradition of Patrick Robinson, Tom Clancy, and Joe Buff. A lifelong student of submarine naval warfare and global geopolitics, he blends real-world tactics, cutting-edge technology, and razor-wire tension to deliver a gripping, authentic story of silent war beneath the waves.

A larger-than-life Western Australian entrepreneur, Ross Smith, earned the moniker "The Wolf of Weed" after becoming the first to list not one, but three medical cannabis companies on the ASX in 2015. Long before that, he'd already made headlines as the founder of Colonial Brewing Co. in Margaret River — one of Australia's pioneering craft beer success stories.

From booze to bud to bullion to books, Smith's ventures have spanned the brewing, telecommunications, technology, and mining sectors — each driven by the same relentless curiosity and risk-taking instinct that define his career.

Now semi-retired, Ross divides his time between his luxury apartment in Perth, a rainforest villa on the island of Koh Samui, and his active gold-mining operations in the Murchison Goldfields, where he still drives heavy machinery and designs processing plants by hand.

Drawing on his globe-trotting life — from Kazakhstan and Cyprus to New York and Stockholm — Ross brings an insider's realism and hard-earned perspective to his debut submarine techno-thriller novel, *Kursk Down*.

A true maverick of modern Australian enterprise, Ross Smith is living proof that reinvention never stops — especially when you're the Wolf of Weed.

Kursk Down is his debut novel in a planned series exploring the shadowy underwater conflicts that threaten global stability.

Fans of Nimitz Class, The Hunt for Red October, and Crush Depth will feel right at home.

AUTHOR'S NOTE & DISCLAIMER

Kursk Down is a work of fiction. While inspired by real-world military history, submarine warfare, and global tensions at the turn of the 21st century, all characters, events, and institutions depicted are fictionalised for dramatic purposes.

Real-life individuals and military figures may be referenced or reimagined within the narrative. These portrayals are entirely fictional and do not reflect the actual beliefs, actions, or reputations of any real person, living or deceased.

This novel is not intended to represent actual events and should be read as a fictional thriller.

The author wishes to express deep respect and admiration for the men and women of the armed forces—past and present—whose service beneath the waves and across the seas remains a cornerstone of peace, duty, and sacrifice.

Ross Smith

ACKNOWLEDGMENTS

I wish to record my gratitude to Captain Peter Sinclair AM CSC, RAN (retired), for his assistance in ensuring the accuracy of submarine operations described in this book. Captain Sinclair was the commander of three submarines, including the 1st and 3nd Collins-class submarines of the Royal Australian Navy, and his experience was invaluable in keeping the technical details correct.

Captain Sinclair, RAN, one of the few Australian officers to pass the Royal Navy's gruelling Perisher command course in Scotland — the world's toughest submarine qualification — earned his dolphins at HMAS Otway before taking command of the Collins-class HMAS *Collins*. His reputation for calm under pressure and precise tactical instincts made him the Navy's go-to man for covert operations in contested waters.

Any errors are, of course, mine alone.

Ross Smith

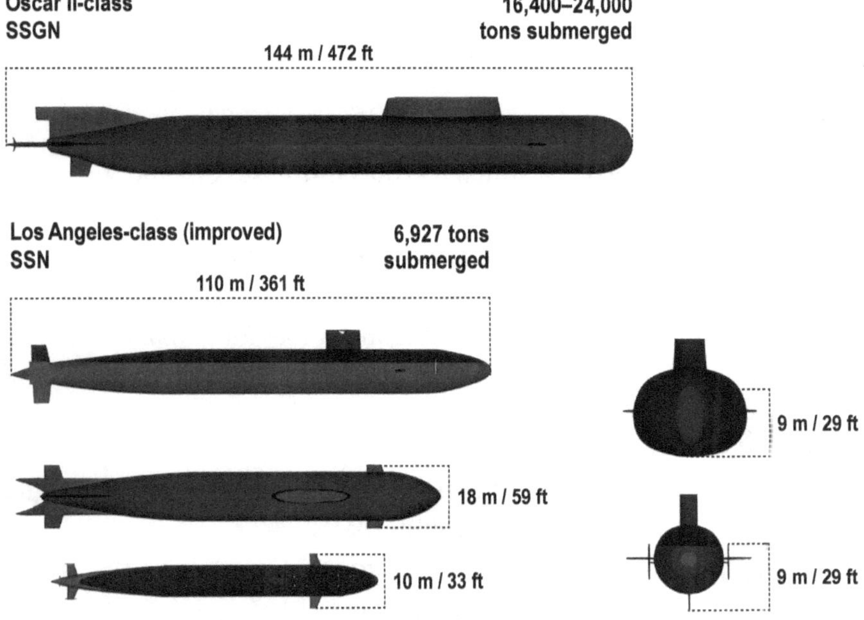

TECHNICAL NOTES

The Russian Oscar-class submarine and the US Los Angeles-class submarine represent two very different naval doctrines and capabilities:

1. Primary Roles

Oscar-class (Russia): Designed as a cruise missile submarine (SSGN), its primary mission is to destroy US aircraft carrier battle groups using long-range anti-ship missiles (like the P-700 Granit).

Los Angeles-class (USA): A fast attack submarine (SSN), primarily built for anti-submarine warfare (ASW), intelligence gathering, and strike missions using torpedoes and cruise missiles.

2. Size & Displacement

Oscar-class: Much larger — around 24,000 tons submerged.

Los Angeles-class: Smaller — about 6,900 tons submerged.

3. Armament

Oscar-class: 24 vertical-launch P-700 Granit supersonic anti-ship missiles (massive, ship-killing weapons). 4 torpedo tubes (533mm) + 2 larger (650mm) for various torpedoes and mines.

Los Angeles-class: 4 x 533mm torpedo tubes (Mk 48 ADCAP torpedoes). Later variants (688i) have 12 vertical-launch tubes for Tomahawk cruise missiles.

4. Speed & Stealth

Oscar-class: Slower (~30–32 knots). Quieter than older Soviet designs but not as stealthy as American counterparts.

Los Angeles-class: Slightly faster (~33–35 knots). Much quieter, especially in later Improved 688i variants with advanced sound isolation and towed sonar arrays.

5. Crew & Automation

Oscar-class: Around 100–120 crew.

Los Angeles-class: Around 130 crew, with more advanced automation.

6. Doctrine

Oscar-class: Built to launch massive missile strikes from long distances and survive retaliatory strikes in high-intensity war.

Los Angeles-class: Built for flexibility, from submarine hunting to land strikes, and excels in stealthy intelligence and special ops delivery.

Summary:

The Oscar is a heavy missile carrier, a "carrier killer" designed for open ocean combat.

The Los Angeles is a nimble, stealthy hunter, optimized for versatility and quiet operations.

ETHOS

Warrior Chief: *"What is best in life?"*

Warrior: *"The open steppe, a good horse, wind in your hair, falcons at your chest!"*

Warrior Chief: *"Wrong. Conan, what is best in life?"*

Conan: *"To crush your enemies, to see them driven before you, and to hear the lamentations of their women."*

Warrior Chief: *"Yes, this is good!"*

THE BEAST UNLEASHED

K-141 Kursk, Severodvinsk Submarine Base, White Sea,
August 11, 2000, 0600 hours local time

The icy wind howled across the Barents Sea, carrying the bitter chill of the Arctic morning sun. Captain First Rank Dmitri Kolesnikov stood atop the conning tower of the K-141 *Kursk*, pitting his broad frame against the frigid gusts whipping across the Severodvinsk Naval Base, at the southeastern end of the White Sea.

The massive Project 949A-class (Oscar II-class) SSGN (Submersible Ship Guided Missile Nuclear) loomed beneath him, its 472-foot hull a black leviathan against the frost-glazed waters, a marvel of Russian engineering cloaked in shadow. At 24,000 tons submerged, the *Kursk* was a titan—powered by twin OK-650 nuclear reactors, each delivering 98,000 shaft horsepower through seven-bladed screws, and armed with 24 P-700 Granit Mach 2.5 supersonic cruise missiles (NATO reporting name SS-N-19 Shipwreck) and the revolutionary VA-111 *Shkval* supercavitating torpedo, a weapon that tore through water at 200 knots via a gas bubble that defied drag.

That morning, her immense bulk strained against the leashes of the towing tugs as she prepared for a classified mission to dazzle a delegation of Chinese admirals aboard the *Pyotr Velikiy*.

Kolesnikov adjusted his Russian *ushanka*, a black bear fur hat with its Red Star, glinting faintly. His navy-black submariner uniform remained crisp. The Order of Nakhimov medal—a recent honour from President Vladimir Putin for a daring Russian mission in the Mediterranean five months prior—gleamed on his chest. It marked Kolesnikov as one of Russia's finest submarine commanders. He had pushed the *Kursk* to its thermal and tactical limits against the Americans and emerged victorious.

Lieutenant Commander Alexei Ivanov, his first officer, stood beside him, breath fogging in the Arctic air as he watched the tugs wrestle the *Kursk's* hull. His uniform mirrored Kolesnikov's, his *ushanka's* flaps tied high against the wind. "Congratulations again, Comrade Captain," he said, eyeing the medal with a wry grin. "Well earned."

Kolesnikov allowed a rare smile; his grey eyes were distant, away in the memory of that Mediterranean night. The *Kursk* had stalked the USS *Abraham Lincoln*, a Nimitz-class supercarrier, as it powered through the Ionian Sea toward Cyprus at 35 knots. The control room had been a crucible of tension, red emergency lights casting stark shadows across sweating faces, the air thick with the tang of ozone from the OK-650 reactors and the metallic bite of hydraulic fluid.

Kolesnikov had stood at the periscope, sweat beading under his *ushanka*, as Sonarman Yuri Pavlov, earphones pressed tight, whispered, "Yankee frigate, bearing zero-four-zero, active ping—no direct contact. Carrier at 50 nautical miles, closing fast."

The *Kursk's* wire transceiver, spooled 500 meters to the surface and pulled in Glonass satellite updates: carrier position; speed; heading.

Kolesnikov had calculated the time vector for the perfect firing solution of the VA-111 Shkval supercavitating torpedo; one hour, nine minutes to enter the Shkval's deadly firing solution range.

"Klimov, throttle the reactors to 10%" Kolesnikov had ordered, engaging a little-used heat vectoring system to mask their acoustic signature—a manoeuvre that would push the *Kursk* to the edge. With the cooling pumps shut off, he circulated reactor coolant using the temperature delta-T between the 300°C super-heated liquid and the 18°C seawater heat exchangers. The twin OK-650 reactors had protested as the thermal limits soared past 120%, with warning lights flashing amber on the control panel and the needle creeping into the red zone.

"Captain, we are red-lining—reactor pressure at 160 bars," Lieutenant Nikolai Klimov, the reactor officer, had warned, his boyish face taut with fear, his hands hovering over the emergency shutdown controls. Kolesnikov had remembered his father, a submariner from the Soviet era: silence is your shield, Dmitri. He had steadied Klimov with a calm nod, his voice low but firm. "Hold fast, comrade. We are invisible."

Lieutenant Viktor Morozov, the weapons officer, stood at his station, his wiry frame rigid with focus. "Captain to weapons," Kolesnikov had said, voice crisp in the red-lit control room. Confirm range and azimuth to target Charlie One. Open forward 533mm torpedo tube one. Check water pressure levels to eject the *Shkval* from the torpedo tube. We want it well clear of our ship before the solid fuel rocket powers up. I want a perfect firing solution."

Morozov replied with military precision: "Range 20,000 yards, Captain, bearing zero-three-five, speed 35 knots. Firing solution confirmed. Tube one open. Tube launch pressure green, sir. *Shkval* is ready."

The supercavitating VA-111 *Shkval* torpedo, a rocket-powered marvel, could reach the carrier in under three minutes—too fast for American countermeasures like their Nixie decoys or defensive measures from its surface and sub-surface escorts. That day, the warhead was conventional, but the *Kursk's* magazine held nuclear-tipped models—0.5 kilotons, capable of vaporising a supercarrier in a cataclysmic blast.

"Firing solution confirmed," Kolesnikov had said, then told Ivanov to make a log entry.

"Boom! You are gone, USS *Abraham Lincoln*. Well done, comrades, mission achieved. If this were not just a test, that American carrier would be heading to the seabed," Kolesnikov said over the submarine's intercom system.

A sonar ping from a Perry-class frigate, closing to 16,000 yards, grazed them, its active sonar scattering through the thermocline. "Sonar, report on those Yankee helicopters," Kolesnikov ordered, his eyes fixed on the sonar plot. Pavlov's voice remained steady: "Negative contact, Captain. SH-60 Seahawks, no change in pattern."

Kolesnikov had adjusted course, slipping beneath a thermocline at 300 meters, the temperature layer diffusing the frigate's pings. The *Kursk's* noise had dropped to a whisper, her massive hull blending with the sea's biologics—shrimp clicks, distant whale calls.

The carrier's signature had faded as the *Kursk* evaded detection; her reactors pushed to the brink by remaining silent. As the American ASW (anti-submarine warfare) screen—frigates, destroyers, and helicopters—continued their futile hunt, Kolesnikov exhaled, and the crew's tension broke in quiet nods of relief.

The *Kursk* had won, a triumph that had echoed in the Kremlin, when the newly elected President Putin pinned the Order of Nakhimov on Kolesnikov's chest in a ceremony steeped in national pride. "For the Motherland," Putin had said, his cold blue eyes locking with Kolesnikov's. "You've shown the Americans we are not to be trifled with."

Pride swelled, but the weight of command lingered—118 lives, a Nation's honour, had depended on his decisions.

"A fine honour. But today, we're the circus act, aren't we?" Ivanov's voice snapped Kolesnikov back to the present, as the last tug released its line with a groan of steel that echoed across the dock.

Kolesnikov chuckled, low and grim, his eyes scanning the Barents Sea, a grey expanse hiding threats beneath its surface. "That is right. Dancing bears for the Chinese aboard the *Pyotr Velikiy*." His tone hardened, voice dropping to a steely edge. "Our orders: evade the Northern Fleet's ASW cordon—Udaloy-class destroyers, Ka-27PL helicopters, active sonar—get within 10 nautical miles of the cruiser, and launch a war-shot *Shkval* at a derelict target. A demonstration to make the Americans sweat from the South China Sea to Washington."

Ivanov smirked and adjusted his cap, the Red Star catching the floodlights' glare. "They want to keep the Yankees guessing. That old carrier they bought from Ukraine—the *Varyag*? Still a rusted hulk, pilots are being taught take-offs and landings on painted steel runways in Liaoning. No catapults, no arrestor cables, no clue."

Kolesnikov laughed, his breath fogging in the biting cold. "We will give them a show they will never forget. But the Americans are out there, Alexei—silent Los Angeles-class subs, sniffing our waters, hunter-killers with Mark 48 torpedoes—are prepping to shadow us as we speak, plotting our acoustic signature. We go slow, 24-hour transit, silent as death."

"Clear the bridge, diving stations comrade," he turned to the conning tower's ladder, his boots ringing on steel, the sound sharp in the predawn stillness. "Gather the officers—officers' wardroom, now."

In the *Kursk's* officers' wardroom, Kolesnikov's key officers—Ivanov, Pavlov, Morozov, Klimov, and Lieutenant Sergei Petrov, a navigation officer with a scar across his cheek from a training mishap, gathered.

"Comrades," he said, "tomorrow we fire a VA-111 *Shkval* for the Chinese, a message to the west: Russia's navy is awake. The *Pyotr Velikiy's* ASW cordon—*Admiral Levchenko, Admiral Kharlamov*, Ka-27PL helicopters with dipping sonars—will test our stealth.

We will transit at 10 knots, maintaining silent running with no errors. The Americans are hunting. A single cavitation, and we are in a shooting war."

Pavlov nodded, his youthful face serious, earphones slung around his neck. "Sonar's sharp, Captain." Morozov, ever dour, added, "*Shkval* has a conventional warhead, and they loaded the nuclear ones in reserve." Klimov shifted uneasily, eyes on the sea. "Reactors are steady, sir, but silent running's a strain—coolant pumps at minimal flow." Petrov, while plotting their course, said, "Glonass has synced, and we have updated bathymetric charts for the Barents' shallows." Kolesnikov's grey eyes met each man's, his voice resolute. "For the Motherland. To your stations."

Belowdecks, the *Kursk* hummed with life —a steel labyrinth of pipes, valves, and glowing screens. The nerve centre was the control room, with green CRT displays flickering Glonass coordinates, and charts mapping the Barents Sea.

The air from the OK-650 reactors carried a sharp tang of ozone. The navigation officer, Petrov, plotted their stealthy 24-hour transit —a ten-knot, silent crawl to evade the ASW nets of Udaloy-class destroyers and Ka-27PL helicopters.

Faintly, the hull creaked, a reminder of the crushing depths. The Barents Sea's noisy currents served as a double-edged sword—both camouflage and threat. As Kolesnikov looked around the control room, the ship's pre-mission preparations intensified. Crew members checked torpedo tubes, securing the *Shkval's* conventional warhead. Engineers monitored the reactors, ensuring that silent running protocols—characterised by minimal pump flow and no cavitation— were in place.

Kolesnikov paused at the reactor panel, Klimov at his side. "Thermal margins?" he asked. Klimov's voice was tense. "Within limits, Captain, but we are at 105% for silent running. Any deeper, and we risk a spike."

The executive officer, Lieutenant Commander Ivanov, nodded; the *Kursk* slipped into the abyss, her fate unwritten but heavy with portent.

...

Kirov-class battlecruiser Pyotr Velikiy, Barents Sea, 12 August 2000, 0600 local time

Aboard the *Pyotr Velikiy* (Peter the Great), the flagship of the Northern

Fleet, Admiral Zhang Wei of the People's Liberation Army Navy (PLAN) stood in a narrow, dimly lit stateroom. A constant reminder of power, the hum of the KN-3 reactors vibrated through the steel deck. The 28,000-ton Kirov-class warship, named for the tsar who forged Russia's naval might, loomed above the Arctic swells, a fortress of nuclear firepower—S-300F missiles, twelve P-700 Granit supersonic cruise missile launchers (NATO designation – *Shipwreck*), and RBU-6000 Smerch-2 rocket launchers bristling from her angular deck.

Tactical maps lined the stateroom's grey bulkheads; one map highlighted the contested Spratly Islands. Admiral Zhang's wiry frame was taut; his crisp PLAN Admiral's uniform stood out starkly against the utilitarian space, his sharp eyes fixed on Captain Li Jun, a covert intelligence operative posing as a Naval Attaché, who stood before the map, his posture rigid with calculation.

"The VA-111 *Shkval* is the key," Zhang said in Mandarin, his voice cold and precise, each word weighted with strategic intent. "No Western navy can counter its 200-knot speed. If we secure the technology, the Americans will hesitate before violating our waters."

"The *Varyag*—that Ukrainian carrier hull we are refitting in Dalian—is a shell, years away from being operational. There are no catapults, no air wing, just pilots stumbling on painted steel runways in Liaoning. The *Shkval* gives us the teeth to deter their Nimitz-class carriers now and to maintain control of the South China Sea," he added.

Li Jun nodded; his mind raced, the weight of his mission pressed against his chest like a lead shroud. A botched PLAN exercise in the South China Sea two years ago had seared his memory—USS *Decatur's* sonar pings had mocked their outdated Type 052 destroyers, and American F/A-18 Hornets had buzzed their fleet unchallenged. It had been a humiliation that had exposed China's naval weaknesses.

The *Shkval* was a fundamental change, a supercavitating torpedo that could shift the balance of power. Their contact, Lieutenant Commander Dmitry Sokolov, a weapons officer on the *Pyotr Velikiy*, was the key—a disillusioned Russian who had been passed over for promotion, and they had bought his loyalty for half a million US dollars.

Li Jun slipped a photo from his pocket: Sokolov's wife and daughter in a Murmansk apartment, their faces for silent leverage if his nerve faltered. "Sokolov's agreed to deliver the schematics—propulsion, guidance, warhead," Li Jun said, his voice clipped and low to avoid the stateroom's faint resonances. "Today, during the *Shkval* demonstration, I will meet with him and get what we have come for, Admiral Zhang Wei."

Zhang paced, his boots clicking on the steel deck, his eyes narrowing as he traced the South China Sea map with a finger. "The *Kursk's* performance will distract the Russians—Admiral Chernov's too busy preening for our delegation and Captain Rostov's focused on the American subs spying on our demonstration. Secure the package before we depart. The Americans are not the only ones watching—British Trafalgar-class subs, Norwegian Ula-class, are all sniffing the Barents Sea for the *Kursk's* trail. Beijing expects results, Li. Our carriers are paper tigers unless we gain the firepower of weapons like the *Shkval*. Fail, and you will answer to the Supreme Council," the Admiral added for good measure.

Li Jun saluted. His hand brushed the concealed blade in his sleeve, a precaution against betrayal. He slipped into the *Pyotr Velikiy's* corridors, blending seamlessly with the Russian crew, his encrypted device—a Kompakt, Chinese-made data extractor—ready to pull the *Shkval* schematics from the ship's systems if Sokolov faltered.

They had set a meeting for the next day, during the *Shkval* demonstration, in a dimly lit maintenance room near the weapons control centre, where the hum of the ship's systems would mask their whispers. Li Jun's mind calculated risks—Sokolov's crumbling nerve, Rostov's suspicious glances.

Meanwhile, Sokolov stood at his fire control station deep within the *Pyotr Velikiy's* armoured weapons control center, his thinning hair damp with sweat, and his hands trembling as he adjusted a radar panel to mask his unease. His decision to betray Russia for dollars gnawed at his conscience. He promised Li Jun the partial schematics, which included the propulsion and guidance systems. The complete warhead data, locked in the *Kursk's* secure servers, would come after the demonstration.

Rostov's earlier scrutiny when he came down to the weapons control center. His piercing brown eyes and curt warning— "Keep your head clear, Dmitry"—had left Sokolov rattled; the spectre of a court-martial or worse loomed large. He glanced at the weapons control tactical screens. The ASW cordon's delta pattern pulsed with *Admiral Levchenko's* and *Admiral Kharlamov's* signatures. He had always been a loyal son of Russia. Born in the frozen outskirts of Murmansk, Sokolov grew up in the shadow of the Soviet Union's naval might, idolising his father, a sonar operator on a Cold War-era Delta-class submarine. His father returned from patrols with stories of silent hunts beneath the Arctic ice, instilling in young Dmitry a fierce patriotism and a dream of serving the Motherland. Sokolov excelled at the Nakhimov Naval School, graduating with honours in 1987 and rising through the ranks as a weapons specialist. By the late 1990s, he served on the *Pyotr Velikiy*, a Kirov-class battlecruiser, and his expertise in torpedo systems and cruise missiles was essential.

But the post-Soviet era had eroded the glory of naval service. Budget cuts, delayed salaries, and outdated equipment crippled the once powerful Russian Navy. Sokolov watched as promotions went to those with political connections rather than merit—men like Captain Rostov, who seemed untouchable despite his brusque demeanour. Sokolov, at 35, with thinning hair and a perpetual scowl etched by years of frustration, had found himself passed over repeatedly. His monthly pay, barely 10,000 roubles (around $350 USD at the time), was a pittance. Inflation devoured what little he earned, and back home in Murmansk, his wife, Elena, a schoolteacher, struggled to feed their 8-year-old daughter, Anya. The family's cramped apartment leaked, while medical bills piled up for Anya's chronic asthma. Sokolov often lay awake during shore leave, staring at the ceiling, wondering how much longer he could endure the humiliation of begging relatives for loans.

The turning point had come during a joint naval symposium in Vladivostok. Captain Li Jun, a polished People's Liberation Army Navy (PLAN) officer posing as a technical Naval attaché, had approached Sokolov there amid discussions on Pacific security and veiled tensions between Russia and China. Li Jun, with his sharp features and impeccable Russian, had struck up a conversation at a reception, complimenting Sokolov's published paper on supercavitating torpedo dynamics. "Impressive work, Lieutenant Commander," Li Jun had said, clinking glasses of vodka. "Russia's innovations could reshape naval warfare if Russia valued them properly."

Over the next few days, Li Jun cultivated the relationship subtly, sharing stories of China's rising navy and the generous incentives for officers who contributed to "mutual progress." He probed Sokolov's frustrations gently—mentioning the delayed Russian fleet modernisations and the stark contrast to China's booming shipyards. Sokolov, emboldened by alcohol and resentment, vented about his stalled career and the navy's neglect. "They treat us like relics," he muttered one evening in a dimly lit bar overlooking the Golden Horn Bay. Li Jun listened intently, then slid an envelope across the table. Inside were photos of Elena and Anya, taken recently in Murmansk—Elena at the market, Anya playing in the snow. "Beautiful family," Li Jun said softly, his eyes cold. "It would be tragic if hardship befell them."

The proposition followed: $500,000 USD—wired to an offshore account in Cyprus—for schematics on the VA-111 *Shkval* torpedo, including propulsion, guidance and warhead designs. Li Jun framed it as a "technical exchange," not betrayal, emphasising that China sought parity against American aggression, much like Russia. "This isn't treason; it's survival," he whispered. "Your navy undervalues you, but we see your worth. Half a million could buy your family a new life—a home in Sochi, medical care for your daughter, security for generations."

Sokolov resisted at first, his patriotism warring with desperation. But as months passed and another promotion slipped away—awarded instead to a connected junior officer—he replayed Li Jun's words. The money represented escape: from poverty, from the navy's indifference, from the fear of Anya's coughs turning fatal without proper treatment. By July 2000, during preparations for the Barents Sea exercise, Sokolov had agreed. Li Jun, embedded with the Chinese delegation aboard the *Pyotr Velikiy*, arranged clandestine meetings in the comms room and maintenance bays, where Sokolov handed over partial data on an encrypted drive. Li Jun had scheduled the entire exchange for the *Shkval* demonstration on August 12.

CHAPTER 1

THE SHADOW GAME

Barents Sea, 180 nautical miles north of Murmansk,
August 12, 2000, 0615 — 0815 hours local time

The *Kursk* glided through the dark waters of the Barents Sea, its 24,000-ton hull a silent predator in the shallow, icy depths. At 472 feet long, the Oscar-class SSGN was a floating fortress, her twin OK-650 reactors humming at 20% power as she prepared for the day's live-fire exercise. Captain First Rank Dmitri Kolesnikov stood in the control room; his broad shoulders squared against the weight of command. At thirty-two, he was young to command a boat of this size, but his grey eyes—sharp, unyielding, and flecked with the steel of a man who had seen the abyss— told a different story.

The red glow of the control room's lights cast shadows across his face as he checked the chronometer: 0615 hours. In less than an hour, they would launch a *Shkval* torpedo at a derelict frigate, a rusted hulk anchored 500 yards off the *Pyotr Velikiy*, to impress the Chinese delegation watching from the battlecruiser.

Ivanov leaned against the plot table. "The Chinese want a show,

Dmitri, but the Yankees are the real audience." Kolesnikov grunted, his eyes on the sonar plot. Lieutenant Nikolai Klimov, a wiry reactor officer, checked the OK-650 gauges, his hands trembling slightly. 'My brother served on the *Komsomolsk*,' he whispered. 'Lost her in '89. This boat feels… heavy today.' Pavlov, at the sonar, forced a grin. 'Just don't let the reactors sing, Nikolai.' The banter faded as Kolesnikov's voice cut through: 'Focus, comrades. We did not come here to lose."

"Range to target?" Kolesnikov barked, his voice cutting through the hum of electronic equipment. "Twenty-two thousand yards, Comrade Captain," replied the weapons officer, Lieutenant Viktor Morozov.

Sonar Officer, Petty Officer Yuri Pavlov's fingers danced over the console. The *Kursk's* MGK-540 sonar suite, a marvel of Soviet engineering, painted a detailed picture of the surrounding sea. "Bearing zero-two-zero. Target locked." Kolesnikov nodded. This was a live-fire exercise, a chance to flex the *Kursk's* muscles for the brass in Severomorsk and the Chinese admirals aboard the *Pyotr Velikiy*. The Northern Fleet had not seen a drill this ambitious in years—not since the Soviet days, when the navy was the pride of the Motherland. He glanced at the weapons officer, Lieutenant Viktor Morozov, a wiry man with a perpetual frown. "Begin firing sequence of *Shkval* from forward 533mm torpedo tube one after pressure check," he said. "Confirm target solution 20,000 yards, bearing 020 set, confirm warhead conventional."

Kolesnikov's mind drifted back to 1995, aboard the Akula-class K-317 *Pantera*. A NATO Spruance-class destroyer had hunted them in the Baltic, its sonar pinging relentlessly. His mentor, Captain Grigory Ivanov, had growled, 'Patience, Dmitri. Let them chase shadows.' Kolesnikov, then a lieutenant, had suggested a daring thermocline dive, masking their signature. The *Pantera* had escaped, and Ivanov's proud nod had stayed with him. Now, on the *Kursk*, that lesson guided him: patience over bravado.

"*Shkval* ready, warhead conventional, aye," Morozov replied, his voice crisp as he input the firing solution commands. The VA-111 *Shkval*, a rocket-powered supercavitating torpedo capable of 200 knots through the water, hummed as its guidance system spun up, a low growl in the forward torpedo compartment. The crew moved precisely, a ballet of steel and sweat, each man knowing the stakes. This was not just a drill but a message to the West: Russia's navy was back, and the *Shkval* was its spear.

The *Kursk's* control room was a maze of steel and screens; the air was thick with the tang of hydraulic fluid. The MGK-540 sonar's green waterfall display flickered with biologics and currents. Weapons officer Lieutenant Morozov checked the *Shkval's* guidance module; it was primed and ready for launch.

Kolesnikov experienced his usual adrenaline rush —the excitement of the hunt —though it was a live-firing exercise. However, a nagging unease lingered in the back of his mind. The Barents Sea was a poor place to hide—shallow, cold, and noisy as hell, with currents that scattered sonar returns like confetti. The Americans were out there, always sniffing around, their quiet Los Angeles-class subs prowling at the edges of Russian waters. He had sensed their presence before, a faint whisper on the sonar, a shadow in the deep. Today, he could not afford to be caught.

"Sonar, report contacts," Kolesnikov ordered, his voice steady but his grey eyes narrowing as he scanned the command screen display.

"No contacts within ten nautical miles, Comrade Captain," Pavlov replied, his voice steady but his hands tense on the controls. "The sea's noisy, currents, biologics, surface traffic. But if the Yankees are out there, they are super quiet."

Kolesnikov nodded. "Keep your ears sharp, Yuri," he said, his tone firm. "We can't afford surprises—not today."

The sound of Pavlov's voice overcame the hum. "Sonar contact! Faint, bearing one-eight-zero. Screw signature matches Los Angeles-class SSN (submersible ship nuclear – attack submarine)."

Kolesnikov's stomach tightened. An American hunter-killer submarine, Naval intelligence had reported an American Los

Angeles-class sub snooping around the Barents Sea before they departed. He gazed across to Lieutenant Commander Alexei Ivanov, his first officer. His concern was reflected in his eyes.

Assigned to the *Kursk* in 1999, their bond had been forged over shared vodka and dreams of naval resurgence.

"Go silent," Kolesnikov ordered. The reactors throttled down, the hum fading to a whisper. The crew stood frozen, breaths held, as Petrov monitored the contact. For ten agonising minutes, the *Kursk* drifted, a shadow in the deep. "Contact fading, Captain," Petrov finally exhaled.

Kolesnikov nodded, but the threat lingered. The Americans were out there, hunting.

The *Kursk's* mission was clear: slip through the Northern Fleet's ASW cordon—a delta pattern of destroyers, frigates, and helicopters designed to flush out intruders—and fire the *Shkval* at the target frigate. The Chinese delegation aboard the *Pyotr Velikiy* wanted to demonstrate the *Shkval's* capabilities, a weapon that could outrun Western countermeasures. But Kolesnikov knew the real test was not the *Shkval*—it was evading the Americans. They would listen if they were out there, recording every decibel of the *Shkval's* acoustic signature. And if they got too close, this exercise could become a shooting war.

USS Toledo, 2000 yards astern of Kursk

Commander Tom Brennan hunched over the sonar scope in the *Toledo's* sonar room, his tall, lean frame taut with focus. The Los Angeles-class SSN was running at five knots, 120 feet beneath the ocean, her hydrophones drinking in every sound from the *Kursk*. At 361 feet long and 6,927 tons, the *Toledo* was a fraction of the *Kursk's* size, her sleek hull, designed for stealth, was dwarfed by the Russian titan. Brennan's orders from the United States Fleet Forces Command (USFFC) in command of the US Atlantic Fleet were clear: get close, record the *Shkval's* acoustic signature, and get out. But two thousand yards was too damn close and Brennan knew it.

"Conn, Sonar," whispered Lieutenant Dave Carter, his voice low but urgent. "Sierra One is increasing speed. Eight knots, bearing zero-four-five. She is prepping something—high-pitched hiss, the *Shkval* torpedo tube's air pressure is building up".

Brennan's pulse quickened. Sierra One was the *Kursk*, a beast they had been waiting for near the entrance of the White Sea for weeks. The *Shkval* supercavitating torpedo was a game-changer—silent until its rocket motor ignited, then unstoppable at 200 knots. If the Russians were testing it live, *Toledo* would need every decibel of data. "Range?" Brennan asked.

"Two thousand yards, sir. Closing slowly," Carter replied, his hands steady on the sonar console.

"Too damn close," muttered XO Paul Reese, a wiry Texan with a perpetual scowl, his cracked rib from a recent training mishap still aching. "If they turn to clear their baffles, we're in their blind spot."

Brennan nodded, adjusting his cap. "Hold course, increase speed to eight knots. We need this." The *Memphis* was out there, ten thousand yards southwest, playing backup. Two SSNs against one Oscar SSGN—odds he would take any day. But the Barents Sea was a lousy place for games, and the *Kursk* was not playing.

Brennan's mind raced as he calculated their position. The *Toledo* was running silent, her reactor was at 15% power, with her screw barely turning to minimise any cavitation noise. The Barents Sea's shallow waters—averaging 750 feet, with some areas as shallow as 300—made hiding a nightmare. Sound travelled too far in these conditions, bouncing off the seabed and scattering through the thermoclines. The *Kursk's* MGK-540 sonar was top-tier, capable of detecting a 50-decibel signal at 20 nautical miles in good conditions. If the *Kursk* turned to clear her baffles, the *Toledo* would expose herself.

"Sonar, any sign of a baffle-clear?" Brennan asked, his voice low but urgent.

"Negative, sir," Carter replied, his eyes fixed on the plot. "She is holding course—zero-four-five, eight knots. But the hissing of the *Shkval* tube's launch pressure is definitely building up."

Brennan concentrated intently. The *Shkval* used a gas bubble created by vented-off rocket exhaust to reduce water resistance, allowing it to reach speeds no conventional torpedo could match. It was silent until it fired, its rocket motor igniting only at launch, but once it did, it was a 200-knot death sentence. If the *Kursk* fired, even in an exercise, a misread signal could turn this into a shooting war.

"Keep us quiet," Brennan ordered, his voice steady. "We're here to listen, not to take part."

"Conn Sonar, Helo contact, bearing zero-one-five, ASW Ka-27PL, deploying a sonar buoy—800 yards to starboard." The control room froze, the ping of the dipping sonar echoing through the hull.

"Chief of the boat, rig for silence, dive to 400 feet, slow to four knots," Brennan ordered. "Sonar, report!' Brennan snapped. Carter's voice was tight. "Listening, Sir." After five agonizing minutes, Carter exhaled. "Buoy inactive, sir." Brennan's jaw remained rigid. 'Too close. Sonar, where did that helo come from?"

"Conn Sonar, Helo likely came from the *Admiral Kharlamov* 40,000 yards, bearing zero-nine-zero, Sir," Carter replied, his attention focused on the plot. "We were lucky the Ka-27PL was just randomly dropping sonar buoys and not using his dipping hydrophones. He would have picked us up straight away, Captain."

"Chief of the boat, resume tracking the *Kursk* in her baffles," Brennan ordered, "Keep us tight at two nautical miles astern of the *Kursk*, slow and steady."

In the engineering compartment, Lieutenant Mark Evans, a 25-year-old nuclear propulsion officer fresh from the Naval Academy, monitored the S6G reactor's gauges with a nervous intensity. His boyish face, framed by a mop of sandy hair, belied his competence—he had graduated at the top of his class at nuclear power school at the Naval War College in Newport, Rhode Island, but this was his first proper mission. The reactor was running at 15% power, and the coolant pumps were on low to minimize noise. "Reactor stable, sir," he reported via intercom, his voice steady despite the butterflies in his stomach. "Coolant flow at 20%, noise levels at 45 decibels."

The assistant weapons officer, Lieutenant Sarah Carter, stood at the comms station, her dark hair pulled back in a tight bun. She had taken over comms after the chief radioman had twisted an ankle during a drill, and her calm efficiency kept the control room grounded. "No new signals on the ULF, sir," she said, eyes scanning the console. "*Memphis* is still on station."

Brennan nodded, his mind on the *Memphis*. Commander John Rourke was out there, a steady hand on whom he could count. They had served together on the USS *Birmingham* SSN-695 three years ago, when Rourke had taken his first command of a Los Angeles nuclear attack submarine, and Brennan was a Lieutenant Junior Grade, fresh from the Academy (class of 1984) and his own nuclear training, served as a junior officer under Rourke's command. Brennan, serving as the assistant weapons officer in 1987, admired Rourke's meticulous command style. Rourke had a knack for getting out of tight spots, and Brennan prayed he would pull through today. But two thousand yards was too close, and the *Kursk* was a beast. If she turned or fired, this could go south fast.

USS Memphis, 14,000 yards southwest of Kursk

Commander John Rourke gripped the edge of the chart table aboard the *Memphis*, his knuckles white against the grey metal. The *Memphis*, another Los Angeles-class SSN, was running ultra quiet at 150 feet, her screw barely turning at five knots. The air in the control room was thick with the tension of being in Russia's backyard. Rourke, a 38-year-old veteran with a square jaw and piercing hazel eyes, had seen his share of close calls, but this mission felt different. The *Kursk* was a monster; the *Toledo* was playing a dangerous game.

"Conn, Sonar," said Lieutenant Mike Hensley, a lanky sonar tech with a knack for hearing whispers in the deep. "Sierra One is flooding a tube. High-pitched hiss—it is the torpedo tubes high-pressure air launch system powering up. Range 14,000 yards, bearing zero-four-five."

Rourke's gut tightened. A flooding tube signalled a torpedo launch, and the *Shkval* rocket-powered torpedo would soon be unleashed, probably during the Chinese delegation's demonstration onboard the *Peter the Great*—Kirov Class Battlecruiser, the flagship of the Russian Northern fleet. He glanced at XO Bill Travers: if the *Kursk* fired, even in an exercise, they were playing for keeps with the Russian Northern Fleet in full ASW (anti-submarine warfare) mode, beating the forest to flush out the foxes, and they were the foxes. "Maintain ultra-quiet," Rourke snapped. "And get me an upgraded firing solution on that bastard—just in case."

Ed Kline, the weapons officer, adjusted a vectored firing solution using the real-time sonar bearing of Seira One–the *Kursk*. "Anything on the UFL comm link to the *Toledo* Ensign?" Rourke asked. Ensign Laura Hayes, *Memphis's* comms officer, a 26-year-old with a sharp mind and a cool head, had joined the Navy to escape a small-town life in Iowa, and now she was in the thick of it. "Nothing from the *Toledo*, sir," she reported calmly.

"Mark 48 ADCAP wire-guided torpedo in tube one, firing solution locked, sir," said Kline.

"Hold it there, enter a firing solution, match bearing ratio, and open the torpedo tube outer doors just in case," Rourke said, though he did not feel the confidence he projected. The *Kursk's* sonar was good, and the Barents Sea's shallow waters made playing hide and seek a nightmare. He tapped the chart table, tracing the *Kursk's* projected course. "She is lining up for her exercise. We hold our position."

Rourke's mind raced as he considered their position. *Memphis* was 14,000 yards southwest of the *Kursk*, a safer distance than *Toledo's* 1,000 yards, but it was still too close for comfort. The *Kursk's* MGK-540 sonar suite could detect a 50-decibel signal at 20 nautical miles in good conditions, and the *Memphis* was running at 45 decibels—quiet, but not invisible. If the *Kursk* turned to clear her baffles or her escorts tightened their ASW net, the *Memphis* could be in the crosshairs.

"Sonar, any sign of escorts?" Rourke asked, his voice low but urgent.

"Surface contacts, sir," Hensley replied, his eyes fixed on the plot. "The *Peter the Great* at twenty-five nautical miles, bearing zero-three-zero. At twenty nautical miles, two Udaloy-class destroyers—*Admiral Levchenko* and *Admiral Kharlamov*—bearing zero-one-five. They are holding a delta pattern, active sonar pinging."

Rourke nodded. *Peter the Great (Pyotr Velikiy)* was a Kirov-class battlecruiser, a 28,000-ton behemoth armed with S-300F missiles and twelve P-700 Granit launchers, a floating fortress capable of dominating a battlefield, and the flagship of the Northern Fleet. With their SRBU-6000 Smerch-2 anti-submarine rocket launcher, Type 53 torpedoes, and RPK-6 nuclear depth charges, the Udaloy-class destroyers hunted submarines as ASW specialists. The delta pattern—a triangular formation of ships and helicopters—was a classic ASW tactic to flush out intruders. The *Memphis* was outside their net for now, but if the *Kursk* fired, the net would close, leaving the *Memphis* in the thick of things.

"Keep us quiet," Rourke ordered, his voice firm. "We're here to back up *Toledo*, not to start a war."

*** USS Toledo, 1000 yards astern of Kursk***

Commander Brennan felt the tension in *Toledo's* control room; the men under his command were consummate professionals, but they were just men at the end of the day. They relied on his calm command style and experience, trusting his judgment in this high-tension, hostile environment. He prayed that he could live up to their trust in him.

The Los Angeles-class SSN remained silent, with its S6G reactor running at 15% power and its screw turning slowly, moving at eight knots to follow the *Kursk*. Brennan stayed focused on the tactical plot as he rapidly calculated their next move.

"Conn, Sonar," said Lieutenant Dave Carter, his voice a whisper as he adjusted his headset. "Sierra One is holding course—zero-four-five, eight knots. But I am picking up a new contact—surface ship, bearing zero-one-five, range twenty nautical miles. Sonar signature identifies it as the *Admiral Kharlamov*—Udaloy-class destroyer."

Brennan's mind raced. The *Admiral Kharlamov* was an ASW specialist. Armed with her RBU-6000 Smerch-2 rocket launchers, 53-65K torpedoes, and multi-launch depth charges designed for submarine hunting. If the *Admiral Kharlamov* launched a Ka-27PL ASW helicopter, the *Toledo's* position would quickly be exposed if they broke cover. She was at the heart of a large ASW net, surrounded by several destroyers and frigates, also deploying dipping sonar Ka-27PL ASW helicopters.

"Sonar, any sign of a helo?" Brennan asked, his voice low but urgent.

"Negative, sir," Carter replied, his eyes fixed on the plot. "But she is capable of launching one. If she does, we will be within her dipping sonar range within ten minutes."

Brennan nodded, his mind racing. "Maintain ultra quiet stations," he ordered, his voice steady. "We need to hold position until the *Kursk* fires. Then we get the hell out."

XO Paul Reese grimaced as he leaned against the chart table. "If they launch a helo, we're in trouble," he said, his voice low. "We can't outrun a dipping sonar at eight knots."

"I know, but we can stop, rely on zero Doppler," Brennan said, his voice steady, though the look on his face darkened with concern. "We have the *Memphis* out there. If it comes to it, they will draw the heat."

At the comms station, Lieutenant Sarah Carter adjusted her headset, her fingers tapping at the ULF console. "Message from *Memphis*, sir," she reported in a calm voice. "They have a firing solution on the *Kursk*— Mark 48 in tube one, ready to fire. They are holding position, awaiting your orders."

Brennan, his mind on Rourke. "Jesus, Rourke, tell them to hold fire," he said. "We are here to listen, not to start World War 3. But if the *Kursk* fires on us, our rules of engagement from USFFC permit him to engage."

Carter nodded, encoding the reply: *MEMPHIS*, THIS IS *TOLEDO*. HOLD FIRE. WE'RE LISTENING, NOT FIGHTING. IF *KURSK* ENGAGES, YOU'RE CLEARED TO FIRE.

Pyotr Velikiy (Peter the Great), 25 nautical miles northeast of Kursk

Admiral Viktor Chernov stood on the bridge of the *Pyotr Velikiy*, located forward and high up, the bridge provided visibility and control for the battle cruisers operations. His meaty hands gripped the chart table as he observed the sonar plot. The Project 1144 Orlan-class battlecruiser, NATO-designated Kirov-class, was the flagship of the Russian fleet. A 28,000-ton behemoth, larger than a WW2 US Navy Ohio-class battleship, with her twin KN-3 nuclear reactors thrumming as she held station. The Russian designation for this type of naval vessel was "heavy nuclear-powered guided missile cruiser, but Western defence commentators had resurrected the term "battlecruiser" to describe them, as they were the largest "line of battle" warships in the world. Her angular radar mast towered over the deck, bristling with twenty P-700 missile launchers, 12 S-300 Fort-M surface-to-air missile launchers, 16 Kortik close-in weapon systems, one 130mm AK-130 dual purpose gun, ten 533mm torpedo tubes and one RBU-1000 rocket launched nuclear depth chargers and with three Kamov Ka-27 helicopters—a variable floating fortress designed to dominate the Arctic seas in the name of Mother Russia. *Pyotr Velikiy* had been the flagship of the Russian Northern Fleet since it entered service in 1998. Chernov, the head of the Northern Fleet, was a towering figure; his broad face, weathered by years at sea, his uniform adorned with the insignia of his rank. Beside him stood Captain Ivan Rostov, captain of *Pyotr Velikiy*, scanning the horizon with thoughtful brown eyes.

Chernov surveyed the bridge, taking in the navigator and officer of the watch, along with the Chinese Admiral delegation, his gaze returning across the choppy Barents Sea.

Admiral Zhang Wei of the People's Liberation Army Navy (PLAN) stood nearby with the Chinese delegation—three PLAN admirals—murmuring in Mandarin, their eyes fixed on the sea where the *Kursk* would demonstrate the power of a silent submarine approach and the launching of an unstoppable super-weapon for their benefit.

"Comrade Admirals," Chernov said, his deep voice a low growl as he turned to Zhang, his cigarette dangling from his lips, ash falling to the deck. "The *Kursk* will fire at 0900. You will see the future of naval warfare—the *Shkval* is a weapon the West cannot match."

Zhang's lips twitched into a thin smile, his sharp features betraying none of the tension he felt. "We look forward to it, Admiral," he said, his voice heavy in accented Russian. "Our submarines need such teeth to keep the Americans out of our waters."

Rostov nodded, his broad face was weathered by years at sea, but his unease was palpable. The Americans were out there—he could feel it. Naval intelligence had reported their silent subs had been sniffing around the Barents for weeks, two Los Angeles-class SSN hunter killers, and the *Kursk's* exercise was a high-profile target. "Captain Rostov," Chernov barked, his voice cutting through the murmurs on the bridge, "tighten the ASW cordon—full active sonar, launch the Ka-27PLs, the works. If any American submarines are sneaking about, I want those Yankees found before they ruin this demonstration."

Rostov saluted; his voice steady despite the tension in his chest. "Sir," he said, relaying the orders to the comms officer, Lieutenant Mikhail Orlov. "Signal the fleet—full ASW sweep. Active sonar, helos dipping sonar, now."

Chernov took a long drag on his cigarette, his dark eyes were burning with determination. The *Kursk* was the pride of the fleet, a symbol of Russia's resurgence under the new President Putin, and he would be damned if he let the Americans interfere. He thought of Captain Dmitri Kolesnikov, a protégé he had mentored for years, a man who embodied the Northern Fleet's future. Kolesnikov was one of the best, but even the best could be caught off guard in

"Lieutenant Sokolov," Rostov called over the intercom. "Ensure the fire control systems are ready. We may need to respond quickly if the Americans interfere."

Sokolov nodded, his hands trembling as he turned to his tactical weapons console. "Aye, aye, sir," he said, his voice cracking slightly.

He had met with Li Jun earlier, agreeing to provide partial *Shkval* schematics—propulsion and guidance systems—for the 500,000 US dollars they had agreed upon. The money was a lifeline, a way out of the navy's post-Soviet decline, but the risk was immense. If Chernov or Rostov found out, he would be court-martialled—or worse.

Below decks, Captain Li Jun moved through the *Pyotr Velikiy's* corridors, his PLAN uniform out of place among the Russian crew; however, his air of authority and purpose discouraged questions. He carried a small encrypted device in his pocket, a tool to extract data from the ship's systems. Sokolov had promised the *Shkval* schematics, and Li Jun intended to collect. He slipped into a maintenance room near the weapons control centre and waited for Sokolov, his eyes darting nervously. A few minutes later, Sokolov entered furtively.

"You have the data?" Li Jun asked in halting Russian, his voice low. Sokolov swallowed hard, his hands trembling as he handed over a USB drive. "Partial schematics—propulsion and guidance systems," he said, his voice cracking. "The rest is on the *Kursk*. I can download it after the demonstration and she surfaces."

Li Jun's eyes narrowed, his hand brushing the concealed knife in his belt. "You'd better," he said, his tone cold. "Half a million dollars is on the line—and your life, if you fail." He pocketed the drive, his mind already on the next step: accessing the *Pyotr Velikys'* comms to intercept any signals about the Fleet's movements. "I need you to get me an officer's uniform and a sidearm. Hide it in the corner here," he added. "What for?" Sokolov asked anxiously. "Just do as I command you, and you will get your money," Li Jun hissed back.

Li Jun was focused entirely on acquiring the *Shkval* technology for China. A weapon capable of forever altering the force dynamics in the South China Sea, giving the PLAN a decisive advantage against the arrogant US Navy.

Captain Li Jun was born in Qingdao, Shandong Province, a coastal city synonymous with China's naval heritage, where the North Sea Fleet's shipyards echoed with the clang of steel and the roar of engines. His father, who had served with distinction in the People's Liberation Army Navy (PLAN), instilled in young Li a profound sense of national pride and the imperative to modernise China's fleet against foreign threats.

Li excelled in academics, graduating from the Naval University of Engineering in Wuhan in 1990 with a degree in weapons systems, his disciplined demeanour marking him as a rising star. By the mid-1990s, at 28, he was a lieutenant aboard the PLAN's Han-class nuclear submarine (Type 091), one of China's first indigenous SSNs, tasked with patrols in the contested waters of the South China Sea amid escalating tensions over Taiwan.

Li's career trajectory shifted dramatically during the Third Taiwan Strait Crisis in 1995-1996, when China conducted missile tests to intimidate Taiwan ahead of its presidential elections. The *Changzheng* 3, Li's Han-class sub, shadowed US naval assets responding to the crisis. In March 1996, as the USS *Independence* and USS *Nimitz* carrier battle groups transited the Taiwan Strait in a show of force—the first such dual-carrier deployment since the Vietnam War—Li's submarine attempted to trail the Nimitz group stealthily through the South China Sea approaches.

US ASW assets swiftly found the Han-class because of its loud reactors and old sonar; P-3 Orion's and Los Angeles-class subs, such as the USS *San Juan*, were used.

What followed was a humiliating cat-and-mouse game that scarred Li profoundly. Over 48 hours, the *Changzheng 3* was repeatedly pinged by active sonar from US helicopters and destroyers, forcing evasive manoeuvres that pushed the sub's aging systems to their limits. Li, as the assistant weapons officer, stood in the cramped control room, sweat-soaked uniform clinging to his frame, as alarms blared from reactor pressure spikes and the crew battled flooding in the torpedo room.

The captain ordered a simulated torpedo launch to assert presence, but US countermeasures—decoys and simulated counterfire—made it clear the Americans had the upper hand. At one point, a US Los Angeles-class sub surfaced nearby in a deliberate display, its sleek hull cutting through the waves like a predator toying with prey, before diving again without incident. Radio intercepts captured American laughter over open channels: "Looks like the dragon's got a cough today."

The *Changzheng 3* was forced to withdraw to shallower waters, aborting the mission and returning to base with morale shattered. China, facing overwhelming US naval superiority, called off further provocations, a retreat broadcast globally as a diplomatic and military embarrassment.

For Li, the incident was a personal humiliation. Promoted to captain shortly after for his composure under fire, he carried the sting of impotence—watching his nation's sovereignty mocked by American technology and bravado.

Currently, China's only naval carrier is the *Varyag*, a derelict carrier

China had bought from Ukraine, being refitted in Dalian, but its air wing is years from being operational. The *Shkval* would give China's navy the ability to deter American carriers from entering contested waters. Li Jun had planted a listening device in the comms room earlier, and he aimed to use it to gather intel on the *Kursk's* movements—and any American subs in the area.

Li Jun had waited long enough to rectify his humiliation.

Udaloy-class Destroyer Admiral Kharlamov, 20 nautical miles north of Kursk

Commander Nikolai Pyotrov stood on the bridge of the *Admiral Kharlamov*, a Project 1155 Udaloy-class destroyer. The 7,900-ton warship, capable of 28 knots, was part of the Northern Fleet's ASW screen, with its missile systems, rocket launchers, and multi-launch depth charges ready to engage any threat. Pyotrov, a grizzled Soviet Naval veteran, scanned the horizon through binoculars, feeling in his gut that the Americans were closer than they appeared.

"Sonar, report," Pyotrov barked, his voice rough from years of shouting over the sea.

"Sir, we have negative contacts," replied Ivan Kuznetsov, the young ensign who was the sonar officer. The *Admiral Kharlamov* sonar suite centred on its MGK-355 Polinom sonar complex, integrating its bow-mounted low-frequency active sonar and a towed passive sonar array. "But the *Kursk* is moving into position—eight knots, bearing zero-four-five, ten nautical miles."

Pyotrov nodded, his eyes narrowing. The *Kursk* was the bait, while the *Admiral Kharlamov* was the hunter, part of a delta pattern designed to flush out any intruders. However, the Barents Sea was a treacherous place, and Pyotrov had a bad feeling about this exercise. The Americans were out there—the pre-mission briefing by Naval Intelligence had been precise. There were two American Los Angeles-class submarines detected in the Barents Sea. Their Los Angeles-class subs were stealthy, featuring anechoic tiles and quiet screws that made them ghosts in the water. If they were shadowing the *Kursk*, they would be close, trying to intercept, listening for the *Shkval's* acoustic signature and any other counter-intelligence they might gather.

"Launch the Ka-27PL Orel," Pyotrov ordered, his voice determined. "Dipping sonar, full sweep. If they are out there, I want those Yankee subs found."

Admiral Kharlamov's deck thundered as the Ka-27PL Orel lifted off, its coaxial rotors clawing the air as it headed south. The Kamov helicopter, named for the falcon, was an anti-submarine specialist; its dipping sonar could pinpoint a submarine at five nautical miles in good conditions. Pyotrov watched the helicopter disappear, his mind on the *Kursk*. Captain Dmitri Kolesnikov was a friend he had served with on a Kilo-class submarine. in the Black Sea Fleet, a decade ago

Born in Vladivostok, joining the navy at 18, Pyotrov had trained at the Pacific Higher Naval School, specialising in sonar and weapons systems, and rose through the ranks with a reputation for precision and calm under pressure, deemed essential for submarine service.

Assigned to a Project 877 *Paltus* Kilo-class submarine based out of Vladivostok, Pyotrov served as a sonar officer under Kolesnikov, who was then a junior officer gaining recognition for his tactical acumen. Their deployment focused on anti-submarine patrols in the Sea of Japan, monitoring US naval movements near the Korean Peninsula amid post-Cold War tensions.

The Kilo, a super silent diesel-electric submarine, known for its stealth and nicknamed the "Black Hole" by NATO, was a cramped vessel where Pyotrov's skill in interpreting faint sonar echoes—distinguishing whale songs from distant Los Angeles-class subs—proved invaluable. A notable mission saw them evade detection by a US Navy ASW group for 72 hours, a feat Kolesnikov credited to Pyotrov's expertise.

Their bond deepened during a tense 1996 exercise when a hydraulic leak forced an emergency surface in stormy seas. Pyotrov coordinated repairs while Kolesnikov maintained morale; their teamwork earned a commendation from the captain. This experience forged a mutual respect, with Pyotrov admiring Kolesnikov's leadership and Kolesnikov valuing Pyotrov's technical prowess.

By 2000, while Kolesnikov commanded the *Kursk*, Pyotrov had moved to the Udaloy-class Destroyer *Admiral Kharlamov*, in a Command role while reflecting on their shared Kilo days with pride—days that shaped his career and highlighted the Navy's reliance on such submarines for coastal defence and intelligence.

"Sonar, keep your ears sharp," Pyotrov said, his voice low. "If the Americans are out there, we must find them.

Kursk, Control Room 25 nautical miles south of the Pyotr Velikiy

Captain Dmitri Kolesnikov stood in the control room; his eyes fixed on the tactical plot as he prepared for the live-fire exercise. The *Kursk* was moving at eight knots, its massive hull gliding through the icy depths of the Barents Sea, powered by its huge twin screws. Kolesnikov knew the Americans were out there, and he could not afford to be surprised—not with the Chinese delegation watching.

"Sonar, any contacts astern?" Kolesnikov asked, his voice steady.

"Negative, sir," replied Sonar Officer Yuri Pavlov, his hands tense on the controls. "But the baffles are blind—we should clear them before the launch."

Kolesnikov nodded, professional concern showing in his face. "Come left to zero-three-zero," he ordered. "Clear the baffles. I want to know what is behind us."

The *Kursk* turned, her giant screws churning as she swung to the new bearing, her sonar sweeping the blind spot astern. Pavlov's hands moved swiftly over the console; his headset pressed tight against his ears. "Conn, Sonar," he reported, his voice tight. "Faint contact—bearing one-eight-zero, range one thousand yards. It is possibly a Los Angeles-class SSN, sir. I cannot be certain."

Kolesnikov's eyes burned with determination. The Americans were conceivably closer than he had expected, shadowing the *Kursk* to gather intel on the *Shkval* demonstration. He could not fire the *Shkval* with an enemy sub so near—it was too risky. "Ahead twelve knots," he ordered, his voice steady. "We will see if the Americans are actually foolish enough to be so close to the *Kursk*."

USS Toledo, 1000 yards astern of Kursk

"Conn, Sonar," said Lieutenant Dave Carter, his voice a whisper as he adjusted his headset. "Sierra One is turning—coming left to zero-three-zero. She is clearing her baffles, sir."

Brennan's heart sank, his face darkening with dread. The *Kursk* was turning to clear her baffles—the blind spot directly astern where her own screws masked incoming noise and exactly where the *Toledo* was positioned. It was a standard manoeuvre the *Kursk* would use to check for threats before firing the *Shkval*. However, it placed the *Toledo* directly in her path, less than a thousand yards astern, in the *Kursk's* blind spot. If the *Kursk's* sonar detected them or the submarine turned too far, they would be exposed—or worse, they would collide.

"Sonar, range to Sierra One?" Brennan asked, his voice low but urgent.

"One thousand yards, sir," Carter replied, his voice tight. "Closing fast—she's at ten knots now."

Brennan's mind raced, his hands gripping the chart table as he weighed his options. "All stop and allow the ship to sink—we'll try to drop out of her path."

The *Toledo* glided to a stop, sinking slowly, her hull a beacon for the *Kursk's* sonar. Brennan's heart pounded; his eyes fixed on the plot as the *Kursk's* turn brought her closer—five hundred yards… four hundred yards… closer and closer. The *Toledo* was sitting silently, trying to make a hole in the water.

"Conn, Sonar," Carter shouted, his voice rising urgently. "Sierra One is speeding up—twelve knots, bearing zero-two-five. She is coming right at us!"

Brennan's blood ran cold, his heart pounding like a jackhammer. "Emergency dive!" he shouted, his voice sharp. "Take us to two-zero-zero feet, ahead flank!

Kursk, Control Room collision with Toledo

Captain Dmitri Kolesnikov felt a sudden jolt ripple through the *Kursk's* massive hull, a minor bump accompanied by a loud metallic screech that echoed through the control room. The 24,000-ton Oscar-class SSGN's reinforced titanium hull barely shuddered. The crew exchanged confused glances, their hands paused on their consoles as they looked to Kolesnikov for answers. No alarms sounded, and no red lights flashed—the *Kursk* was unscathed, but the noise was unmistakable.

"What the hell was that?" Kolesnikov barked, his grey eyes narrowing as he steadied himself against the console, his mind racing.

"Unknown, sir," replied the damage control officer; his voice sounded puzzled. "There was no damage reported. But it felt like a minor impact—contact with the US Los Angeles-class submarine, sir?"

Kolesnikov scowled, his mind raced. An American submarine, the ghost they had picked up on sonar—they had been out there the whole time, shadowing the *Kursk* and gathering intel. The collision confirmed his worst fears; they were a direct threat at this range. The *Shkval* in tube one was ready for the demonstration. Still, it was useless in close-quarter combat—its high speed and lack of manoeuvrability made it unsuitable for submarine-to-submarine fights. He needed a weapon that could track and kill at this range.

"Sonar, confirm the contact astern," Kolesnikov ordered, his voice cold and precise.

"Contact astern, right behind us, sir," Pavlov reported, his voice tight. "It is a Los Angeles-class SSN, sir. The submarine appears to have sustained substantial damage; it sounds like its nuclear reactor has scrammed."

Kolesnikov's lips curled into a grim smile, his grey eyes burning with determination. "Weapons, load tube two with a 53-65K torpedo," he ordered. "Confirm warhead conventional. Snapshot—fire on my command."

"Tube two loaded, 53-65K ready, warhead conventional, aye," Morozov replied, his hands moving swiftly over the console. The 53-65K, a wake-homing torpedo designed for anti-submarine warfare, spun up with a low hum. Once launched, it would lock onto the turbulence signature of the American submarine and attack it.

"Fire tube two," Kolesnikov ordered, his voice steady. "Let's send the Yankees a message."

The atmosphere inside the *Kursk* changed slightly as a high-pressure jet of air pushed the 53-65K out of the tube. The 53-65K propeller spun up and immediately carried out a 180-degree turn, locking onto the *Toledo* at 45 knots. The turbulence created by the damaged Los Angeles-class sub formed a deadly target.

USS *Toledo*

Commander Tom Brennan felt the *Toledo's* hull shudder violently as the *Kursk's* massive bow slammed into her, the impact was a deafening screech of steel on steel that reverberated through the sub. For the smaller Los Angeles-class SSN, the collision was catastrophic. The crew of the *Toledo* were thrown against bulkheads as equipment crashed to the deck, and the sub pitched violently to starboard. Alarms blared, red lights flashed as the control room descended into chaos.

Brennan was slammed against the periscope stand, and his left shoulder dislocated with a sickening pop. A gash opened above his left eyebrow as his head struck the metal. Blood streamed down his face; his vision swam from the pain. Around him, the crew suffered similar fates—Lieutenant Dave Carter slammed his head against the chart table, leaving him concussed; XO Paul Reese clutched his chest, likely cracked ribs, gasped as breathing exacerbated his injury; and several enlisted men sustained cuts and bruises from flying debris.

Petty Officer James Carter, the corpsman, was overwhelmed triaging the wounded on the deck with a medical field kit, his hands stained with blood. At the same time, he bandaged a young ensign's gashed forehead.

"Damage report!" Brennan shouted, his voice hoarse as he clung to the railing, blood streaming down his face.

"Reactor scrammed, sir!" reported Lieutenant Mark Evans from the engineering compartment, his voice trembling over the intercom. "Major structural damage. We are on battery power, zero knots, five-degree list to port."

"Engineering, please check the sail for damage by raising the periscope," he requested. Brennan's mind raced. The *Kursk* had collided with them—a devastating blow for *Toledo*. Her smaller hull had proved no match for the Oscar-class giant. The Russian sub must know they were here, and the Northern Fleet would come for them. "Sonar, status on Sierra One?" he barked, wiping blood from his eye.

"Conn, Sonar," Carter replied, his voice shaky as he held a cloth to his bleeding forehead. "Sierra One is… she is behind us, sir. No significant change in her acoustic signature—she seems fine, sir."

"Captain, we are not getting anything from the periscope; everything is offline. We believe the sail is severely damaged and possibly gone," engineering reported.

USS Memphis, 8,000 yards southwest of Kursk and the Toledo

Commander John Rourke stood in *Memphis's* control room. His heart pounded as the tactical plot lit up with the new situation; staring at the plot, he quickly considered the shift.

"Conn, Sonar," said Lieutenant Mike Hensley, his voice sharp with urgency. "Collision detected—Sierra One just hit something hard. Range eight thousand yards, bearing zero-four-five. It is the *Toledo*, sir—she has taken a major hit."

Rourke's blood turned icy as his heartbeat roared in his ears. The *Kursk* had struck the *Toledo*—potentially catastrophic. Before he could react, Hensley's voice interrupted again. "Sierra One is opening a second torpedo door! I hear a 53-65K spinning up—it is live, sir. Torpedo in the water—bearing zero-two-five, speed 45 knots!"

Rourke frowned, his mind racing. The *Kursk* had fired a 53-65K—a wake-homing torpedo, likely in self-defence after the collision. With the *Kursk* right on top of her, the *Toledo* had seconds to react, and her damaged state made evasion unlikely. Rourke could not wait for confirmation—she was already a sitting duck. "Weapons, snap-shot tube one—Mark 48, target Sierra One," Rourke ordered, his voice like steel. "We are not letting them finish her. They will probably launch a second. Come on, Brennan, launch countermeasures."

The *Memphis* water-ram torpedo ejection system, a rapid pulse of high-pressure water, forced the Mark 48 torpedo out the launch tube with a slight pressure change within the hull, streaking toward the *Kursk* at 55 knots, its wire-guided system feeding data back to the sub. Rourke's hands gripped the plot table as he calculated the time to target.

The *Kursk* was a beast; its titanium hull and advanced sonar made it a formidable target. But the Mark 48 was a killer, its 650-pound shape-charged warhead capable of punching through even the *Kursk's* double hull. Rourke thought of Brennan, his friend and fellow commander, fighting for survival on a crippled sub. He would do whatever it took to get them out of this alive.

Con, Sonar, *Toledo* has launched multiple countermeasures," Hensley's voice called out.

"Four minutes and nineteen seconds to Sierra One, sir," called Ed Kline, the weapons officer. "It's going to be really close," Rourke responded, "continue to provide the range and bearing to Sierra One."

Rourke remembered it was only a few weeks ago when he had sat across the table from Tom Brennan, his former junior officer from the USS *Birmingham*, in the dimly lit briefing room at Naval Station Norfolk. Charts of the Arctic Circle lined the walls, and a grainy satellite image of the K-141 *Kursk* had loomed on the screen—its 472-foot hull a black leviathan poised to dominate the White Sea. The intelligence briefing had been clear, delivered by a stern-faced admiral with a voice like gravel: the *Kursk*, under Captain Dmitri Kolesnikov, was no ordinary Oscar-class SSGN. Kolesnikov, a decorated veteran with a Nakhimov Medal for a daring Mediterranean stalk of the USS *Abraham Lincoln*, was a tactician of rare skill, blending Soviet-era cunning with modern ruthlessness. His crew was tight-knit, his *Shkval* torpedo a game-changer capable of outpacing any US countermeasures at 200 knots.

Rourke's mind churned as he recalled the admiral's orders: "You are to shadow the *Kursk* during her exercise with the Chinese delegation. The *Memphis* and *Toledo* will operate in tandem, closer than protocol allows—within five nautical miles of each other and the target."

The room had gone silent, the absurdity hung heavy. Submarine doctrine demanded separation to avoid collisions and maintain stealth, yet here they were, tasked with breaking every rule. Brennan shifted uncomfortably, his voice low: "Sir, that's a collision course waiting to happen." Rourke nodded in agreement. "Aye, Tom. But it is a calculated risk. Intel suggests Kolesnikov's testing more than missiles—he and the Russian admiralty are probing our resolve."

The briefing had detailed Kolesnikov's profile: a man who had pushed the *Kursk's* OK-650 reactors to 120% thermal limits to evade detection in the Mediterranean, a commander who had successfully outmanoeuvred the entire Battle Carrier Group's ASW screens with heat-vectoring tricks. Rourke respected the skill but sensed the danger. The admiral's last words echoed: "This is about deterrence. We must show the Russians that we are not intimidated. Rourke's gut twisted—years of instinct from the USS *Birmingham* patrols screamed against it. Operating so close risked not just detection but catastrophe, especially with the *Kursk's* 24 P-700 Granit missiles and that damned *Shkval*. And now the risk had become reality.

USS Toledo, directly astern of Kursk

The *Kursk* collision had disastrous consequences: it had destroyed the conning tower; knocked the reactor out of commission; and severely injured the crew. About half of the crew had injuries such as concussions, broken bones, and cuts from flying debris.

"Conn, Sonar," Carter gasped, his voice shaky as he held a cloth to his bleeding forehead. "Torpedo in the water—bearing zero-two-five, range—she is right on top of us, speed 45 knots! It is a 53-65K, sir!"

Brennan's heart stopped; his eyes were wide with terror. The *Kursk* had fired a 53-65K—a wake-homing torpedo, likely in self-defence after the collision. At this distance, they had seconds to react. "Launch countermeasures!" Brennan shouted; his voice sharp. "Full spread—now!"

The *Toledo* launched a cloud of acoustic decoys and bubble generators; the devices darted north to mimic a fleeing sub. The 53-65K torpedo veered off, chasing a decoy, its sonar pings fading as it lost lock. Brennan exhaled, his body trembling with adrenaline, but the relief was short-lived. The *Kursk* would fire again—or worse, the Northern Fleet would come for them.

"Get me *Memphis* on the ULF," Brennan ordered, his voice hoarse as he wiped blood from his face. "We need to get the hell out of here—now."

Kursk, Control Room

The control room of the *Kursk* was a whirlwind of confusion. The crew's voices created a cacophony of uncertainty as they attempted to understand the minor bump that had jolted the 24,000-ton Oscar-class SSGN. Captain First Rank Dmitri Kolesnikov stood at the centre of the chaos. His eyes burned with intensity as he assessed the situation.

"Sonar, status on the torpedo?" Kolesnikov ordered.

"It is veering off, sir," replied Sonar Officer Yuri Pavlov, his voice tight as he adjusted his headset. "It is chasing decoy-countermeasures. The contact astern is still there, bearing one-eight-zero, directly behind us, range 500 yards. It is the Los Angeles-class SSN, sir."

Kolesnikov's lips curled into a grimace. The US submarine had used countermeasures to lure the torpedo away. She was still out there, wounded, and vulnerable after the collision—he could finish her. He was about to order another torpedo loaded when Pavlov's voice cut through the control room like a knife.

"Conn, Sonar!" Pavlov shouted. "New contact—torpedo inbound! Bearing one-three-five, range 1000 yards, speed 55 knots! It is a Mark 48, sir!"

Kolesnikov's blood ran cold, his heart slammed against his ribcage as the words sank in. A Mark 48—American, wire-guided, and deadly, with a 650-pound warhead capable of punching through the *Kursk's* double hull. They had less than thirty-two seconds to react at one thousand yards, closing in at 55 knots. The torpedo must have come from a second submarine—he had not even considered the possibility of another American SSN out there, waiting in the shadows. "Emergency, blow all ballast, all ahead full" Kolesnikov shouted, his voice sharp as he clung to the console, his mind desperately seeking a way out. "25-degree bubble, full rise of the forward planes, 30 knots, shut aft openings, rig for torpedo hit! Do it—now!"

The *Kursk's* crew acted, their hands moving quickly across the controls as the ballast tanks emptied with a roar. At a 25-degree angle, the sub surged upward. The 24,000-ton titanium hull moaned in protest under the sudden strain, its twin reactors pushing the screws to the limit as she tried to get away.

Kolesnikov's eyes darted to the sonar plot, his breath ragged as he tracked the incoming Mark 48—400 yards... 300 yards.... too close. "Countermeasures!" Kolesnikov barked, his voice hoarse with desperation. "Launch decoys—full spread!"

The *Kursk* launched a cloud of acoustic decoys and bubble generators; the devices darting in all directions to mimic the sub's signature, but the Mark 48 was wire-guided, its firing solution already locked onto the *Kursk's* massive hull. The Mark 48 torpedo slammed into the *Kursk's* forward torpedo room. A cataclysmic explosion ripped through the sub's hull and ignited the *Shkval's* rocket fuel in tube one, causing a massive explosion that registered as a 4.2-magnitude seismic event. The *Kursk's* forward section was obliterated, the control room destroyed in an instant, killing Kolesnikov and most of the crew.

Kolesnikov's quick action in securing the aft compartments meant the aft section remained intact, while the submarine sank to the shallow seabed at 350 feet. Remarkably, 23 men survived in compartment nine. The flooding and pressure sealed their fate. The *Kursk* was gone, its 118 souls lost to the icy depths, a tragedy that would echo across the world.

CHAPTER 2

THE HORNETS' NEST

Barents Sea,
August 12, 2000, 0815 — 1015 hours local time

The *Pyotr Velikiy* (Peter the Great) stood as a sentinel in the icy waters of the Barents Sea, its 28,000-ton hull slicing through the choppy waves. As the flagship of the Northern Fleet, it was a floating fortress bristling with missile launchers and a formidable array of anti-submarine-warfare weaponry. Her radar masts towered over the deck, scanning the horizon for threats, while her crew of 727 moved with the precision of a well-oiled machine. But on the bridge, the atmosphere was anything but calm.

Admiral Viktor Chernov felt the shockwave before he heard the report. A low rumble shuddered through the *Pyotr Velikiy's* 28,000-ton hull and set the bridge crew on edge. Chernov's attention was on the sonar plot; he gripped the chart table as the reality of *Kursk's* fate became clear.

"Comrade Admiral," the sonar officer, Lieutenant Mikhail Orlov, said, his voice trembling as he adjusted his headset, "massive explosion—bearing two-one-five, range twenty-five nautical miles. It is… the explosion came from the last known bearing of the *Kursk*, Admiral."

Chernov's face turned to stone, but his dark eyes burned with rage, the cigarette in his hand forgotten as ash fell to the deck. "The *Kursk*?" he growled, his deep voice a low snarl that made Orlov flinch. "What do you mean, explosion?"

"Sonar signature matches a catastrophic detonation," Orlov replied, his hands shaking as he pointed to the plot. "Debris field expanding—metal fragments, possible *Kursk* sinking to the bottom, no emergency signal from her, however. The explosion was… massive, sir. Seismographs have picked it up as 4.2 seismic event."

Chernov's fist clenched, crumpling the chart in his hand, the paper tearing under the pressure. "Pizdetz, the Americans," he spat, his voice dripping with venom. "It must be. They were here the whole time—I told you we should have tightened the ASW cordon Rostov." He turned to Captain Ivan Rostov, the *Pyotr Velikiy's* CO, whose thoughtful eyes betrayed a flicker of doubt. "Launch another Ka-27PL helicopter, head straight out on the *Kursk's* last known bearing, full sweep. Signal the fleet: every ship, every helo. Find out what has happened and whether there is an American submarine in the theatre."

Rostov hesitated for a fraction of a second; his calm demeanour countered Chernov's rage. "And the *Kursk*, sir?" he asked, his voice laced with concern.

Chernov's eyes softened, but only briefly; his thirst for vengeance drowned the flicker of humanity. "Dispatch the *Smolensk*," he ordered, his tone clipped. "She is closest"—Krivak-class frigate, named for the city of Smolensk. "Find the *Kursk*, look for survivors. But if it is the Americans, they are going to pay dearly." He lit another cigarette, the smoke curling around his head like a storm cloud, his mind already on the hunt.

Chernov's rage was a palpable force, a storm brewing on the bridge of the *Pyotr Velikiy*. He had known Dmitri Kolesnikov for years— a protégé, a friend, a man who embodied the Northern Fleet's resurgence under Putin's leadership. Kolesnikov had been one of the best, the submarine commander who had outsmarted the Americans in the Mediterranean just six months ago. Chernov's blood boiled with the need for vengeance. The Americans must have been shadowing the *Kursk*— he suspected they had been snooping around for weeks, with intelligence reports confirming US submarine activity in the Norwegian and Barents Seas. But he had not expected this— an American submarine, a catastrophic explosion that had turned the *Kursk* into a tomb.

The *Kursk*—the pride of the fleet, an Oscar-class SSGN that had been the centrepiece of today's demonstration—had just been destroyed.

Chernov's fist slammed the chart table, rattling the coffee mugs and sending a pencil rolling to the deck. "Pizdetz, those Yankee bastards," he growled, his deep voice reverberating through the bridge. "A quiet Los Angeles-class submarine shadowing us like a wolf." He turned to the three Chinese admirals standing nearby, their faces pale despite their stoic masks.

Admiral Zhang Wei, the senior PLAN officer, stood at the forefront, his sharp features betraying a flicker of unease. Beside him, Captain Li Jun, his intelligence operative posing as a naval aide, kept his expression neutral, though his mind raced with the implications of the *Kursk's* loss.

"Gentlemen," Chernov said, his tone barely concealing his rage, "you have not seen the *Shkval's* power, but now you see the enemy's treachery. You are no longer safe here."

Zhang Wei nodded curtly, his voice steady and accented in Russian. "We must return to Beijing. This changes everything."

"Helicopter, now!" Chernov barked. Rostov relayed the order, and within minutes, the deck thundered with the roar of a Ka-27 Helix helicopter. The Chinese admirals clutched their briefcases tightly as they hurried aboard. Li Jun lingered on the deck, scanning for Lieutenant Commander Dmitry Sokolov, the Russian weapons officer he had compromised to steal the *Shkval* schematics.

"Captain Li," Zhang called from the helicopter, his tone sharp. "We are leaving. You have your orders."

Li Jun nodded. His plans had been thrown into chaos. But he couldn't get on the helicopter. Sokolov had provided him with a Russian naval officer's uniform, complete with a Makarov PM pistol in a holster as a contingency. As his colleagues moved towards the helicopter, he slipped into an alcove and started to get changed. He needed to maintain a low profile and blend in with the crew of *Pyotr Velikiy*. Sokolov had provided partial schematics—propulsion and guidance systems—but the complete data, including the *Shkval's* warhead design, was on the *Kursk*. With the sub gone, Li Jun needed to extract what he could from the *Pyotr Velikiy's* systems before departing. He slipped below decks as the Ka-27 Zvezda lifted off and banked south toward Murmansk.

Chernov watched the helicopter disappear, his mind already on the hunt. "Launch another Helix," he snapped, turning to Rostov. "Ka-27PL—I want your best team up there searching. Find those American rats." He turned to his communications officer, a young ensign named Mikhail Orlov. "Signal the fleet—every frigate, every destroyer. Search and destroy. I want that American submarine on the bottom."

"Admiral, we don't know exactly what has happened to the *Kursk*, and we certainly don't know if there is an American submarine involved," Rostov calmly pointed out.

"Sonar, report," Chernov barked, his voice a low growl as he turned to Lieutenant Orlov.

"Debris field expanding, sir," Orlov replied, his hands trembling as he adjusted his headset. "Metal wreckage, no emergency transmissions from the *Kursk*. But I am picking up a faint active sonar signal— American submarine, designated Target One, likely Los Angeles-class. Range twenty-five nautical miles, bearing two-one-five, Target One is extremely noisy, potential damage from the *Kursk* Admiral." Orlov was utilising the Kirov-class battlecruiser's largest and most capable

Soviet surface-ship sonar systems; its role is broader compared to the Udaloy-class destroyers' pure ASW focus. One of the most powerful in the Northern Fleet, the ship's MGK-355 "Polinom" sonar complex cues ASW RPK-6 Vodopad, RPK-2 Vyuga, torpedoes and its ASW rocket weapons systems through the ship's extensive fire control.

Chernov's dark eyes burned with rage, his cigarette forgotten as ash fell to the deck. "The Americans," he growled, his voice dripping with venom. "They planned this—shadowed us, waited for their moment. They will pay for this day." He turned to Rostov, his rage barely contained. "Signal the *Admiral Levchenko* and *Admiral Kharlamov*—Udaloy-class destroyers. Inform them we are dealing with a potential Los Angeles-class SSN submarine. I want it on the bottom."

Rostov nodded, relaying the orders, but his mind was elsewhere. The *Kursk's* loss was a devastating blow, not just to the Northern Fleet but to Russia's naval ambitions. The *Shkval* demonstration was meant to showcase Russia's technological edge, to secure Chinese investment in the Northern Fleet's modernisation. Now, the *Kursk* was a wreck, and the Americans were to blame.

Rostov's gaze shifted to Lieutenant Commander Dmitry Sokolov, whom he had encountered earlier during his ship's inspection. Deep within the *Pyotr Velikiy's* 28,000-ton hull, a heavily armoured weapons control centre housing all the controls for the weapons systems that the massive battlecruiser could bring to bear against any foe. Sokolov, his face pale and his hands nervously fidgeting, had seemed out of sorts, and Rostov's suspicions only grew. He had seen Sokolov with Captain Li Jun, the PLAN operative, talking on the bridge earlier, and the timing felt too convenient.

USS Toledo, 1000 yards south of Kursk

Brennan's eyes darkened as he weighed his options; the pain in his dislocated shoulder was excruciating. The *Toledo* could not survive on battery power alone—not with the Northern Fleet closing in. They had to get the reactor back online; it was their only chance. "Engineering, prepare for an emergency reactor restart," Brennan ordered, his voice masking the concern he had of the surrounding chaos. "We need power now. Make it happen."

Lieutenant Mark Evans, in the engineering compartment, struggled to stabilise the *Toledo's* systems, his hands trembled as he monitored the gauges. The S6G reactor had automatically scrammed during the collision, with the control rods fully inserted to halt the chain reaction, leaving the sub on battery power. "Battery at 80%, sir," Evans reported via intercom, his voice tight. "We have got maybe two hours at this speed—five knots, two hundred feet."

"Emergency reactor restart," Brennan ordered, "I need power, Lieutenant."

The emergency reactor restart was a gamble, but it was their only shot. A scrammed S6G reactor needed a careful sequence to get back online: withdrawing the control rods to reach criticality, restarting the coolant pumps to control heat, and spinning up the turbines to produce power—all while avoiding a thermal spike or further damage to the already stretched systems. The noise would be deadly in these waters. The coolant pumps alone would produce a distinct hum, and the turbines would add a high-pitched whine—together, a symphony of sound that would echo through the shallow Barents Sea. But they had no chance if it failed. "Emergency reactor restart, aye, aye, sir," Evans replied, his voice tight as he began the procedure.

Evans's hands moved swiftly over the control panel; sweat matted his sandy hair as he initiated the restart sequence. "Control rods withdrawing—initiating at 5% per minute," he reported, his voice steady despite the tremor in his hands. The control rods made of neutron-absorbing hafnium began to lift from the reactor core, allowing the nuclear chain reaction to resume. The neutron flux gauge ticked upward, a faint hum filled the engineering compartment as the reactor approached criticality. "Reactor criticality achieved... neutron flux stable at 10^14 neutrons per square centimetre," Evans said, his eyes darting between the gauges.

"Coolant pumps to 20%," he continued, activating the primary coolant pumps to circulate water through the reactor core, absorbing the heat generated by the fission reaction. The pumps whirred to life, the sound was a low rumble that reverberated through the *Toledo's* hull, the noise level spiking to 80 decibels—a whisper in open air, but a shout in the silent sea. "Primary coolant temperature rising—300 degrees Celsius and climbing... heat exchangers online," he reported, as he monitored the temperature gauges for any sign of a spike. A thermal runaway could overheat the core, risking a meltdown, but the *Toledo's* systems held steady. "Turbines engaging," Evans said. His hands trembling as he activated the steam turbines, which converted the reactor's heat into electrical power for the sub's propulsion and systems. The turbines spun up with a high-pitched whine, the noise level spiked at 90 decibels as power surged through the *Toledo's* grid. The reactor's steam generators hissed, the sound a was sharp contrast to the silence of battery power, and the sub's screw began to churn with renewed vigour. "Reactor at 35%, sir," Evans reported, his voice steady despite the fear in his chest. "Power restored—propulsion online, but we are very loud. Noise levels at 90 decibels across all frequencies."

Brennan's mind raced as he calculated the odds. The reactor restart had given them power, propulsion, sensors, and life support—but it had also painted a target on their back. The *Toledo's* noise signature would be detectable up to 40 nautical miles in these shallow waters, a beacon for the Northern Fleet's ASW net. "Sonar, any contacts?" he asked, his voice low but urgent.

"Conn, Sonar," Carter replied, his voice tight as he adjusted his headset, still woozy from his concussion. "Surface contact—bearing zero-one-five, range twelve nautical miles. It is the *Admiral Kharlamov,* an Udaloy-class destroyer. She is speeding up, sir—likely heard us."

Udaloy-class destroyer Admiral Kharlamov, ten nautical miles north of Kursk

Commander Nikolai Pyotrov stood on the bridge of the *Admiral Kharlamov.* The 7,900-ton Udaloy-class destroyer was moving at 15 knots, away from her position in the Northern Fleet's ASW screen, with her Shtil-1 missile system and RBU-6000 Smerch-2 rocket launchers ready to engage any submerged threat.

Pyotrov's face turned ashen as his sonar officer Ensign Ivan Kuznetsov, reported the news "Bearing zero-four-five, range ten nautical miles. Seismic event—4.2 magnitude. It is the *Kursk,* sir—she is gone."

Pyotrov's thought of Captain Dmitri Kolesnikov, a friend he had served with in the Black Sea Fleet a decade ago. The Americans had killed him, and Pyotrov would make them pay. "Signal the *Pyotr Velikiy,*" Pyotrov ordered, his voice tight with emotion. "*Kursk* is down—possible torpedo strike. Request orders."

The comms officer conveyed the message, and within moments, the reply arrived: *KURSK* ATTACKED BY UNKNOWN US SUBMARINE. FULL ASW SWEEP. MAXIMUM AGGRESSION. SINK THE AMERICANS.

Pyotrov's lips curled into a grim smile, his face twisting with the motion. "Flank speed—set course for the *Kursk's* last known position, bearing zero-four-five," he ordered, his voice steady. "Launch the Ka-27PL Orel (Eagle)—dipping sonar, full sweep. I want those Yankees found."

With her screws churning at 25 knots, the *Admiral Kharlamov* surged forward toward the *Kursk's* last known location. The deck thundered as the Ka-27PL Orel lifted off, its coaxial rotors clawing the air as it headed south. The Kamov helicopter was an ASW specialist; its dipping sonar was capable of pinpointing a sub at five nautical miles in good conditions. Pyotrov watched the helicopter disappear into the pale Arctic twilight, his mind on the *Kursk's* crew.

"Conn, Sonar," Kuznetsov reported, his voice sharp and urgent as he adjusted his headset. Extremely difficult to hear anything on our active sonar suite, sir; however, new contact—bearing zero-four-five, range twelve nautical miles. Noisy reactor, 80 decibels—a Los Angeles-class SSN, sir. Very loud, sir. It has sustained damage. The turbulence signature indicates significant damage." Pyotrov's pulse quickened, his dark eyes burning with determination—the American submarine—the sub that had sunk the *Kursk*. The Americans had sunk his friend, and now the Americans were wounded, limping through the Barents Sea like a dying animal. "Signal the *Pyotr Velikiy*," Pyotrov ordered, his voice cold. "Report the Yankee submarine's position and status."

The comms officer relayed the message, his voice steady over the encrypted channel: *PYOTR VELIKIY*, THIS IS *ADMIRAL KHARLAMOV*. CONTACT DETECTED IS LOS ANGELES-CLASS SSN, BEARING ZERO-FOUR-FIVE, RANGE TWELVE NAUTICAL MILES, NOISY REACTOR, DAMAGED. REQUEST ORDERS.

Within moments, Admiral Chernov's voice came through, a low growl: *ADMIRAL KHARLAMOV*, THIS IS *PYOTR VELIKIY*. SINK THAT YANKEE SUBMARINE. FULL SPEED—ENGAGE WITH EXTREME PREJUDICE. NO MERCY.

"Weapons, prepare tubes one and two—53-65K wake homing torpedoes, sonar seek a firing solution," Pyotrov ordered, his voice steady. "Communications, signal the Ka27PL Orel helix, give them the coordinates and order them to attack."

The weapons officer swiftly moved while the hum of the torpedo tubes filled the bridge, loading tubes one and two with 53-65K torpedoes. Pyotrov's eyes remained fixed on the sonar plot, but his thoughts were with Kolesnikov. A friend, a brother-in-arms, now gone. The American submarine would pay; he owed it to him.

USS Toledo, 2000 yards south of the Kursk wreck

Commander Tom Brennan clung to the periscope stand in the *Toledo's* control room, the red lights cast harsh shadows across his gaunt face. With the reactor back online thanks to Lieutenant Mark Evans's efforts, the *Toledo* was limping at eight knots, 150 feet down, her hull groaning with a five-degree list to port. The helm crew were busy working the bow planes to level the submarine.

Brennan's left arm hung limp, but he ignored the pain, His focus was on his ship and crew's survival. His XO, Paul Reese, clutched his cracked ribs, his breathing was shallow, but his eyes remained sharp. Consoles sparked, screens flickered, the air was thick with the stench of ozone and fear. The corpsman, Petty Officer James Carter, treating men on the control room deck with a medical field kit.

"Carter, for god's sake, get over here and put my arm back into my shoulder," Brennan commanded. Carter swiftly came over. He enlisted an ensign to help, "Sorry, sir, this will hurt. Ensign, hold the Commander steady." He grabbed Brennan's arm and lifted it, then pulled it out and down simultaneously, allowing the ball of the arm to slip back into place. "Frack!" Brennan cried out in extreme pain, but instantly felt relief from the excruciating agony.

"Thank you, Evans, carry on with the crew, please." "Aye, sir," Carter replied quickly, assisting those who needed his attention. "Conn, Sonar," gasped Lieutenant Dave Carter, his voice strained as he adjusted his headset. "Helo sonar buoy, three nautical miles north. They are on to us."

Brennan's stomach dropped. "Battle stations, Rig for ultra-quiet. Depth two-zero-zero, come left to one-eight-zero." The *Toledo* creaked as she turned, her damaged hull shuddered under the strain. He glanced at Reese, whose face was a mask of sweat and fear. "If they drop an APR-3E torpedo, we're done."

"*Memphis* is out there," Reese said, his voice hollow. "They will step up."

"They'd better," Brennan muttered. He had seen the Mark 48 launch on sonar—the *Kursk* was gone; her debris field a grim testament to the *Memphis's* retaliation. It was a fight to survive, and the *Toledo* was a wounded beast in a sea of hunters. "Engineering, can I have flank speed yet?" Brennan asked over the coms link.

Lieutenant Mark Evans monitored the reactor in the engineering compartment as he adjusted the coolant flow. The reactor was at 40% power, he fine-tuned the pumps to minimise noise, but the *Toledo's* systems were strained. A pipe had burst during the collision, and the compartment was a haze of steam and sweat. "Reactor holding, sir," Evans reported via the intercom, "But we can't push her much harder."

At the comms station, Lieutenant Sarah Carter decrypted a ULF message from the *Memphis*. "Sir, *Memphis* reports they are ready to cover us. They are asking for our status."

"Tell them we're limping at eight knots, sail's gone, crews banged up, and we have limited reactor power," Brennan said, wiping blood from his eye. "Request immediate cover."

Carter nodded, encoding the reply: "*MEMPHIS*, THIS IS *TOLEDO*. LIMPING AT 8 KNOTS, TWO-ZERO-ZERO FEET, SAIL DESTROYED, CREW INJURED, LIMITED REACTOR POWER. REQUEST IMMEDIATE COVER."

Brennan calculated their chances. The *Toledo* was a wreck—her sail gone, her reactor strained, and half her crew injured. Triggering a chaotic chain reaction, the glancing blow from the collision with the *Kursk* was a disaster. The *Kursk* had fired a torpedo in self-defence—a 53-65K that had missed, distracted by the countermeasures launched— but the *Memphis* retaliated with a Mark 48, sinking the Russian sub and dooming her crew. Brennan thought of the *Kursk's* men. The guilt weighed on him like a lead shroud, but there was no time for remorse. The Northern Fleet hounds were coming, and the *Toledo* was the fox.

Ka-27PL Orel nine nautical miles southwest of the Admiral Kharlamov

Lieutenant Alexei Volkov gripped the controls of the Ka-27PL Orel. The helicopter's sonar buoy dangled below, its hydrophones actively pinging to locate the US submarine in the depths. The Barents Sea stretched out beneath, a grey expanse concealing killers. Volkov, a 32-year-old pilot with a buzz cut and a scar across his right eyebrow from a training accident, had flown ASW missions for a decade, but this was personal.

"Contact," said Lieutenant Mikhail Orlov, the co-pilot's voice sharp as he adjusted the sonar console. "Bearing two-one-zero, range three nautical miles. Submerged, moving slow—eight knots."

Volkov's pulse spiked. "American?"

"Very noisy for an American Los Angeles-class submarine, but it's the only contact out here, it must be," Orlov replied, his fingers flying over the controls. "Los Angeles-class, maybe. Depth two-zero-zero feet."

"Raise the buoy," Volkov ordered. The winch whined, and the sonar buoy furled back up into the Ka-27PL's underbelly. "*Admiral Kharlamov*, this is Orel. Possible Yankee sub, three nautical miles southwest. Engaging."

The radio crackled back: "Confirmed matching our sonar contact, weapons free. Sink it."

Volkov armed the APR-3E torpedo slung under the chopper's belly. The APR-3E, an anti-submarine torpedo powered by an "Eagle" rocket with a turbo pump engine, was designed to hunt submarines ruthlessly. The torpedo required at least 100 metres of water depth for the initial drop, which is not an issue in this case.

Volkov's hands tightened on the controls. He thought of Kolesnikov, the nights they had spent in Severodvinsk, toasting to the Motherland's glory. Kolesnikov had been a mentor, a friend, a brother-in-arms. Volkov would make the Americans pay. He waited to close the gap; he did not want the Yankee submarine to have any chance of survival or escape.

"Volkov, second contact, submerged and moving very fast two nautical miles, 270 degrees," Orlov called. Just then, Orlov noticed a splash and a flash off to their west. "Volkov, what is that?" he asked as Volkov banked the Ka-27PL to get a closer look. It was the last thing they would see or do.

USS *Memphis, two nautical miles southwest of the Kursk wreck*

Commander John Rourke stood in the *Memphis's* control room as he watched the tactical plot. The *Kursk* was a smoking hole in the seabed, the Mark 48's warhead having ripped her apart. Rourke had fired to save the *Toledo* after the collision, but the secondary explosion—a massive blast from the *Shkval's* rocket fuel—had been unlike anything he had ever heard.

Now, as the *Memphis's* sonar listened to the *Kursk's* death throes post-collision, Rourke's thoughts flashed back to Norfolk. The brief had underestimated Kolesnikov's edge—and the recklessness of their orders. "Damn fools," he muttered, hands steady on the periscope. "We're paying for their gamble now." With the *Toledo* crippled and the Russian northern fleet mobilising, Rourke's resolve kicked in, channelling that briefing's weight into action—saving Brennan's crew would be his defiance of a mission gone awry.

"Conn, Sonar," said Lieutenant Mike Hensley, his lanky frame hunched over the sonar console. "Helo Ka-27PL, two nautical miles north. Second contact—surface ship, 10 nautical miles, bearing zero-three-zero, 25 knots, and closing fast. It is the Admiral *Kharlamov*—Udaloy-class destroyer."

Rourke frowned. The Ka-27PL would launch its APR-3E torpedo at any second at the retreating *Toledo*: "Kline, Sea Lance firing solution, weapons lock on to that Ka-27PL ASW helo."

"Tube one, Sea Lance, locked on the helo's position," replied Weapons Officer Ed Kline, a stocky man with a buzz cut and a no-nonsense demeanour. "Solution ready, aye."

"Fire tube one," Rourke snapped, his voice steel. The *Memphis* shuddered as the Sea Lance—a torpedo-launched, rocket-boosted missile—raced into the dark ocean depths and burst out of the water like a geyser. It streaked upward, locked onto the Ka-27PL Orel's heat signature, and slammed into the helicopter, vaporising it in a fireball that lit up the twilight sky. Debris rained down into the sea, a smoking epitaph for Lieutenant Alexei Volkov and Lieutenant Mikhail Orlov.

Rourke thought back to early July, with the sun hanging low over the Naval Station in Norfolk, casting long shadows across the tarmac as he had stepped out of the briefing room, his mind a whirlwind of strategy and unease. The orders had been explicit: shadow the K-141 *Kursk* during its *Shkval* torpedo demonstration in the Barents Sea, with the USS *Memphis* and USS *Toledo* operating in unprecedented proximity—five nautical miles from each other and the target. The briefing had painted Kolesnikov as a formidable adversary, a captain whose Mediterranean triumph over the USS *Abraham Lincoln* showcased his ability to push the *Kursk's* limits with heat-vectoring manoeuvres and reactor overdrives. Rourke, at 49, with nearly three decades of submarine warfare under his belt, felt the weight of the admiral's words: "Show the Russians we're not intimidated." But the directive to break every rule of submarine operations had gnawed at him.

As the briefing adjourned, Rourke had exchanged a glance with Brennan, whose furrowed brow mirrored his own concern. "We'll talk later, Tom," Rourke had. "I need to dig deeper into this." Brennan had nodded, then headed off to prep the *Toledo*, while Rourke turned toward the submarine base arsenal, a sprawling complex of steel hangars and secure bunkers. He needed an edge, something to tip the scales if Kolesnikov's *Shkval* turned this shadow game into a firefight. Accompanying him was Lieutenant Commander Ed Kline, the *Memphis's* weapons officer, a wiry 38-year-old weapons specialist and a steady hand under pressure.

The arsenal's interior was a cavern of controlled chaos—racks of Mk 48 ADCAP torpedoes, Harpoon missiles, and experimental prototypes lined the walls, guarded by armed sentries. Rourke's commanding officer's clearance allowed him to access the restricted section, where they kept innovative developments. A grizzled chief petty officer, Master Chief Masterson, greeted them with a curt nod. "What brings you here, Captain?" he asked, his eyes narrowed with curiosity.

"I need to see anything that can give us an advantage against potential ASW air threats," Rourke replied, his tone leaving no room for debate. "We're sailing into a potential hornet's nest."

Masterson led them past rows of conventional munitions to a sealed vault. Its door hissed open to reveal a sleek, cylindrical weapon shrouded in a protective casing. "This is the Sea Lance," he said, gesturing to the torpedo-like device. "Subsurface-launched air-defence-system. Developed for the Seawolf-class subs—state-of-the-art, top secret."

Rourke's interest piqued as Masterson elaborated. The Sea Lance was a revolutionary hybrid, blending the dimensions of a Mk 48 torpedo with a subsurface-launch capability from a conventional torpedo tube for air defence. Designed to counter low-flying threats—such as Russian Ka-27 helicopters or anti-submarine aircraft—it deployed a high-speed rocket-powered projectile that breached the surface and engaged targets with a heat-seeking warhead. "It's got a range of 5 nautical miles and can hit speeds of Mach 2.5 once airborne," Masterson explained. "The Seawolf's fire control system integrates the targeting and launch sequence natively, but we've been testing a plugin module for older platforms like the Los Angeles-class."

Kline leaned in, inspecting the schematics displayed on a nearby console. "Dimensions match the *Memphis's* Mk 48's 21-inch tube," he noted, tracing the blueprint. "With a plugin for our fire control, we could load it out?"

"Exactly," Masterson confirmed. "The Seawolf system uses an advanced combat management suite, but we have adapted a portable integration tablet. It is not plug-and-play yet—it requires calibration—but it'll work with your BQQ-5 sonar and weapons control. You would need to train on it, though."

Rourke's mind raced. The *Shkval's* supercavitating speed of 200 knots posed a lethal threat underwater, but the *Kursk's* escorting surface ships and helicopters could be just as dangerous if Chernov's fleet reacted aggressively. Sea Lance offered a counterpunch, turning the *Memphis* into a multi-domain threat. "How many can we take?" he asked.

"Six units are ready," Masterson replied. "We have got the plugin tablet and a training module. It is experimental, Captain—untested in combat."

Rourke nodded, his decision instantaneous. "Load out six Sea Lance torpedoes. Kline, get familiar with the targeting and launch sequence. Use the tablet and run simulations until you can do it blindfolded."

Kline accepted the tablet, a sleek device with a glowing interface, and began scrolling through the manual. "I'll have it down by departure, sir," he said, already absorbed in the technical details. The balance of the *Memphis's* weapons load-out would remain Mk 48 ADCAP torpedoes—reliable workhorses for anti-submarine and strike missions—but the Sea Lance addition felt like a trump card, a hedge against the unknown.

Back at the *Memphis* berth, Rourke had overseen the loading process. The crew worked had with precision, hoisting the Sea Lance units into the torpedo room with cranes, their matte-black casings gleaming under the dock lights. Kline set up a temporary station in the control room, connecting the plugin tablet to the fire control system. The interface flickered to life, displaying a 3D sonar map and a launch sequence protocol. "It's syncing with the BQQ-5," Kline reported, adjusting parameters. "I will carry out a dry run—targeting a simulated Ka-27 at five nautical miles."

Rourke watched, arms crossed, as Kline executed the simulation. The tablet's screen projected a virtual helicopter, its heat signature pulsing red. With a few taps, Kline locked the target and initiated the launch sequence. A digital Sea Lance breached the surface; its rocket ignited in a burst of pixels and tracked the target with uncanny accuracy. "Hit confirmed," Kline said, a rare grin breaking through. "Range and speed are spot-on."

"Good work," Rourke said. His mind was already on the Barents Sea. The Sea Lance's potential was clear, but its untested nature gnawed at him. He thought of Kolesnikov's crew, the *Shkval's* devastating speed, and the Chinese delegation aboard the *Pyotr Velikiy*—witnesses to a demonstration that could escalate beyond exercises. The admiral's orders to "show resolve" felt reckless, a provocation that might ignite Chernov's wrath. Rourke's experience told him proximity bred accidents—collisions, misfires, war.

That night, in his quarters aboard the *Memphis*, Rourke had sat with a cup of black coffee, the Sea Lance tablet on the desk. He scrolled through its manual, memorising the launch protocols himself. The device's integration with the Seawolf system hinted at a future where submarines could dominate both sea and sky, but its reliance on the plugin module worried him. A glitch mid-mission could render it useless—or worse, expose them to retaliation. He thought of his son's submarine models and daughter's drawings, their innocence a stark contrast to the stakes ahead. "For the *Thresher's* lost," he whispered, echoing his father's sacrifice, a mantra that steadied his resolve.

The next morning, Rourke convened the senior staff. "We've got a new tool," he announced, holding up the tablet. "Sea Lance—subsurface air defence. Kline's training on it, and we have loaded six units. Our Mk 48s handle the underwater fight, but if the Russian Northern Fleet helicopters or destroyers close in, this gives us an edge. I want every officer running simulations—discretion is our shield, but readiness is our sword."

Lieutenant Commander Sarah Carter, the navigation officer, raised a hand. "Sir, operating this close to the *Toledo*. It is a tight box. If Kolesnikov detects us, or if we misjudge a turn—"

"I know," Rourke cut in, his voice firm. "It is a damn fool's errand, but we are not the ones calling the shots. We will mitigate the risk—Kline, I want a fail-over protocol for the Sea Lance if the plugin fails. Carter, plot evasion patterns at five-nautical-mile intervals. We are not here to start a war, but we will finish one if it comes."

The crew dispersed, and Rourke lingered, staring at the Barents Sea chart. The Sea Lance was a wild card, a technological leap that could save them—or doom them if mishandled. He recalled the Norfolk admiral's cold assurance: "Kolesnikov's a shark, but you're the hunter." Rourke was not so sure. The *Kursk's Shkval*, with its 10 nautical mile range and nuclear potential, made Kolesnikov the predator, and the close-proximity orders had turned the *Memphis* and *Toledo* into bait. Yet, with Sea Lance, Rourke felt a flicker of hope—a chance to turn the tables if the Russian northern fleet turned hostile.

Over the next week, Rourke had drilled the crew relentlessly. Kline's simulations grew sharper; the Sea Lance tablet had become an extension of his hands. They had practised launch sequences in the simulator bay, targeting virtual Ka-27s and MiG-29Ks, adjusting for sea state and thermocline interference. Rourke had joined in, mastering the tablet's interface, his fingers moving with the precision of a pianist. "Speed is survival," he had told Kline during a late-night session. "If we are under attack from above, you've got 30 seconds to lock and fire."

The departure date loomed, and Rourke spent his final shore leave with his family. Rachel, his wife, sensed his tension, her hands lingering on his as they watched their children play. "Come back to us," she whispered. Rourke nodded. "I will," he promised, though the uncertainty gnawed at him.

When the *Memphis* had cast off from the Norfolk naval base. Rourke stood on the conn, with the Barents Sea ahead, a grey expanse of potential conflict. The crew had stowed the Sea Lance units and readied them; they had primed the Mk 48s, and Kline had synced his tablet. "All stations, silent running," he ordered. The briefing's recklessness, Kolesnikov's prowess, and the Sea Lance's untested power converged in his mind. "Let's hope we don't have to use them," he repeated to himself, a prayer against the storm brewing beneath the waves.

And now, his worst fear has become a reality. "Weapons, confirm the hit," Rourke ordered, his voice steady.

"Confirmed, sir," Kline replied, his voice steady. "Helo down—sonar confirmed, explosion and splash detected." Rourke nodded, but the victory was short-lived.

The *Admiral Kharlamov* was closing at 25 knots. "Firing solution?" Rourke asked, his voice calm despite the cold sweat trickling down his spine.

The sonar screen lit up with new contacts—four additional Ka-27PL helicopters, launched from the *Pyotr Velikiy* and her escorts, their dipping sonars forming a deadly net. The *Admiral Kharlamov* was closing in rapidly, her 53-65K torpedoes posing a serious threat to the *Toledo*. "We've got the entire Northern Fleet bearing down on us," Rourke said, his voice low. "Let us go deep and avoid them. Dive to 400 feet, ahead two-thirds."

The *Memphis* nosed down fifteen degrees, her screw churning as she descended into the colder, denser water; her hull groaned under the pressure. Rourke turned to Kline, his mind already on the next move. "Weapons, get me a firing solution on every frigate and destroyer within 25 nautical miles. Reload tube 1 with Mark 48 conventional war-shot and slave all four Mark 48 war-shots to the tactical plot. Designate *Admiral Kharlamov* as Sierra 1."

Kline worked fast, and the fire control system calculated a solution for *Admiral Kharlamov*. "Solutions locked, sir," he reported. "Tubes one through four loaded with Mark 48s, ready to fire."

"Hold fire for now," Rourke said, "We will use them if we must. But for now, we hide."

Rourke analysed his tactical situation. The *Memphis* was intact, had several more Sea Lances available, a full complement of Mark 48 torpedoes, her reactor was running at optimal power, and her screw was pushing the ship forward at 15 knots as she dived to 400 feet. However, the Russian fleet was closing in, a net of steel and sonar that stretched across the Barents Sea. The *Pyotr Velikiy* was 25 nautical miles north. Her escorts were even closer—the *Admiral Kharlamov* was closing fast, and the *Admiral Levchenko* was 15 nautical miles away, bearing down at 25 knots. Their active sonar pings lit up the water like a thunderstorm, a relentless drumbeat that promised death. Their additional ASW Ka-27PLs presented a clear and present danger for *Toledo* and the *Memphis*.

Krivak-class Frigate Smolensk, one mile north of the Kursk wreck

Captain Sergei Ivanov stood on the bridge of the *Smolensk*; his weathered face etched with grief as he guided the frigate towards the stricken *Kursk*. The 3,575-ton warship was fast and agile, her Silex missile system and RBU-6000 rocket launchers ready for action, but Ivanov's mission was one of mercy, not war. Kolesnikov had been a mentor, a friend, a brother-in-arms. They had served together on a Kilo-class SSK diesel electric submarine in the Black Sea Fleet years ago. Now he was likely dead, and Ivanov's heart ached with the loss.

"Sonar, anything?" Ivanov called, his voice rough with emotion as he gripped the binoculars, scanning the grey expanse of the Barents Sea.

"Wreckage at three-five-zero feet," replied the sonarman, Ensign Alexei Pyotrov, a young officer with a nervous tic, adjusted the MGK-335 sonar suite. "Debris field—metal hull signature. *Kursk* is sitting on the bottom. No emergency pod yet, sir. A lot of background noise—biologics, ships, helos."

Ivanov cursed under his breath, his greying beard quivered as he fought to maintained his composure. He thought of Petty Officer Yuri Pavlov, the sonar officer who had been on the *Kursk*, a young man with a quick smile and a talent for detecting the faintest signals in the deep. Pavlov had been a family friend since childhood—could he still be alive? Ivanov clung to the hope of an escape pod, but the forward section, where the pod was located, was likely a mangled ruin. The aft hatch was their only chance, but at 350 feet, with flooding and pressure, rescue was a race against time. If any crew had survived, that is.

Ivanov thought about a six-month deployment in the Black Sea, a theatre buzzing with NATO exercises following the Soviet collapse. The K-123, under Captain Oleg Grigorev, had been tasked with shadowing a US Los Angeles-class submarine near the Bosporus, a mission requiring stealth and precision. Ivanov, as first officer, had overseen the navigation and tactical planning, while Pavlov manned the MGK-400 sonar suite, his earphones pressed tight as he tracked the Americans' faint propeller beats. A tense moment had arisen when the US sub altered course, closing to within 10,000 yards. Pavlov's whispered report— "Bearing zero-two-zero, speed 15 knots, passive contact only"— had alerted Ivanov as Second Officer, who had ordered a silent dive to 200 meters, exploiting a thermocline to mask their signature. During a simulated torpedo run, Pavlov had detected a decoy, saving the K-123 from a costly error, while Ivanov's quick change of the boat's trim had kept them undetected.

"Keep searching," Ivanov ordered, his voice steady despite the tears in his eyes. "We don't stop until we find the escape pod—or confirm it never made it to the surface."

A fireball erupted on the horizon, several nautical miles to the west, and the Ka-27PL from the *Admiral Kharlamov*, their eyes in the sky, was obliterated. Ivanov's heart sank. The Americans were fighting back. "Signal the *Pyotr Velikiy*," he ordered, his voice tight. "Ka-27PL Orel's is down—probable missile strike. The Yankees are still out there."

Ivanov's mind raced as he processed the implications. The Americans had a weapon they had not anticipated—a subsurface-to-air missile, capable of taking out ASW helicopters. The Ka-27 Orel's loss was devastating, not just to their ASW net but to the Northern Fleet's morale. Ivanov thought of the *Kursk's* crew. They were gone, and the Americans were to blame. The Northern Fleet would come for blood, and Ivanov would be part of the hunt—but first, he had to find the *Kursk's* wreck and confirm the fate of her crew.

Udaloy-class destroyer Admiral Kharlamov, eight nautical miles north of the Kursk wreck

Pyotrov stood on the bridge of the *Admiral Kharlamov*. His Ka-27PL helicopter, call sign "Olan," had just exploded in the air, downed by an unseen American weapon that defied all his naval instincts. He leaned against the chart table, eyes narrowing as he listened to the sonar operator's frantic report: a sudden spike, a high-pitched whine, and then silence as the Ka-27PL Olan's transponder blinked out.

The helicopter, carrying torpedoes and dipping sonar, had been sent to hunt the damaged American submarine, and its crew of two were now presumed lost.

The *Admiral Kharlamov's* Rastrub-B missile system and MGK-355 Polinom sonar had not detected any surface threat; however, the Ka-27PL had been obliterated mid-flight, 12 nautical miles from the destroyer, which was impossible.

"Status report!" Pyotrov barked, his voice a low growl over the intercom. The weapons officer, Lieutenant Grigori Sokolov, hesitated before responding. "Sir, it is… it's gone. No debris, no ejection.

Something launched from below—subsurface, high-speed, airburst signature. American, likely from the Los Angeles-class submarine."

Pyotrov's stomach churned. A subsurface-to-air weapon system? The Americans had always held an edge in submarine stealth, but this was unprecedented. His mind raced back to the Black Sea exercises with Kolesnikov, where surface-submarine coordination had been their strength. Now, that advantage seemed reversed. The *Kursk's* sinking had shaken him. And now this: a technological ambush that mocked his command.

"Analysis!" he snapped, turning to the sonar chief, Petty Officer Alexei Kuznetsov. The man's face was pale as he adjusted the MGK-355 controls. "Sir, the trace suggests a rocket-assisted projectile. Launched from depth, breached the surface, and tracked the Ka-27PL Orlans' heat signature. Estimated speed... Mach 2.5. It is not a standard SAM—too fast for a Harpoon derivative."

Pyotrov's dismay deepened. The Seawolf-class submarines were rumoured to carry next-generation systems, but a torpedo-launched air defence weapon—he was pretty sure they were not dealing with one of the new deadly silent Seawolf-class American submarines—but this challenged everything he knew about naval warfare. The Ka-27PL, a workhorse of Russian ASW, had been his eyes above the waves, and its loss left the *Admiral Kharlamov* vulnerable to further American attack. Denisov's face flashed in his mind—eager, green, trusting Pyotrov's orders—and guilt gnawed at him. He had sent the helicopter into a trap.

"Chernov will have our heads," muttered Sokolov, referring to Admiral Viktor Chernov, whose aggressive stance against the US Navy now seemed justified. Pyotrov ignored the comment. "Plot the launch point," he ordered. "Triangulate from the last sonar ping. If it is the American submarine, we will flush her out." The crew scrambled, but the sonar returned only faint biologics—whale calls and shrimp clicks— masking the American sub's retreat.

Pyotrov's hands clenched the railing, his breath fogging in the cold. The

Kursk's implosion had been a tragedy; this was an insult. The Americans had turned the underwater domain into a multi-threat arena, and it had blindsided him. His Black Sea days with Kolesnikov had taught him to expect surface threats, but this subsurface innovation exposed a gap in his preparedness. "They've outplayed us," he murmured, the weight of command pressing down. Losing the Ka-27PL Orlan was not a tactical setback; it was a personal failure, a crack in the armour of his pride.

As the *Admiral Kharlamov* adjusted course, Pyotrov vowed retribution. The Sea Lance's existence, though unknown to him by name, fuelled his resolve to adapt. He had seen Kolesnikov's tenacity firsthand—now he would channel it, turning this dismay into a hunt for the mysterious American submarine, no matter the cost to his career or Chernov's wrath.

"Con sonar, I have detected a submerged contact, sir," replied the sonar officer, Lieutenant Ivan Kuznetsov. "Bearing two-one-zero, range ten nautical miles. Moving slowly—eight knots. It is the damaged US Los Angeles-class submarine."

"Launch torpedoes—two 53-65Ks, active sonar, full spread," Pyotrov ordered, his voice steady. "Let's finish what the Orel started."

"Captain, ten nautical miles is the most extreme range of the 53-65 torpedoes; a long transit time will give the US sub plenty of time for countermeasures," weapons officer, Lieutenant Grigori Sokolov, stated.

"Do it," Pyotrov hissed, "Sokolov track the torpedo progress, it will take 13 minutes for them to get close enough to that Yankee sub to lock on to its wake signature", he added.

"Aye sir," Sokolov replied.

The *Admiral Kharlamov* launched the torpedoes. They immediately sped up to 45 knots searching for the Los Angeles-class submarine's wake signature as they streaked toward the US submarine. Pyotrov watched the plot, his mind on the *Kursk's* crewmen he had known, men he had trained with. "The Americans would pay for this day," he assured the bridge crew standing watch.

"Sonar, track those torpedoes," Pyotrov ordered, his voice steady. "And signal the *Admiral Levchenko*—I want them coordinating with us in this search and destroy mission for this US submarine."

The *Admiral Kharlamov* comms officer relayed the order, and within minutes, the *Admiral Levchenko* launched her own Ka-27PL—Ka-27 Sokol (Falcon)—its coaxial rotors clawing the air as it headed south. Pyotrov watched the plot, his mind on the *Kursk*.

"Sir, report from Admiral Chernov on *Pyotr Veliky*," the *Admiral Kharlamov* comms officer called out. "There are two American Los Angeles-class submarines in theatre; he orders them both sunk, sir", the comms officer practically yelled.

"Pizdetz, two Yankee submarines. It must be the second one that just took out Orel. Coms contact the *Admiral Levchenko* and warn their Ka-27PL Falcon to stay clear," Pyotrov ordered. "Message them that Yankee submarines can shoot ASW helicopters out of the sky."

USS *Toledo, 12 nautical miles south of the Kursk wreck*

Commander Tom Brennan stood in *Toledo's* control room, his shoulder still throbbing as he clung to the railing, his eyes fixed on the tactical plot. The *Toledo* was at 200 feet, limping along at eight knots; his ship was struggling under the strain of the damage from the collision with the *Kursk*. The control room was still a chaos of red lights and flickering screens, with the air thick with the stench of ozone and burnt plastic. He needed to steady the men in his command if they had any chance of survival.

"Conn, Sonar," said Lieutenant Dave Carter, his voice tight as he adjusted his headset. "Torpedoes in the water—bearing zero-one-zero, range eight thousand yards, speed 45 knots. They are active and closing—ETA five minutes."

Brennan's heart pounded, his eyes darkening with dread. The *Admiral*

Kharlamov had fired two 53-65K wake-homing torpedoes, their sensors picking up their wake signature as they hunted the *Toledo*. At eight thousand yards, they had minutes to react. "Launch countermeasures!" Brennan shouted; his voice sharp. "Full spread—now!"

The *Toledo* launched another cloud of acoustic decoys and bubble generators, the devices darted north to mimic a fleeing sub. The 53-65K torpedoes wavered, one veering off to chase a decoy, but the second stayed locked on, its propeller noise growing louder. Brennan's mind raced, his hands gripping the railing as he weighed his options. "Come left to one-five-zero," he ordered, his voice steady. "Increase to 10 knots—we'll have to risk the noise."

The *Toledo* turned, her screw cavitating as she sped up, the turbulence from the missing sail created a low rumble, a beacon for the torpedo. The second 53-65K stayed locked on, its proximity growing louder, a death knell in the silent sea. Brennan's heart pounded; his eyes fixed on the tactical plot as the torpedo closed the gap—three thousand yards… two thousand yards.

"Conn, Sonar," Carter shouted, his voice rising urgently. "Torpedo at two thousand yards, ETA 79 seconds!"

Brennan made a split-second decision. "Emergency surface!" he shouted, his voice sharp. "Blow all ballast tanks! Angle up the bow planes—25 degrees up bubble, all ahead flank!"

The *Toledo* shuddered as high-pressure air blasted into the ballast tanks, forcing the 6,927-ton sub upward. Her screw was powering her to 40 knots—a reckless speed for a damaged boat, but they had no choice. The sudden ascent threw the crew against bulkheads, equipment, and anything not screwed down flew everywhere as the sub breached the surface like a whale, her hull slicing through the icy, choppy waters at a 25-degree angle. Spray exploded around her; the shallow sea frothed in her wake as the *Toledo's* black hull broke into the arctic air and settled on the surface.

The 53-65K torpedo lost its lock in the surface clutter, its wake homing guidance systems became confused by the scattering in the rough waves. It circled once, twice, then self-destructed in a muted explosion, its deadly warhead detonating harmlessly 100 feet below the surface. Brennan exhaled, his body trembling with adrenaline, but the relief was brief. The *Toledo* was on the surface, exposed, and the Russian fleet was closing in.

"Dive, dive!" Brennan shouted; his voice was hoarse as he clung to the railing. "Take us to 150 feet, ahead two-thirds!"

The *Toledo* slipped beneath the waves, its reactor humming at 35% power, its screw churning as it descended to 150 feet. The hull moaned under the pressure, the damage from the collision was taking its toll. Brennan glanced at XO Paul Reese, his face grim. "We are not out of this yet," he said, his voice low. "The Russians know where we are now, and every radar would will a lock on us. We're lit up like a beacon, and they will come for us with everything they have."

Brennan clung to the periscope stand aboard the USS *Toledo*, his knuckles white as he recovered from the near-miss of the two torpedoes. The emergency surfacing had been a violation of every submerged instinct, a move that exposed the *Toledo* to surface threats, but it had been their only shot.

Brennan exhaled, sweat beading under his cap, his mind flashed to the Norfolk briefing where he and Rourke had questioned the close-proximity orders, but survival demanded focus. The sonar crackled with activity: the *Admiral Kharlamov's* MGK-355 Polinom sonar pinged aggressively, and beyond, the Northern Fleet's signature loomed— destroyers, frigates, and possibly a nuclear depth charge threat. Brennan's options were narrowing fast.

"Damage report," he ordered, steadying his voice. Chief Engineer Lieutenant Mark Hensley's response was grim: "Hull integrity at 85%, sir. Cooling pumps are failing—reactor temperatures are climbing. We have maybe six hours before we must shut down or risk a scram. The *Toledo* had lost its stealth capabilities, and its acoustic signature had become a beacon in the frigid depths. Brennan's gaze shifted to the plot—Rourke's *Memphis* had bought them time, taking out the Ka-27PL ASW helicopter, but the Russian response was mobilising. The Russian Northern Fleet's vengeance, fuelled by the *Kursk's* loss, promised no mercy.

Brennan weighed his choices. Option one: dive and evade, slipping beneath the thermocline. The damaged pumps made this risky—prolonged submersion could lead to a reactor meltdown, stranding them. Option two: limp to the surface and signal for rescue, a humiliating surrender that would expose them to the Russian Fleet's air assets, including the Ka-27PLs they might redeploy. Option three: make haste westward, toward Norwegian territorial waters, where NATO could intervene. The last was the least suicidal, but it meant outrunning the Northern Fleet's closing net—frigates like the Udaloy-class and the Kirov-class cruiser *Peter the Great*, all armed to the teeth with ASW assets.

"Carter, plot a course west at flank speed," Brennan decided. "Max depth 150 feet—keep us under the layer but above the critical zone. Hensley, rig emergency cooling with seawater bypass if the pumps fail." The crew sprang into action, the *Toledo's* seven-bladed screw churned at 35 knots. Brennan knew the move invited detection—flank speed was noisy—but lingering invited annihilation. The Northern Fleet's sonar blooms on the plot were 10 nautical miles out, closing at 25 knots. Time was their enemy.

He recalled Rourke's mentorship on the USS *Birmingham*, the 1987 Pacific patrol, where silence had saved them. Silence was a luxury lost. The Sea Lance system Rourke had loaded onto the *Memphis* flickered in his mind—subsurface air defence that had downed the Ka-27PL helicopter. If the Russians deployed more air assets, the *Toledo* would be defenceless. Brennan ordered the weapons officer, Lieutenant Dan Rivera, to ready two Mk 48 ADCAPs. "If they close to six thousand yards, we will engage the *Admiral Kharlamov*," he said, a bitter taste in his mouth. Self-defence was their only justification, but it risked war. "Sonar, designate the *Admiral Kharlamov*, Sierra One, Lieutenant Rivera, lock in a firing solution and fire on my orders."

Radar from the *Admiral Kharlamov* would have locked onto him, Brennan figured, its Rastrub-B missiles were a looming threat. He ordered evasive zigzags, the sub's hull groaned as it danced through the depths. The sonar plot logged a new contact—another Russian frigate, fifteen nautical miles and gaining. The Russian Northern Fleet was a noose tightening, and Brennan's crew, already shaken by the *Kursk* collision, faced exhaustion. He thought of his wife, Emily, and their kids—10-year-old Jake and 7-year-old Lily—waiting in Groton. Surviving this mission, born of reckless orders, now hinged on his choices.

"Status of the pumps?" he asked Hensley. "Bypass is online, sir, but it is a patch. Temp's at 280°C—red line is 300. We have got four hours, max." Brennan nodded, his mind racing. The Norwegian coast was 150 nautical miles west—a six-hour sprint at flank speed, if they held together. He activated the ELF transceiver, sending a coded distress signal to NATO, hoping Rourke's *Memphis* could draw fire. "All hands, brace for pursuit," he announced over the 1MC. "We're heading home, but it's going to be rough."

As the *Toledo* plunged back to 250 feet, Brennan stared at the tactical plot. *Admiral Kharlamov's* torpedoes had been a wake-up call; the Northern Fleet's advance was a potential death knell. His successful surfacing tactic had saved them, but haste was now their only chance for salvation. He muttered, "For the crew," echoing Rourke's USS *Thresher* mantra, steeling himself for the gauntlet ahead. The sea held their fate, and Brennan's next move would define it.

CHAPTER 3

FOXES AND HOUNDS

Barents Sea, August 12, 2000, 1015 — 1215 hours local time
Udaloy-class destroyer Admiral Kharlamov,
12 nautical miles north of Toledo

Commander Nikolai Pyotrov stood on the bridge of the *Admiral Kharlamov*, scowling, his binoculars gripped tightly in his hands.

"Sonar, report on those torpedoes!" he barked.

"First torpedo missed, sir," replied Ensign Ivan Kuznetsov, his voice tense as he adjusted his headset. "It chased a decoy—bearing zero-three-zero. The second torpedo… it lost lock. At ten nautical miles, the S-T 53-65 torpedoes were at their most extreme range, sir. Target one executed a rapid surfacing manoeuvre confirmed by sonar and radar. She surfaced at coordinates 70 degrees north, 31 degrees east, then rapidly dived to two and fifty hundred feet. It is the American sub, sir—Los Angeles-class SSN."

Pyotrov's blood ran cold. First, they had lost their Ka-27PL Orel ASW helicopter, and now the Americans had evaded both of the 53-65K torpedoes they had launched. The Americans were cunning; their wounded submarine was fighting to survive despite the odds. Pyotrov thought of his friend Kolesnikov, dead at the bottom of the Barents Sea with the *Kursk's* crew.

"Signal the *Pyotr Velikiy*," Pyotrov ordered. "Report the Yankee sub surfacing at 70 degrees north, 31 degrees east, and then a rapid dive to two hundred feet. Advise Admiral Chernov of our Ka-27PL destruction by a submarine-to-air super-weapon. The US Los Angeles subs can shoot ASW helicopters out of the sky from the depths. Note that she has evaded two of our torpedoes. Request orders."

The comms officer relayed the message. Admiral Chernov's low growl replied over the radio: *ADMIRAL KHARLAMOV*, THIS IS *PYOTR VELIKIY*. RE-ENGAGE IMMEDIATELY. FULL ASW SWEEP—DEPTH CHARGES, TORPEDOES, ACTIVE SONAR. SINK THAT SUB.

Pyotrov smiled to himself; it was time to get serious. Admiral Chernov was as angry as a hornet. "We can't launch the second Ka-27PL Volk," he said, his voice steady. "We run the risk of losing it along with its flight crew. Sound general quarters, man torpedo stations and RBU teams, set the Combat Information Center (CIC) to ASW intercept mode."

The *Admiral Kharlamov's* CIC housed the Lesorub suite and the weapons-control centre, and was located inside the central superstructure, just below and immediately aft of the bridge, within the ship's protected superstructure citadel.

The CIC crew jumped to their assigned tasks at the combat systems consoles. The fire control operators, consisting of radar, sonar, ESM repeaters, and comms, worked in unison to hunt the American submarines.

Weapons-control functions were integrated into the ship's combat information system. The CIC fire control consoles, radars and optics were distributed on the superstructure and forward decks. The ship and crew were primed and ready for the task of hunting and destroying the enemy submarines.

"We will launch a standoff strike," Pyotrov ordered, "CIC, pattern-fire a SS-N-14 Silex salvo immediately along the last known track of that American Los Angeles-class submarine."

"CIC con, sir, target one range covers ten nautical miles. They might launch a torpedo counter-defence strike. We suggest you execute irregular manoeuvres as an anti-torpedo defence while we use intermittent active pings to refine the target firing solution."

"Officer of the watch, slow to 15 knots, irregular manoeuvres, CIC get me a firing solution on that Yankee sub for immediate SS-N-14 Silex launch," Pyotrov ordered.

The *Admiral Kharlamov's* Silex ship-launched rocket missiles were delivery systems, whose primary ASW role was to carry and place a lightweight homing torpedo or depth charge into the water near a submarine contact.

With an effective range of 48 nautical miles, and the delivery vehicle travelling at Mack 0.9 the American submarine would come under attack in under 2 minutes. After splashdown, the missiles released their torpedoes, whereby they powered up and began searching for the target, utilising active sonar.

Pyotrov was burning with a desire for revenge on that US submarine.

Kursk 350 feet down on the bottom of the Barents Sea

The *Kursk* was a tomb before she hit the seabed, her 24,000-ton hull a shattered relic of Russia's naval pride. The Mark 48 torpedo from the USS *Memphis* had slammed into her forward torpedo room, its 650-pound shape-charged warhead punching through the double hull like a sledgehammer through glass. The initial detonation had been a white-hot flash, vaporising steel and men in milliseconds. Standing in the control room twenty feet aft, Captain First Rank Dmitri Kolesnikov never stood a chance. The blast wave turned the compartment into a blender of fire and steel, killing the forward crew of sixty men instantly. The command module was obliterated, and its consoles, charts, and men were reduced to ash in the inferno.

The *Kursk's* twin OK-650 reactors, housed midships, however, had been built to withstand hell. Their reinforced bulkheads had held, shielding the rear section from the inferno. Twenty-three men in the aft compartments—engineers, cooks, and a junior officer— had survived the initial blast, thrown against bulkheads as the sub pitched violently nose-down. Now, at 350 feet, the *Kursk* lay on the seabed, its survivors, trapped in the reactor control and engineering compartments, fought to stay alive in a world of darkness and cold.

Lieutenant Ivan Federov, a 28-year-old reactor technician, coughed blood from his cracked ribs into his sleeve. The compartment was dark, lit only by a flickering emergency lamp that cast eerie shadows across the steel walls. Cold as death, water seeped through a cracked seam, pooling at his boots and numbing his legs. Around him, men groaned, men prayed, their voices were a desperate chorus. The air was thick with the acrid stench of burning insulation and the metallic tang of blood, the oxygen levels dropped with every passing minute.

Federov's hands trembled as he grabbed a wrench from the tool rack, his fingers slick with sweat and blood. He banged it against the hull—three short, three long, three short. SOS. The sound echoed dully; a plea swallowed by the abyss. He did not know if anyone could hear, but he would keep tapping until his strength gave out. Beside him, Petty Officer Yuri Pavlov, the sonar officer who had been off-duty in the aft section, clutched a broken arm, his face pale but determined. "Keep going, Ivan," Pavlov rasped, his voice barely a whisper. "They'll find us."

Federov nodded, though he was not so sure. The *Kursk* was at 350 feet—shallow for a submarine, but deep enough to make rescue a race against time. The escape pod at the rear of the control room was inaccessible, buried under tons of twisted steel. The aft hatch was their only hope, but the flooding and pressure made it a long shot. Federov tapped again, his rhythm faltering as the cold seeped into his bones. He thought of his wife, Elena, back in Severomorsk, and their newborn son, Alexei. He had promised to be home for the boy's first birthday. Now, that promise felt like a cruel joke.

The compartment was a hellscape of twisted metal and flickering lights, the emergency lamp's glow cast long shadows across the faces of the survivors. The air was growing thinner, each breath more of a struggle. The water level was up to Federov's knees, the icy liquid numbed his legs and sapped his strength. He tapped again—three short, three long, three short—his hands trembling as the wrench slipped from his fingers and clattered to the deck. He reached for it, his movements sluggish, his vision swam as the cold and lack of oxygen took their toll.

Federov thought of Captain Kolesnikov, a man he had admired since joining the *Kursk* two years ago. Kolesnikov had been a steady hand, a commander who had led with courage and precision. Earlier, Federov had been in the control room, watching Kolesnikov, sharp with focus, prepare for the *Shkval* demonstration. Now Kolesnikov was gone, along with the forward crew, and Federov was trapped in a dying sub, his only hope a faint SOS signal that might never be heard.

Pyotr Velikiy (Peter the Great), 25 nautical miles northeast of the Kursk wreck

Lieutenant Commander Dmitry Sokolov stood in the *Pyotr Velikiy's* weapons control centre, his hands trembling as he watched the sonar plot. The *Admiral Kharlamov's* Ka-27PL Orel's destruction confirmed his worst fears—the Americans were not only present but fighting back with advanced weaponry. Sokolov, a 35-year-old weapons officer with thinning hair and a perpetual scowl, had been on edge all morning, his deal with the Chinese weighed on him like a death sentence. He had given Captain Li Jun partial *Shkval* schematics—propulsion and guidance systems—but the complete data, including the warhead design, was on the *Kursk*. Now the *Kursk* was gone, and Sokolov was trapped between a vengeful Russian navy and a Chinese operative who would not take no for an answer.

Li Jun stepped into the weapons control centre, his new Russian naval officer's uniform and sidearm blending in among the Russian crew. He carried a small encrypted device in his pocket, a tool to extract data from the ship's systems. "Sokolov," he hissed in halting Russian, his voice low. "The *Kursk* is gone. I need the rest of the data—now."

Sokolov's face paled, his eyes darting to the door. "I told you—the warhead schematics were on the *Kursk*," he said, his voice trembling. "I can get you the *Pyotr Velikiy's* ASW data, but that's all I have."

Li Jun's eyes narrowed, his hand brushing the concealed knife in his belt. "That's not enough," he said, his tone cold. "You promised the *Shkval*. Find a way, or I will make sure Chernov knows about your little side deal."

Sokolov swallowed hard, his mind racing. He accessed the ship's database, pulling up the *Pyotr Velikiy's* ASW protocols—sonar frequencies, torpedo guidance algorithms, and depth charge patterns. It was not the *Shkval*, but it was valuable. He copied the data to a USB drive, his hands shaking as he handed it to Li Jun. "This is all I can do," he said, his voice cracking. "Get out before they catch us." The *Pyotr Velikiy's* ASW protocols contained sonar frequencies, torpedo guidance algorithms, and depth charge patterns—but only partial data on the *Shkval*. He knew Li Jun would probably come for him again, possibly to kill him to save the USD500,000 payment and keep it for himself. The thought made his stomach churn.

Li Jun pocketed the drive, his mind already on his next move. The Chinese delegation had evacuated, but he had planted a listening device in the comms room, intercepting the signals between the *Pyotr Velikiy* and the fleet. He had heard of the ULF transmissions—two American subs, not one. He would relay that intel to Zhang Wei before they reached Murmansk, ensuring China's advantage in the unfolding chaos.

Li Jun's mission was clear: acquire as much intel as possible before exfiltrating. The *Shkval* was lost, but the *Pyotr Velikiy's* ASW protocols were a valuable consolation prize. He knew the Russians would be too focused on the Americans to notice his actions, at least for now. But he needed to move fast. The Northern Fleet was on high alert, and if Chernov or Rostov discovered his espionage, he would be a dead man. He slipped into the *Pyotr Velikiy's* comms room under the towering bridge and adjusted the listening device he had planted earlier. The small, encrypted device intercepted ULF signals between the American subs, confirming what he had suspected: two US submarines were in the area. The communications crew and officer of the watch ignored him in his Russian naval officer's uniform. To them, he was just another command officer doing his watch check, and they wanted to look busy rather than face a reprimand for idleness. He had relayed the intel to Admiral Zhang Wei via a secure channel, ensuring China's advantage in the unfolding chaos. But Li Jun's mission was not over. He needed to extract more data from *Pyotr Velikiy's* systems before finding a way off the ship.

Li Jun's mind raced as he accessed the comms terminal, his fingers flew over the keyboard and bypassed the security protocols with a preloaded exploit. The data, including fleet movements, sonar frequencies, and ASW patterns, began downloading. It was not the *Shkval*, but it was valuable—a prize that would advance China's naval ambitions. The Russians were distracted but he needed to move fast, access to the engineering systems in particular would enable him to extract detailed technical information on the two KN-3 nuclear marine propulsion units with their GT3A-688 steam turbines—valuable intelligence for the rapidly growing Chinese Naval fleet.

USS *Toledo, 12 nautical miles south of the Kursk wreck*

"Conn, Sonar," said Lieutenant Dave Carter, "I am picking up faint tapping. Hull strikes, SOS pattern. Aft section of the *Kursk*—there appear to be survivors, sir." Brennan's stomach twisted, a wave of guilt crashed over him. Survivors. Trapped in a dying sub, at 350 feet, with no hope of rescue. He had been the one to get too close, to trigger this nightmare by colliding with the *Kursk* during her baffle-clearing manoeuvre. The Russian sub had fired a torpedo in self-defence—a miss, thank God—but the *Memphis* had retaliated with a Mark 48, sinking the *Kursk* and dooming her crew. Brennan thought of the men in the aft section, with families waiting back home. But he could not do anything—not now, not with the Russian fleet closing in.

"Keep listening," Brennan said quietly, his voice hoarse. "But our priority is survival. We cannot help them now."

The *Toledo* was far from what he would describe as mission capable — her sail gone, her reactor strained, and her crew severely knocked around. The collision with the *Kursk* had been Brennan's worst nightmare come true. The Norfolk command orders had bordered on insanity. Brennan thought of the *Kursk's* men—now at the bottom of the Barents Sea. The guilt weighed on him like a lead shroud, but there was no time for remorse.

USS *Memphis, ten nautical miles southwest of the Kursk wreck*

In the *Memphis's* control room, the sonar replays still echoing in Rourke's ears. The Mark 48 had done its job—too well. The secondary explosion from the *Kursk's Shkval* rocket fuel and the ordinance in the *Kursk's* torpedo room was unlike anything he had heard, a roar that drowned out even the *Kursk's* death throes. The Russian sub was gone, and with her, 118 men. Rourke, a 38-year-old veteran with a square jaw and piercing hazel eyes, felt the weight of those lives on his shoulders. He had fired to save the *Toledo* and its crew, but this was a massacre.

"Conn, Sonar," said Lieutenant Mike Hensley, "Debris field confirmed. *Kursk* is… she is on the bottom, sir. But I am picking up faint tapping—SOS signals from the aft section."

Rourke's hazel eyes darkened. Survivors. He thought of the men trapped in the *Kursk's* aft section, with families waiting back home. But he could do nothing—not with the Russian fleet closing in. "Status on *Toledo*?" he asked, his voice steady despite the turmoil in his chest.

"Still with us," Hensley replied. "Bearing one-eight-zero, range two nautical miles. She is noisy, but moving—eight knots."

"Set course to put us between the *Toledo* and the Russian northern fleet," Rourke ordered. "We will cover her retreat." He glanced at XO Bill Travers, whose face was pale but resolute. "The Russians will come for us now. We need to be ghosts and get the hell out of here, while covering the *Toledo's* retreat."

"Hayes, message *Toledo*. Can you request a status update?" Rourke ordered. At the comms station, Ensign Laura Hayes adjusted her headset. "Message sent to *Toledo*, sir," she reported, her voice steady. "They're requesting cover—they're in bad shape."

"Rig for ultra-quiet, battle stations," Rourke said, his mind racing. "Ahead one-third, come right to zero-nine-zero. We will draw the Russian fleet away from the *Toledo* and draw fire if we must."

Rourke assessed their tactical situation. The *Memphis* had several Sea Lances remaining and a full complement of Mark 48 torpedoes, although he doubted the Russians would risk another Ka-27PL after his Sea Lance demonstration. Still, the Russian fleet was closing in, a net of steel and sonar extending across the Barents Sea. The *Pyotr Velikiy* was 25 nautical miles north, but her escorts were closer—the *Admiral Levchenko* and *Admiral Kharlamov* were bearing down fast at 25 and 15 knots respectively. Their active sonar pings illuminated the water like a thunderstorm, a relentless drumbeat that promised death. Both Russian destroyers carried a formidable array of rocket-propelled depth charges and light homing torpedoes that could be lobbed at their position at any time. The *Admiral Kharlamov* was behaving in a way that it looked very likely she was preparing to launch her deadly SS-N-14 Silex anti-submarine rockets.

Rourke thought of his wife, Rachel, and their two children, Sarah and Michael, back in Groton, Connecticut. He had promised to be home for Sarah's birthday next month. Now, that felt like a distant dream. The sinking of the *Kursk* was a tragedy, but it was also a declaration of war.

Ka-27 Zvezda (Star), en route to Murmansk

Admiral Zhang Wei sat in the cramped cabin of the Ka-27 Zvezda, his hands clasped tightly around his briefcase as the helicopter headed south toward Murmansk. Zhang's mind was anything but calm, despite the smooth ride of the Kamov. The sinking of the *Kursk* had thrown their plans into disarray. The *Shkval*—a supercavitating torpedo that could revolutionise China's naval strategy—was partially lost, its secrets buried in the Barents Sea. However, Captain Li Jun, his intelligence operative, had stayed behind on the *Pyotr Velikiy*.

Zhang's sharp features were set in a mask of determination as he opened his briefcase, revealing a secure satellite phone. He dialled a number, his voice low in Mandarin as the connection crackled to life. "General Chen, this is Zhang Wei," he said, his tone steady. "The *Kursk* is lost—torpedoed by the Americans. Li Jun has partial *Shkval* schematics and ASW data from the *Pyotr Velikiy*. He has confirmed two US submarines in the operations area—likely the *Toledo* and *Memphis*, as our naval intelligence indicated."

General Chen, head of PLAN intelligence, replied in a clipped tone. "Good work, Admiral," he said, his voice steady. "The *Shkval* data is a start, but the ASW protocols are just as valuable. Ensure Li Jun extracts safely—we will need that intel to counter the Americans in the South China Sea."

"Understood," Zhang said, his mind already on the next steps. The sinking of the *Kursk* was a tragedy for the Russians, but for China, it was an opportunity. The Americans and Russians would be too busy pointing fingers to notice China's quiet acquisition of their secrets.

Zhang's sharp mind raced as he considered the implications. A fundamental change in military technology, the *Shkval* outran any Western countermeasure. The *Varyag*, a scrapped carrier China had bought from Ukraine, was being refitted in Dalian, but its air wing was years from becoming operational. The *Shkval* would give China's navy the teeth needed to deter American carriers from entering contested waters. Li Jun's intel—partial *Shkval* schematics and the *Pyotr Velikiy's* ASW protocols—would be a start, but Zhang knew they needed more. He had instructed Li Jun to extract as much data as possible before exfiltration, and he prayed the operative would make it out alive.

Zhang thought back to a previous mission with Li Jun, one of his most skilled covert operatives.

Operation Sea Serpent's mission was to steal advanced sonar technology. The *Oyashio*-class was a series of Japanese diesel-electric attack submarines built by Kawasaki, with a crew of 70, including ten officers. The submarine featured an Oki ZQQ-6 hull-mounted sonar and flank arrays, as well as a towed array. Chinese Naval intelligence had discovered that the Japanese were integrating a next-generation towed array sonar, the OQR-3, capable of detecting China's noisy Han-class subs at unprecedented ranges—a threat to PLAN operations in the East China Sea.

Admiral Zhang had tasked Li with leading a small team to infiltrate the facility, extract the sonar blueprints, and exfiltrate undetected, all while evading JMSDF patrols and American Navy oversight from nearby Yokosuka.

Li had assembled a four-man unit, including a demolitions expert, a communications officer, and a diver, and had trained them in a secluded bay near Qingdao. The plan hinged on a nighttime insertion via a disguised fishing trawler, with Li posing as a merchant sailor to approach the Japanese coast. The stakes were astronomical: success would give China a technological edge, but failure risked diplomatic fallout, especially with the USN 7th Fleet stationed nearby. Zhang's orders were explicit: "No traces, no witnesses. This is for the Motherland's future."

On July 15, 1994, under a moonless sky, Li's team launched from the trawler three nautical miles off Yokosuka. The diver, Petty Officer Chen, swam ashore with a waterproof satchel, planting a micro-drone to scout the facility. Li had monitored the operation from a concealed inflatable raft, as JMSDF P-3C Orion aircraft circled overhead, their sonar buoys dropping into the water. The drone relayed images of the prototype hangar, guarded by two sentries and a motion-sensor grid. Li's demolitions expert, Lieutenant Wei, neutralised the sensors with an EMP pulse, allowing Chen to breach the perimeter.

Once inside, Chen photographed the OQR-3's schematics—detailed blueprints of its hydrophone arrays and signal processing algorithms. A patrol boat's spotlight nearly compromised the team's exfiltration when it swept the beach. Li, reacting instinctively, ordered a diversion: Wei detonated a small charge offshore, drawing the JMSDF's attention. As the alarms blared, Chen swam back, the satchel clutched tightly. Li guided the raft through a kelp bed, evading the base's radar sweeps, but a USN Sea Ark Force Protection Small Craft, FPSC, rapidly moved at 35 knots from the other side of the bay. Its intense spotlights, linked to M2 50-calibre machine guns, swept the water. Li held his breath; he had killed the electric engine as a precaution, and they all lay flat on the hull. The raft's rubber hull blended with the sea noise until the American harbour patrol craft withdrew.

Within two days, the team returned, giving the blueprints to Zhang. The mission's success earned Li a promotion to captain and Zhang's trust, though the admiral's praise was curt: "You have proven your worth, Li.

Do not falter." The OQR-3 data sped up China's sonar development, enhancing the Type 093 submarine program. However, the close call with the US Navy harbour patrol craft reinforced Li's humiliation from Western superiority, a wound reopened by the later South China Sea incident. This mission had taught Li Jun the value of audacity and the cost of exposure, shaping his later approach to Sokolov—using leverage and secrecy to secure the *Shkval* intelligence.

For Li, Operation Sea Serpent was a crucible, blending pride in his success with a burning desire to erase the memory of his near capture. Under Zhang's mentorship, he honed a ruthless edge, viewing every mission as a step toward China's naval ascendancy—a mindset that drove him to the Barents Sea in 2000, where the *Kursk's* secrets became his next prize.

Zhang hoped Li Jun would make it out of this mission alive.

Pyotr Velikiy, 25 nautical miles northwest of the Kursk wreck

Chernov's face twisted with rage, his voice a low snarl as he turned to Rostov. "The Americans," he growled, his hands trembling with fury. "They have sunk the *Kursk*. What Akula hunter-killer submarines do we have in the western region of the operations area in the Barents Sea?"

Rostov's mind raced, his brown eyes narrowing as he recalled the fleet's deployment. "The K-335 *Gepard* Akula-class hunter-killer submarine, sir," he replied, his voice steady despite the tension on the bridge. "Captain Yuri Volodin's command—she is positioned twenty nautical miles southwest of the *Kursk's* last known position." Chernov's dark eyes burned with determination, his voice a growl as he issued his orders. "I know Captain Yuri Volodin, an aggressive commander, perfect. Contact the K-335 *Gepard* immediately," he barked, his cigarette falling to the deck. "Advise Volodin to find those Yankee Los Angeles-class submarines—the damaged one and her accomplice. Search and destroy with extreme prejudice. I want them on the bottom of the Barents Sea, Rostov."

Rostov nodded, relaying the orders to the comms officer. "Signal the K-335 *Gepard*," he ordered, his voice steady. "*Kursk* is down—Two American Los Angeles-class submarines in the area. Search and destroy with extreme prejudice."

Chernov's rage threatened to overwhelm him as he stared at the tactical plot. He knew his future was at stake here; it would be a success or a public court-martial.

Akula-class Submarine K-335 Gepard, 40 nautical miles northwest of the Kursk wreck

Captain Yuri Volodin stood in the control room of the K-335 *Gepard*; his dark eyes fixed on the sonar plot as the encrypted message from the *Pyotr Velikiy* came through. The Akula-class submarine, named for its speed and agility, was at 200 feet, moving at ten knots, her MGK-500 sonar suite scanning the noisy Barents Sea for any sign of the enemy. Volodin's shaved head gleamed under the dim red lights; a full-length scar across the right side of his face gave him a somewhat menacing appearance—a memento from a near-fatal training accident in 1995— he scowled as he processed the orders.

"Con, Comms," reported Lieutenant Alexey Bulavin, a young officer originally from Moscow, his voice steady despite the tension in the room. "Message from the *Pyotr Velikiy*: KURSK SUNK BY HOSTILE AMERICAN LOS ANGELES-CLASS SUBMARINES. SEARCH AND DESTROY WITH EXTREME PREJUDICE. TARGETS IN THE WESTERN REGION OF THE OPERATIONS AREA."

Volodin's pulse quickened, his dark eyes burning with fury as he acknowledged the order. "Message received," he growled, his voice cold and precise. "Signal the *Pyotr Velikiy*: GEPARD ACKNOWLEDGES.

COMMENCING SEARCH AND DESTROY MISSION." He turned to his crew, his scar twisting with the motion. "That explains that massive explosion; the *Kursk* is gone, and our mission is to sink the two Yankee submarines that are responsible for the *Kursk's* destruction and the deaths of our comrades. Come right to zero-nine-zero—turn east. Increase speed to thirty knots. Battle stations, we are hunting those Yankee bastards."

The *Gepard* turned east, her single screw powering the Akula hunter-killer to thirty knots, her titanium hull slicing through the icy depths of the Barents Sea. Volodin's thoughts were on Dmitri Kolesnikov, his close friend since their days at the naval academy in St. Petersburg. They had graduated together in 1988, two ambitious young officers determined to restore Russia's maritime glory. Volodin, now 38, was a rising star in the Northern Fleet, his tactical brilliance had earned him command of the *Gepard* in 1998.

However, the scar on his face was a constant reminder of how easily things could go wrong— in that case, a torpedo loading mishap during a training exercise that had killed two of his crew and left him with a permanent memento of the event. Kolesnikov had pulled Volodin from the wreckage, a debt he could no longer repay.

Now Kolesnikov was gone, Volodin would make the Americans pay dearly. "Sonar, full sweep," Volodin ordered, his voice steady but laced with venom. "Find those Los Angeles-class subs. They will not escape us."

Sonar Officer Lieutenant Ivan Kuznetsov, a 29-year-old prodigy who had joined the navy to escape a childhood marked by poverty in Murmansk, where his father, a fisherman, had drowned during a storm when he was ten, adjusted the MGK-500 suite, his hands steady despite the pressure. The navy had given him purpose, but losing his father had left him with a deep-seated fear of failure. "Aye, aye, sir," Kuznetsov replied, his voice tight as he focused the sonar array eastward. "Sweeping now—active pings at 50 decibels, passive listening prioritised."

At Volodin's side stood Executive Officer Commander Alexei Morozov, a 35-year-old veteran with a stocky build and a perpetual frown, who monitored the crew's performance. Morozov had served with Volodin for two years on the *Gepard* where a bond had been forged during a harrowing mission in 1999 when the *Gepard* evaded a NATO ASW net in the Norwegian Sea. Morozov's wife, Elena, had died of cancer two years ago, leaving him with a teenage daughter, Sofia, whom he rarely saw. The navy was his life now, and he channelled his grief into his duty. "Crew efficiency at 92%, sir," Morozov reported, his voice gruff. "Weapons officer, status on tubes?"

Weapons Officer Lieutenant Viktor Popov, a wiry 31-year-old with a buzz cut and a quick temper, responded from his station. Popov had grown up in a military family in Vladivostok, and his father, a retired admiral, had pushed him into the navy. Popov resented the pressure but excelled under it, his skill with torpedoes was unmatched in the Northern Fleet. "Tubes three and four loaded with 53-65K torpedoes, sir," Popov replied, his voice sharp with determination. "Guidance systems active—ready to fire on your command."

Volodin nodded, his dark eyes burning with a predator's focus. The *Gepard's* crew was a well-oiled machine. Kolesnikov's death had hit them all hard—Volodin most of all—but they would channel that rage into the hunt. Volodin would ensure that the American submarines would be destroyed.

USS Toledo, eight nautical miles south of the Kursk wreck

Commander Tom Brennan stood in *Toledo's* control room. He fixed his eyes on the condition of his men. Half the crew had sustained injuries: Lieutenant Dave Carter had a concussion from slamming his head against the sonar console in the forward comms room and was barely functioning; yet in the current emergency, he could not let him leave his post. XO Paul Reese gasped in pain from his cracked rib every time he moved. his cracked rib aggravated by the impact. Several enlisted men had suffered cuts, bruises, and broken bones from being thrown around the control room. Yet, they were still functioning as a solid, disciplined team and he felt proud to lead them.

Conn, Comms," said Lieutenant Sarah Carter, her voice steady despite the chaos. "Message from *Memphis* on the ULF: *TOLEDO* TWO 53-65KS EVADED—DECOYS AND RAPID SURFACING CONFIRMED. *MEMPHIS* DESTROYED KA-27PL ASW HELO WITH SEALANCE. STAY QUIET AND GET OUT OF DODGE. WE WILL LEAD THE RUSSIANS AWAY."

"Carter, we are close enough to *Memphis* for direct ship-to-ship dialogue, correct?" Brennan asked Carter. "Correct, Captain, do you want me to patch you through to the *Memphis*?" said Lieutenant Sarah Carter.

"Make it so, Coms," Brennan replied.

"Commander Brennan, actual, Commander Rourke, actual," came Rourke's answer. Brennan stood in the dimly lit control room of the USS *Toledo*; the faint hum of the HVAC and control screens a steady pulse beneath the tension crackling through the crew. The ultra-low-frequency (ULF) communications system, a lifeline for submerged subs, crackled to life as Brennan leaned into the microphone, his voice steady despite the stakes.

"Tom, this is *Memphis* Actual," Rourke transmitted, the ULF signal penetrating the depths to reach the *Toledo*. "I am aware of your close call with those *Admiral Kharlamov* torpedoes. Decoy saved the first, and that surfacing trick was damn gutsy—well done. We have got your back." He paused, "The *Admiral Kharlamov* is being joined by a swarm of Udaloy-class destroyers closing from the north. *Toledo's* position, exposed by the surfacing, is a beacon to Chernov's vengeful Northern Fleet."

Rourke continued, his tone shifting to a grim update. "*Memphis* engaged and took out an ASW Ka-27PL with Sea Lance. Likely a wake-up call for the Russians. They will be scrambling to adapt, but it bought us a window. However, the Northern Fleet, are now alerted to this new capability and will redouble their efforts."

Con sonar, "Sir, three Udaloy IIs—*Marshal Shaposhnikov*, *Admiral Tributs*, and *Vice-Admiral Kulakov*—bearing zero-one-zero, 25 nautical miles, closing at 28 knots. Active pings are increasing." Brennan nodded. Chernov's destroyers, armed with SS-N-14 Silex missiles and 53-65K torpedoes, were bearing down. Brennan's damaged sub, with failing reactor pumps, could not outrun them silently.

Rourke made his call. "Tom, I am going noisy—full flank speed to draw their fire. *Memphis* will act as a decoy and pull the swarm off you. Head west to Norwegian waters, 150 miles out. Rourke out." He switched to the mic. "All hands, battle stations!

The ULF crackled with Brennan's reply: "Copy that, John. Pumps are critical—no more than four hours. Thanks for the cover. Good luck." Brennan felt the weight of their USS *Birmingham* days, the mentor-student bond now a lifeline.

He turned to Carter. "Plot an erratic course—zigzag at 10-degree intervals. Keep us behind the *Memphis* and the Udaloy's." The *Toledo* surged forward, her hull groaning as active sonar pinged back, revealing the 25 nautical mile range.

Brennan knew that *Memphis* going noisy was an invitation to a torpedo and rocket attack. Still, Rourke was a master tactician— and better the *Memphis*, with its intact systems, than the limping *Toledo*.

The first SS-N-14 splash was spotted at 20 nautical miles; its rocket-assisted launch captured the sonar crews' full focus. Brennan held the tactical plotting table, thinking of his family, his crew, and Rourke. "Good luck, John," he muttered, steering the *Toledo* away from danger and towards the safety of the Norwegian coast. The Northern Fleet's wake-up call had begun, and Rourke's loud sacrifice was the *Toledo's* only hope.

Brennan exhaled, his body trembling with adrenaline as he processed Rourke's message. The *Memphis* would play decoy, drawing the Russian surface fleet away with noisemakers and increased speed. The *Admiral Kharlamov's* sonar pings faded as the destroyer turned north, chasing the *Memphis's* false signatures. He hoped the three other Russian Udaloy-class destroyers would follow the *Admiral Kharlamov's* lead.

The *Toledo* slipped away from immediate danger, her noisy reactor and damaged hull no longer the fleet's primary target. "Maintain two hundred feet, ahead five knots, slow and as silent as we can manage," Brennan ordered, his voice steady. "Let us put some distance between us and the Russians while Rourke buys us time."

The *Toledo* crept west at five knots, her hull groaned as she moved through the icy depths of the Barents Sea. Brennan fixed his eyes on the sonar plot and breathed a sigh of relief. They had evaded the immediate threat, but the Northern Fleet would not stop hunting. The *Memphis* had given them a chance, and Brennan would make the most of it—he had to get his crew home.

In the aft section of the ship, Lieutenant Mark Evans wiped the sweat from his brow, the confined air in the engine room thick with the metallic tang of overheating machinery and the low hum of the S6G reactor struggling against its wounds. The USS *Toledo*, had barely escaped annihilation in the icy Barents Sea, her hull still reverberating from the emergency surfacing that dodged the second 53-65K torpedo from the *Admiral Kharlamov*. Evans was the reactor department head, a Virginia Tech graduate with a knack for coaxing life from nuclear hearts under duress. His hands, callused from years of drills and deployments, hovered over the control panel as alarms flickered amber, warning of the failing cooling pumps that had been damaged in the collision with the *Kursk*.

The intercom crackled, and Captain Tom Brennan's voice cut through the din, steady but edged with urgency. "Evans, this is the captain. Report to the conn immediately."

Evans acknowledged with a crisp "Aye, sir," and made his way forward through the narrow corridors, dodging crewmen securing loose gear. The *Toledo's* 130 souls were on edge, the *Kursk's* sinking a grim reminder of their own fragility. Reaching the control room, Evans found Brennan at the tactical plot table, eyes scanning the tactical plot where Rourke's *Memphis* was drawing fire like a sacrificial lamb.

"Lieutenant," Brennan said without preamble, his voice low to avoid carrying. "We're heading west, full stealth, toward Norwegian waters. One hundred fifty nautical miles to safety, but the Russian Northern Fleet is closing the noose. The *Memphis* is going noisy to pull the, *Admiral Kharlamov* and *Admiral Levchenko*, off us— but more Udaloy-class destroyers, *Shaposhnikov*, *Tributs*, and *Kulakov* are joining the hunt. They are 20 nautical miles out and gaining. Our position's compromised from that surfacing stunt, but it saved us."

Evans nodded. The emergency blow had vented the ballast tanks explosively, propelling the sub to the surface in an emergency ascent, and disrupting the Russian torpedo's wake-homing target acquisition software. But the manoeuvre had stressed the already battered pumps, and their bearings were grinding audibly—a death knell in submarine warfare where noise was the ultimate betrayer.

"I need you to get those reactor pumps settled and as quiet as possible," Brennan continued, his gaze locking on Evans. "Any transient, any cavitation, and we're lit up like a Christmas tree. The *Admiral Kharlamov's* Polinom sonar suite is state-of-the-art, and they are hunting us, and those Udaloy's have Rastrub-B missiles ready. We are in no condition to fight—hull integrities at 85%, and the reactor temperatures are pushing 280°C. Bypass is holding, but if we redline, we're dead in the water."

"Sir, the primary pump's impeller is misaligned from the collision," Evans replied. "The secondary's compensating, but the vibrations at 15 hertz—enough to echo through the thermocline. I will rig a manual dampener, isolate the flow using auxiliary valves, and manually recirculate coolant through the heat exchangers. It'll drop the noise by 20 decibels, but we'll lose 5 knots in efficiency."

Brennan placed a hand on Evans's shoulder, a rare gesture in the high-stakes world of sub command. "Make it happen. Every man aboard is counting on you. Hensley's assisting in the torpedo room—get him on it too if needed. We are diving to 150 feet, under the thermocline layer. West at eight knots, silent as we can be, to safety, I am relying on you, Evans."

"Aye, Captain," Evans said, saluting sharply before heading back. The reactor's glow casting eerie shadows through the shielding as he descended into the engine spaces. The crew there—Petty Officer Ramirez at the throttles, Seaman Lee monitoring pressure—looked to him with expectant eyes. "Listen up," Evans ordered. "Captain's directive: west to Norway, stealth mode. Pumps need to whisper. Ramirez, isolate pump one—reroute through the secondary loop. Lee, monitor delta-T; keep it under 50°C differential."

As they worked, Evans' thoughts drifted to his wife back in Groton, her letters tucked in his bunk. The *Toledo* was not built for this—her 110-meter hull was optimised for ASW, not fleeing a fleet. But Brennan's leadership, honed under Rourke's wing, inspired confidence. The pumps protested one last time before settling into a muffled purr and the noise signature dropped to near-undetectable levels.

Back on the conn, Brennan watched the sonar as the *Memphis's* decoys flared, pulling the Russian swarm north. "Good work, Evans," he muttered over the intercom. The *Toledo* slipped westward, a shadow evading giant, her fate hinging on silence in the deep.

Udaloy-class Destroyer Admiral Kharlamov, 18 nautical miles northeast of Toledo

The *Admiral Kharlamov* cut through the Barents Sea swells at 15 knots, her hull groaning under the strain of irregular manoeuvres designed to evade any lurking threats. Captain Pyotrov gripped the bridge railing, his eyes scoping the horizon where the American Los Angeles-class submarine had last been spotted on radar—surfaced, vulnerable, but now vanished into the depths with that telltale transient noise echoing through the sonar feeds.

"Con sonar, report!" Pyotrov barked, his voice cutting through the cacophony of alarms and crew confirmations in the Combat Information Center (CIC) below.

"Transient confirmed designated Target 1, Captain. High-speed screw cavitation, bearing 045, range eight nautical miles and increasing. Possible evasion manoeuvre—submarine diving deep."

Pyotrov's lips curled into a grim smile. The Americans thought they could play cat and mouse in Russian waters? Not today. "Weapons, firing solution locked?"

"Affirmative, sir. Barrage configured: eight depth charges via Silex payloads. Launch sequence initiated."

The destroyer shuddered as a salvo of SS-N-14 Silex missiles erupted from her forward quad launchers, flames licking the morning sky like a dragon's breath. Their solid-fuel boosters ignited with a thunderous roar that vibrated through the ship's superstructure. Each SS-N-14, a sleek 7.6-meter behemoth weighing over three tons, arced skyward on a parabolic trajectory, guided by the ship's fire-control radar. At the apex, they would release their deadly cargo—a UMGT-1 homing torpedo or, in this case, depth charges set for a patterned spread to saturate the target area.

Pyotrov watched the exhaust trails fade into the polar sky as the missiles' inertial navigation systems plotted a course to the submarine's last known position. The *Admiral Kharlamov* carried two quad launchers—eight missiles ready in total, with reloads in the magazine below decks. But a whole barrage like this was a statement: overwhelm, do not chase.

In the CIC, Lieutenant Commander Nadia Volkova monitored the tactical display. Sweat beaded on her forehead despite the chill air pumping through the vents. "Missiles away, time to impact: two minutes. Sonar pings show the target altering course—erratic, but they're not fooling us."

The ship heeled to port as the helmsman executed another zigzag, Pyotrov's orders keeping them unpredictable. Overhead, the Ka-27 helicopter—callsign "Volk", meaning Wolf—throttled up on the aft deck, its rotors whipping the sea spray into a frenzy. " Volk, deploy dipping sonar. Bracket the impact zone."

"Acknowledged, Captain. Lifting off."

"Standoff well clear of Target 1, transient Volk," Pyotrov ordered, "I don't want a repeat of losing another Ka-27PL ASW asset and flight crew."

As the helo rose, the second quad launcher rotated with a hydraulic whine, aligning for follow-up if needed. Pyotrov's mind raced through the intel briefs: the American LA-class sub, likely an SSN-688 variant, was fast and quiet, equipped with a single screw. However, that noisy transient—perhaps a decoy launch or mechanical glitch—had betrayed its location.

A muffled boom echoed across the waves as the first Silex reached its drop point. The missile's payload separated cleanly, the depth charge plummeting into the abyss on a parachute retarder before detonating at 300 to 500 feet.

Hydrophones registered the shockwave—a deep, resonant thud that propagated a water column designed to crush hulls or force a sub to surface.

"Detonation confirmed," Volkova reported. "Secondary transients— possible hull stress on target. Wait... active sonar return! Submarine ascending rapidly, bearing 050, range six nautical miles."

Pyotrov's pulse quickened. "All hands, brace for counterfire. Torpedo tubes, stand by with countermeasures." The Barents Sea was a graveyard of Cold War relics, and tonight might add another. The

Admiral Kharlamov's sister ship in the task force—the nearby *Admiral Levchenko*—signalled readiness, their own ASW suites lit up. Pyotrov would not share the glory. "Weapons, prepare torpedo tubes. If it surfaces, we finish it."

The ship shuddered again, this time from the ocean's retaliation: a distant underwater explosion rippled through the hull, possibly a countermeasure or self-inflicted damage from the sub. Volk radioed in: "Dipping sonar active. Target signature weakening—possible flooding."

In the bowels of the destroyer, the engineering team monitored the twin gas turbines as they pushed the ship through the chop. Chief Engineer Sergei Ivanov wiped grime from his face, barked the order to maintain speed. "Keep her steady! If we lose propulsion now, we're sitting ducks."

Back on the bridge, Pyotrov scanned the radar scopes. No surface contacts had been made yet, but the air hummed with tension. The remaining four Silex missiles waited in their tubes, ready for a second barrage. Each carried a single payload—conventional high explosive depth charges—but in volley, they formed an inescapable net. The Udaloy's design excelled here: anti-submarine warfare was her raison d'être, with RBU-6000 rocket launchers for close-in defence if things got hairy.

Minutes stretched like hours. Then, a breakthrough: "Con sonar, target breaching! Surfacing at four nautical miles, emergency blow!"

Pyotrov grabbed the binoculars. There, amid the foaming whitecaps, the dark silhouette of the LA-class sub broke the surface, listing slightly, steam venting from her sail. "Gunnery, target the conning tower. Destroy them now."

The 130mm AK-130 turret swivelled, belching shells that splashed harmlessly ahead of the sub.

The sky lite up again as the *Admiral Kharlamov's* second Ka-27PL Volk exploded in a fireball. "Pizdetz, another ASW Helo and flight crew destroyed. XO Weapons prepare for torpedo attack and counter measures. That lunatic in command of that American submarine is a real cowboy." Pyotrov vented.

Memphis, eight nautical miles northeast of the Admiral Kharlamov

Commander John Rourke gripped the periscope handles in the USS *Memphis*'s control room; his eyes locked on the sonar waterfall display as his Los Angeles-class submarine thrummed at flank speed. His bold decision to go noisy had worked—drawing Admiral Viktor Chernov's vengeful armada away from the westerly retreating *Toledo*, her damaged reactor pumps a ticking clock. The *Memphis*, at 35 knots, surged north, her seven-bladed screw churning a deliberate acoustic trail that screamed "here we are" to the enemy's sonar arrays.

"Captain, *Admiral Kharlamov* is eight nautical miles northeast, bearing zero-four-five, closing at 15 knots," reported Sonar Chief Petty Officer Dan Willis, his voice taut over the headset. They appear to be making way under irregular manoeuvres sir, possibly as a self-defence counter measure." The Udaloy-class destroyer, armed with its MGK-355 Polinom sonar and Rastrub-B missile systems, led the swarm—*Admiral Levchenko* was a further 15 nautical miles away, closing at 25 knots, their combined weapons systems a wall of Soviet-era armament.

Rourke nodded, his mind a tactical chessboard honed from decades of Cold War patrols. "Steady as she goes, XO. Keep drawing them north—away from Brennan." Lieutenant Commander Bill Travers, the executive officer, acknowledged with a crisp "Aye, sir," as he stood next to the Chief-of-the-boat at the helm station adjacent to the navigation plot. The *Memphis*'s diversion was a sacrificial play, buying the *Toledo* precious miles toward Norwegian territorial waters, where NATO air cover might intervene.

Suddenly, the sonar console erupted in alerts—transient spikes pierced the ambient ocean noise. "Con, sonar—multiple Silex launches detected! Two salvos, eight rockets each," Lieutenant Mike Hensley called out, his face paling under the red battle lights. The SS-N-14 Silex, a rocket-propelled anti-submarine weapon, streaked from the *Admiral Kharlamov's* launchers, their subsonic flight carrying payloads that could be UMGT-1 homing torpedoes or depth charges. At this range, Rourke could not discern—passive sonar only caught the ignition transients, not the warhead signatures.

"Rig for depth charges!" Rourke ordered, his voice a steady anchor amid the rising tension. "XO, prepare torpedo countermeasures— Nixie decoys on standby." The crew scrambled, securing loose gear and donning impact harnesses. The *Memphis* had no choice but to sit and wait for the splashdown as the Silex rockets arced overhead in a deadly parabola, their 185-kilogram payloads designed to plunge into the sea and hunt.

Seconds stretched into eternity. "Con, sonar—splash detected! Multiple entries, depth charges confirmed," Hensley shouted. The ocean above erupted as the charges hit the water, sinking toward preset detonation depths. Rourke thought quickly, recalling Russian ASW tactics from intelligence briefs: dispersed patterns to blanket convergence zones, standard settings for submarine operational depths of 300 to 500 feet. The *Memphis* hovered at 400 feet, right in the kill box.

"Emergency blow—front planes to 25 degrees up! XO, all ahead flank. Engineering, give me 110% power, get us above 300 feet now!" Rourke commanded, channelling the lessons from his days in USS *Birmingham*. The control room lurched as the chief engineer throttled the S6G reactor beyond redline. The turbine screamed as 34,000 shaft horsepower drove the screw. Compressed air blasted into the ballast tanks, expelling water in a violent rush. The bow planes angled sharply, and the 6,900-ton sub catapulted upward, aided by the emergency blow and raw propulsion.

Below and behind them, the Silex depth charges initiated their detonation sequences—controlled explosions rippling through the water column in a patterned grid, designed to crush hulls with hydrostatic shock. The first blasts hammered the *Memphis's* stern, shock waves propagating like thunderclaps, further propelling the ascending hull beyond 45 knots towards the surface. The sub bucked wildly. Alarms wailed. Pressure gauges spiked.

The *Memphis* breached the surface with a massive splash; her sail erupted through the waves casting geysers of foam and spray. The crew clung to the handrails and consoles, their bodies were thrown against their restraints as the boat slammed back down, and rolled in the choppy sea. "Hang on!" Rourke yelled, his own frame braced against the periscope stand. The shock waves from the underwater detonations slammed against the hull and violently rocked the surfaced sub as if it were a wine cork in a storm.

"XO, damage report!" Rourke barked as the chaos subsided.

Bill Travers scanned the boards, his voice steady amid the groans of settling metal. "A few cuts and bruises, sir—minor electrical shorts in auxiliary, but the ship's fine. Hull integrity holding at 100%. Reactor stable."

Rourke exhaled, wiping a trickle of blood from a split lip. "Emergency dive—get us under, 200 feet, rig for ultra quiet." The planes angled down, and the *Memphis* slipped beneath the waves, her acoustic cloak partially restored.

But respite was fleeting. "Con, sonar—sir, radar contact while surfaced: another Ka-27PL, five nautical miles northeast," Willis reported. The Russian ASW helicopter, NATO-coded Helix-A, hovered with its dipping sonar and torpedo payload, a persistent thorn in their evasion.

Rourke's lips curled in a grim smile. "Don't they ever learn? Weapons, Kline—firing solution on that Ka-27PL. Immediate launch of Sea Lance."

Lieutenant Commander Ed Kline, at the fire control console, tapped the plugin tablet synced to the BQQ-5 array. "Confirmed, Captain. Sea Lance in tube one, armed and ready. Full firing solution—range 4.5 nautical miles, bearing zero-five-zero."

"Fire," Rourke ordered.

For the second time in military history, the Sea Lance erupted from the torpedo tube. Breaching the surface in seconds, it streaked skyward at Mach 2.5, and homed on the Ka-27PL's heat signature. The helicopter's two-man crew were oblivious until the warhead detonated and their helicopter, spiralled into the sea.

"Con, sonar—Helix destroyed, splashdown confirmed. Well done, weps," Willis announced. A ripple of relieved, muted cheers echoed through the conn.

Rourke allowed a brief nod, but the Northern Fleet's swarm, alerted by the surfaced breach, would redouble their hunt. The *Memphis* had drawn blood, but the Russian Northern Fleet's vengeance loomed. "Steady west-northwest, 25 knots, depth 400 feet, take us under the thermocline," he commanded. "We have given Brennan his window— now let's make ours."

The *Memphis* glided deeper into the Barents' cold embrace, a temporary shield in the escalating shadow war.

CHAPTER 4

THE NOOSE TIGHTENS

Barents Sea,
August 12, 2000, 1215 — 1415 hours local time

Memphis glided through the icy depths of the Barents Sea; her 6,927-ton hull creeping at five knots, 400 feet down, her screw barely turning to minimise cavitation noise. The control room's red lights casting harsh shadows across the tense faces of the crew.

Commander John Rourke stood within the control center, watching the tactical plot. The Russian fleet was closing in—a net of steel and sonar stretched across the Barents Sea, led by the *Pyotr Velikiy*, the Kirov-class battlecruiser named after Peter the Great, the tsar who had modernised Russia's navy. The tactical situation was grim. He had narrowly avoided having his ship destroyed by a barrage of Silex depth charges launched from *Admiral Kharlamov*. But it could have been worse. He had successfully drawn away the Russian Northern Fleet from the crippled *Toledo*, risking his ship and crew in doing so.

The Northern Fleet was relentless, their active sonar pings illuminating the sonar screens like a thunderstorm. The *Admiral Kharlamov* and

Admiral Levchenko were 12 nautical miles away, closing at 15 knots; they slowed alternately to eight knots to activate their bow-mounted active sonar. Four more Ka-27PL helicopters, launched from the *Pyotr Velikiy* and its escorts, formed a deadly net, their dipping sonars probing the depths for the American sub. "Comms, get me *Toledo* on the ULF," Rourke ordered, cold sweat trickling down his spine. The ultra-low-frequency system was a top-secret lifeline, designed for SSN-to-SSN communication in the deepest, most hostile waters. It was slow at this range—messages would take minutes to transmit and decode—but it was their only option without breaking stealth.

"Aye, aye, sir," replied Ensign Laura Hayes, the *Memphis's* comms officer, her fingers flying over the ULF console. TOLEDO, THIS IS *MEMPHIS* ACTUAL. RUSSIAN FLEET CLOSING—ENTIRE NORTHERN FLEET INBOUND. CONTINUING TO EVADE. STATUS?

The ULF signal pulsed into the deep; its ultra-low-frequency waves undetectable. Rourke waited, his eyes scanned the sonar screen, each second felt like an eternity. The *Admiral Levchenko* was about to present as much of a problem as the *Admiral Kharlamov*. The *Memphis* had drawn considerable attention with the Sea Lance strikes. Still, the Russians were relentless—they would utilise their RPK-6 Vodopad anti-submarine missile torpedoes once they could get a firing solution. The only saving grace at present was that the relatively shallow and choppy Barents Sea created a lot of background sonar noise, meaning the destroyers would be having a difficult time achieving a reliable sonar lock on the *Memphis*.

The ULF receiver beeped, and a faint green light on the comms console signalled a message from *Toledo*. MEMPHIS, THIS IS *TOLEDO ACTUAL*. PROPULSION ONLINE, SAIL DAMAGE CAUSES NOISE ABOVE 5 KNOTS. MAINTAINING STRICT ELECTRONIC EMIS-SION CONTROL (EMCOM). CAN NOT EGRESS FAST. HEADING WEST OUT OF THE OPERATIONS ZONE. YOUR PLAN?

Rourke paced the control room, thinking about his reply, the red battle lights casting stark shadows on the crew's tense faces. The Barents Sea's continental shelf stretched beneath them, a shallow expanse of 400 to 900 feet cluttered with bottom echoes, shipping noise, and fractured sea ice—conditions that shortened detection ranges and turned every contact into a nerve-wracking puzzle.

The *Memphis* was silent at 8 knots, her hull and flank arrays vigilant. He had ordered the TB-29 thin-line towed array streamed astern, a silent sentinel, its hydrophones trailed hundreds of meters piercing the ambient clutter.

Rourke's noisy decoy run had pulled Chernov's Northern Fleet northward, away from the retreating crippled *Toledo*. Then, the sonar waterfall suddenly bloomed with an additional threat. "Con, sonar—new contact, designated Sierra Three. Akula-class submarine, bearing two-seven-zero, charging southwest at 35 knots. Range estimate: 18 nautical miles on that bearing. Captain they are moving to intercept the *Toledo*," Chief Petty Officer Dan Willis reported. The Akula, a Project 971 Shchuka-B, was bow-on to the *Toledo*, her twin reactors pushing her at maximum speed—loud with flow noise and machinery hum, but deadly with her 533mm torpedoes and SS-N-16 Stallion missiles.

Rourke's mind raced through the environmental calculus: there were no convergence zones in this shelf water; battle tactics were bottom-limited and patchy. The towed array had picked up the narrow-band tonals first—propeller blade-rate frequencies at high revs, the turbine whine, reduction gears, and reactor coolant pumps. The sophisticated sonar suite that the *Memphis* carried included a detailed library of unique tonal signatures of Russian submarines. Each one having a unique tonal "fingerprint" — in this case, the Akula, a Project 971 Shchuka-B. It was too far away and there was too much biological noise for the *Toledo's* hull/flank arrays to have picked it up. Rourke quietly congratulated himself for having ordered the towed array deployed.

Relative closure: 35 knots minus *Toledo's* 8 knots equals 27 knots head-on—time to contact: roughly 40 minutes at current range, Rourke calculated.

"Confirm classification," Rourke ordered, leaning over the plot. Willis nodded. "Akula signature confirmed—seven-bladed screw, tonals matching K-335 *Gepard*. She's racing toward *Toledo's* retreat path." The Toledo, limping west at silent speed with reactor issues, was vulnerable. "Weapons, check for a firing solution on Sierra Three," he added for good measure.

Rourke activated the ULF transmitter, the ultra-low-frequency system, their only submerged link. "*TOLEDO*, THIS IS MEMPHIS ACTUAL. AKULA-CLASS ATTACK SUBMARINE, NORTHEAST OF YOUR POSITION, CHARGING SOUTHWEST AT 35 KNOTS. RANGE TO YOU APPROXIMATELY 20 NM - CLOSING IN UNDER 45 MINUTES. MAINTAIN COURSE AND PREPARE TO DEFEND YOURSELF.

Weapons Officer Lieutenant Commander Ed Kline ran the firing solution. "Captain, Sierra Three's outside our attack window—geometry is off for Mk 48 snapshot. Bearing rate too high for reliable intercept at this range." Rourke grimaced. Any torpedo launch would reveal the *Memphis* without guarantee of a hit. "*Toledos* on her own," he transmitted. "Attention XO and Chief of the Boat, there's the potential for other Akulas in the area—Northern Fleet deploys in packs. Maintain 8 knots; rig for ultra-quiet operation. Sonar, pay close attention to the side array and the towed array signals for any other submerged threats that may be present. We do not want to be ambushed like the captain of the Akula is attempting on the *Toledo*—flank arrays for broad coverage, towed for long-range tonals. Ride the layer—below if present—to mask transients."

Rourke watched the plot as Sierra Three's bearing shifted, her 35-knot sprint a thunderous giveaway in the cluttered shelf. "She's bow-on to *Toledo*—hear her before she hears you," he thought, echoing unclassified tactics. The Akula's noise at maximum speed—over 110 dB from the flow alone—would light up *Toledo's* BQQ-5 towed array at 12-20 nautical miles, giving Brennan evasion time. But if she slowed to creep, her quiet rafting could turn the tables.

The sea held its breath, the Akula's tonals grew louder—a predator in the deep, unaware of the watchers in the shadows

USS *Toledo, 35 nautical miles west of the Kursk wreck*

Commander Tom Brennan received the warning with increased concern; his crew was already at battle stations. "Evans, status on pumps?" he whispered over the intercom. Lieutenant Mark Evans, in engineering, replied, "Quiet as we can get, sir—vibration damped too minimal. Running at 5 knots, our noise signature is low." Brennan addressed the crew standing watch in the control room and sonar room: "Gentlemen, silent vigilance. Side arrays sweep flanks; towed array astern for tails. Possible multiple Akulas—any noise betrays us. I do not want to fight; we are in no condition. We're ghosting to Norway."

Brennan stood in *Toledo's* control room, his shoulder throbbed as he thought about the sudden change in the tactical situation. As if he did not have enough to contend with — a crippled ship and half his crew injured — and now a deadly Russian Akula seeking to destroy his ship and crew. The *Toledo* was creeping at 5 knots, 150 feet deep and heading west out of the Russian Northern fleet operations area. Her reactor hummed softly, and the cooling pumps were functioning optimally, thanks to Lieutenant Mark Evans, who had done an incredible job of settling them down after the emergency reactor start, which had saved the entire crew from destruction. Brennan made a mental note to commend Evans' role in the emergency and recommend him for a Naval citation.

The control room was no longer a chaos of red lights and injured men; everything had settled down, and they were moving steadily and stealthily further west with each passing minute.

"Conn Sonar, can you see the Akula SSN 15 nautical miles northeast of our position?" he asked. "Conn, Sonar," Carter replied, "subsurface transient detected, bearing forty-five, range 15 nautical miles confirmed, sir. It is a K-335 Akula SSN vectoring in our direction at eight knots, sir. Akula will be in range for a firing solution once they close to six nautical miles, acknowledge?"

"Eight knots?" Brennan exclaimed. "The Akula has slowed down and must be actively searching for our sonar signature using its combined spherical bow, flank, and towed arrays. He will vector towards us in a zig-zag path to allow him to use his full sonar suite. Sonar con, keep a close eye on it and keep the XO up to date," Brennan ordered. "Reply to *Memphis* Carter," Brennan said. "Acknowledge the Russian Akula; however, our priority is to stay hidden. We will engage with extreme prejudice if threatened."

Carter nodded, encoding the response: *MEMPHIS*, THIS IS *TOLEDO ACTUAL*. WE HAVE ACQUIRED THE AKULA AND WILL ATTEMPT TO EVADE. SHOULD THAT FAIL, WE WILL ENGAGE. THE CAPTAIN ASKS THAT YOU DO THE SAME.

Brennan turned to XO Paul Reese, his face grim, as he transmitted the message. "We will creep at 3 knots, bearing two-seven-zero. It is our only shot to stay quiet. But if they find us…" He did not finish the thought; the unspoken truth hung heavily in the air.

Lieutenant Mark Evans monitored the S6G reactor in the engineering compartment as he adjusted the coolant flow. The reactor was operating at 15% power, with the pumps set low to minimise noise, but *Toledo's* systems were strained. "Reactor stable, sir," Evans reported via intercom, his voice steady despite the chaos. "But we are leaking in three compartments. The pumps are barely keeping up."

At the coolant control panel, Petty Officer First Class Emily Chan checked the gauges: "Coolant flow at 25%, sir. Noise levels at 45 decibels—we're as quiet as we can get without shutting down again, sir."

Brennan's mind now turned to his tactics in case the Russian Akula found them and attacked.

Akula-class submarine K-335 Gepard, 15 nautical miles southwest of Toledo, 0727 hours

Captain Yuri Volodin stood in the control room of the K-335 *Gepard*; his dark eyes fixed on the tactical plot as his team worked in tense silence. Her MGK-500 sonar suite—a marvel of Soviet engineering—scanned the turbulent Barents Sea. Volodin's shaved head gleamed under the dim red lights as he awaited updates.

"Sonar, anything?" Volodin barked with venom.

Sonar Officer Lieutenant Ivan Kuznetsov adjusted the MGK-500 suite. He had developed a reputation for detecting faint signatures in noisy environments, a skill honed by running multiple algorithms to isolate anomalies against background noise. "Running full biological sonar signature analysis, sir," Kuznetsov replied, as he initiated the protocols. "Filtering against Barents Sea environmental noise— currents, biologics, surface traffic… Algorithms Alpha-3 and Delta-7 engaged." Kuznetsov's team—three junior sonar techs—worked in sync, their screens displaying the processed data while the algorithms sifted through the chaotic soundscape of the Barents Sea.

A faint anomaly emerged, a rhythmic hum cutting through the background noise. "Contact detected—bearing zero-four-five, range fifteen nautical miles," Kuznetsov reported, his voice rising with urgency. "Confirmed reactor transient, 45 decibels—a Los Angeles-class SSN, sir. I detect something else. The turbulence signature shows damage. She is the crippled Yankee submarine."

Volodin's pulse quickened, his dark eyes burning with a predator's focus. The damaged American submarine—the one that must have collided with the *Kursk*, setting off the chain of events that led to her destruction. Kuznetsov's team had isolated her signature, a testament to their genius. "Stow the towed array, flank speed—classic Wolf Trot," Volodin ordered, his voice cold. "Close the distance, then coast in silence. Deploy the towed array once we are coasting."

The *Gepard* surged forward, its giant screw propelling the Akula to 35 knots—flank speed—as she raced toward the *Toledo's* position, bearing zero-four-five. Volodin's tactic, the "Wolf Trot," was a classic manoeuvre taught at the Russian Naval College: run fast to close in on the target, then coast in silence to avoid detection while deploying the towed array sonar in combination with the central forward sonar sphere in the bow of the Akula. The towed array—a long cable with hydrophones—extended behind the *Gepard*, providing a wider detection range, while the bow sonar sphere offered pinpoint accuracy. "Speed down to five knots—coast now," Volodin ordered after fifteen minutes, the *Gepard's* noise signature dropping as she glided silently, her sensors active.

"Towed array deployed," Kuznetsov reported, his voice steady but his hands trembling with adrenaline. "Bow sonar sphere active... confirming target—bearing zero-four-five, range six nautical miles. It is the American submarine, sir. Hopefully, we have picked her up before she has detected us."

Volodin's lips curled into a predatory smile, his scar twisting with the motion. This was a deadly game of who detected whom first and who got off the first shot. The *Gepard's* crew knew the stakes—failure meant death, either by the Yankee subs' torpedoes or Chernov's wrath. "Weapons, firing solution—now," Volodin ordered, his voice sharp.

Weapons Officer Lieutenant Viktor Popov, moved swiftly over the controls, his buzz cut damp with sweat. "Firing solution established, sir," Popov reported. "Tubes three and four—53-65K torpedoes, wake homing, locked on target by its sonar signature. Ready to fire on your command."

Volodin's dark eyes burned with focus. The *Gepard* had the *Toledo* in its sights. One shot would avenge Kolesnikov's death. However, Volodin knew the Americans were cunning—survival depended on striking first.

USS Toledo, six nautical miles west of the Akula - Gepard

"Conn, Sonar," reported Lieutenant Dave Carter, his voice shaky as he adjusted his headset, still woozy from his concussion. "New contact— bearing two-two-five, range ten nautical miles and closing, speed 35 knots! It is the Akula-class SSN, sir—onrushing, directly at us!"

Brennan's heart stopped, his eyes wide with dread. Admiral Chernov, commander of the Russian Northern Fleet, would have ordered the Akula-class submarine to hunt them down. At 35 knots, the Akula was closing fast, using the classic Russian "Wolf Trot", he suspected, to close the distance before coasting silently.

Her noisy, damaged hull made the *Toledo* a sitting duck; someone had detected her long before she could evade. "Battle stations!" Brennan shouted; his voice sharp. "Rig for silence—now!"

The *Toledo* crew sprang into action, their hands flying over the controls as the sub went silent. The crew reduced coolant pumps to 10%, dropped reactor power to 20%, and shut down all non-essential systems, which caused the noise level to fall to 30 decibels—a faint whisper.

Brennans scanned the chart for a tactical advantage. "Sonar, any undersea valleys nearby?" he asked, his voice low but urgent. "We need to suppress our sonar signature—find me something to work with."

Carter's hands trembled as he analysed the sonar data. His concussion blurred his vision, but he pushed through the pain. "Undersea valley— bearing one-eight-zero, range five nautical miles, depth six hundred feet," Carter reported, his voice tight. "It's narrow, sir, but it might mask our signature if we arrive on time."

"Set course one-eight-zero, ahead five knots," Brennan ordered, his voice steady despite the fear in his chest. "Weapons, firing solution on that Akula—now."

Weapons Officer Lieutenant Blake Phillips, his dark hair cut in a regulation Navy crewcut, worked swiftly at his station, his hands steady despite the tension in the control room. "Firing solution established, sir," he reported, his voice sharp with determination. "Tubes one and two—Mark 48 torpedoes, wire-guided, locked on target Sierra 1. Ready to fire on your command."

The *Toledo* slowly moved towards the undersea valley, its hull gliding through the water at five knots, with its noise signature partially masked by the rocky walls of the valley. Brennan's eyes burned with focus, his mind on the Russian hunter sub. The Akula was undamaged, fully armed, and closing in quickly—a superior predator in every way. The *Toledo* was crippled, her crew battered, and her systems stretched to the limit. It was a game of hunter and hunted. Failure meant death—not just for Brennan, but for everyone on board. They had to fire first, or they would end up at the bottom of the Barents Sea.

Krivak-class frigate Smolensk, Kursk wreck location, 1130 hours local time

Captain Sergei Ivanov stood on the bridge of the Russian frigate *Smolensk*, as it sliced through the choppy waves of the Barents Sea under a leaden sky. The orders from Admiral Viktor Chernov were clear: search for the stricken K-141 *Kursk* and scan for survivors in the emergency escape pod. The *Smolensk*, which had a 130-meter hull and an advanced sonar suite, was equipped for ASW operations, but this mission carried the weight of national tragedy. Ivanov, at 37, a seasoned commander with a square jaw and eyes hardened by years in the Northern Fleet, felt the burden acutely. His crew of 180 worked in grim silence, the air thick with the salt of the sea and the metallic hum of the ship's engines.

"Captain, sonar contact," reported Senior Sonarman Petty Officer Yuri Pavlov from the sonar room, his voice crackling over the intercom. "Bearing zero-one-five, range 500 yards, depth 350 feet, sir. Faint metallic tapping—rhythmic, like Morse code. It's the *Kursk's* hull signature, confirmed."

Ivanov leaned over the chart table, his uniform crisp despite the fatigue. "Survivors," he muttered. A flicker of hope pierced the dread. The *Kursk* lay at 350 feet, its massive Oscar-class frame a tomb on the seabed. The tapping—desperate signals from trapped men—echoed the real-world horror of submariners clinging to life in compartments sealed against the crush. But without the escape pod deploying, rescue was impossible. Russia's deep-diving Mir submersibles were days away, and foreign aid was politically taboo under Putin's new regime. "Poor souls," Ivanov thought, picturing Kolesnikov's crew reduced to faint and futile knocks in the deep.

He summoned Lieutenant Oleg Vesnen, his navigation officer, to the bridge. Vesnen, 28, with a lean build and a perpetual frown from his Murmansk upbringing, arrived swiftly with the sonar logs clutched under his arm. The two had served together on the K-123 in the Black Sea five years prior. "Oleg, walk me through it again," Ivanov said, gesturing to a quiet corner away from the crew.

Vesnen unfolded the sonar printouts, his voice low. "We were in proximity, Captain—10 nautical miles from the exercise zone when it started. The initial transient: a grinding collision, metal-to-metal. *Kursk's* double hull versus an American Los Angeles-class. The signatures matched—OK-650 reactors on *Kursk*, S6G on the LA. It was no accident; the American submarine was shadowing too close."

Ivanov nodded, recalling the jolt that had shaken the *Smolensk*. The Barents Sea exercise, meant to impress the Chinese delegation on the

Pyotr Velikiy, had turned deadly. "Then the escalation," he prompted.

Vesnen traced the timeline on the log. "*Kursk* fired first—a 53-65 torpedo in self-defence—wake-homing, 400kg warhead, aimed at the intruder's stern. But the Americans evaded, using decoys or manoeuvres. Then, out of nowhere, a second U.S. sub—another LA-class—launched a Mk 48. It struck the *Kursk* forward, right in the torpedo room."

"We felt it here," Ivanov said, tapping the deck. "A thunderclap from 250 feet down. The hydrophones overloaded for seconds."

"The sonar crew recorded everything—timestamps, frequencies, bearings. Collision at 0800, *Kursk's* 53-65 launch at 0801, Mk 48 impact at 0804, major explosion at 0805. It is irrefutable. When the investigation comes—and it will, with Putin demanding answers—this tape is our shield."

Ivanov rubbed the rough stubble on his chin. The Kremlin would spin the narrative: accident; torpedo malfunction; anything but American aggression. But Chernov's fleet was already mobilising for vengeance, depth charges and helicopters hunting the intruders. "It could save our careers," Ivanov agreed. "Proves we had nothing to do with it—too far to intervene, no orders to engage. We were observers, not actors."

Vesnen hesitated. His mind flicked to the coded postcard from his defector friend, Sergei Kuznetsov, urging him to contact American handlers. The fibre optic cables Kuznetsov had mapped—vulnerable lines on the seabed—had been his friend's lottery ticket out of Soviet poverty, but Vesnen kept the thought buried. Loyalty to Ivanov, his mentor from the K-123, outweighed temptation.

"The tapping... It's compartment nine, aft. Maybe 23 men left, hammering for help."

Ivanov sighed, the weight of command pressing. "Signal Chernov: *Kursk* located, survivors detected, no pod. Request deep rescue assets." But he knew the response—delay, denial, cover-up. The *Smolensk* circled the site, her Ka-27 helicopter dipping buoys, but at 350 feet, hope faded with each tap. The disaster's truth, etched in sonar logs, would haunt them —a testament to the Cold War beneath the waves.

As the sun was reaching its zenith, Ivanov stared at the horizon. The Mk 48's strike had escalated a shadow game to slaughter, and the *Smolensk's* recordings were the only witnesses. "For the Motherland," he whispered, but the words rang hollow against the faint, dying echoes from below.

Below deck, Vesnen slipped into a storage compartment near the ship's stern. He had decided, his hands trembling as he pulled a concealed commercial satellite phone from his pocket. Vesnen's secret burden traced back to his childhood friendship with Sergei Kuznetsov, a naval architect stationed at the Severomorsk Naval Base in Russia's Murmansk Oblast. Born in Murmansk, he had grown up in the shadow of the Northern Fleet, where Arctic winds and submarine silhouettes defined his world. His father, a diesel mechanic on the Victor-class subs, had died in a 1989 dockyard accident, leaving Oleg with a fierce loyalty to the navy but a quiet scepticism of its post-Soviet decay. Enlisting at 18, Vesnen trained in navigation operations at the Severomorsk Academy, his acute eyesight and analytical mind had since earned him postings on elite crews.

Sergei Kuznetsov, two years older and from the same neighbourhood, was Vesnen's closest confidant. They shared a childhood code—a simple substitution cipher based on Murmansk Street names—which they had first used for notes during school pranks. Kuznetsov had pursued engineering, rising to a classified role at Severomorsk by the late 1990s, where he had gained access to design blueprints for naval infrastructure, including the locations of submarine communication fibre optic cables. These undersea lines, laid in the Barents and Norwegian Seas, were critical for secure fleet comms and linked bases like Severomorsk to subs like the *Kursk*. Kuznetsov's work had exposed him to the navy's vulnerabilities—outdated tech, corruption, and the Kremlin's incompetence under Boris Yeltsin.

In July 1999, during a vacation in Istanbul, and disillusioned by his delayed salary and a colleague's arrest for justified dissent, and posing as a tourist, he had contacted the U.S. Embassy and discreetly met with a mid-level diplomat from the Department of State, Michael Harper. Driven by fears for his family's future amid Russia's economic turmoil, over tea, Kuznetsov had hinted at the extent of his access. Harper, recognising the intelligence goldmine, had arranged an exfiltration. Kuznetsov had defected that night along with digital copies of Russian base plans and cable coordinates via an encrypted drive hidden in his luggage. Kuznetsov had resettled in Virginia under a new identity, and provided ONI (Office of Naval Intelligence) with details that could disrupt Russian sub ops in a crisis for years to come.

Before vanishing, Kuznetsov had sent Vesnen a postcard from Istanbul, disguised as a tourist memento. Using their childhood code—where "fish market" meant "opportunity" and "spices" signified "escape"—the message read: "The spices here are incredible, better than home. The fish market is thriving. If you find rare herbs, call this merchant: 1-202-555-0199." Decoded, it praised the defection ("better than home") and urged Vesnen to contact the number—a secure CIA line—if he had vital info. Vesnen, stationed on a coastal naval patrol craft, received it weeks later. He had burned the card but memorised the number, torn between loyalty and the allure of escape.

By 2000, aboard the *Smolensk* under Captain Sergei Ivanov, Vesnen's awareness of Kuznetsov's defection weighed heavily on him. During the *Shkval* demonstration, as tensions rose with the US vessels, Vesnen reflected on the detailed sonar records of the *Kursk* sinking and the evidence of American involvement—explosive information that might be his ticket out.

Vesnen, a wiry man with a gaunt face and haunted eyes, had been disillusioned with the Russian navy for years. The post-Soviet decline had left him underpaid, overworked, and bitter, his dreams of a proud naval career had been reduced to a series of humiliations. He had first-hand knowledge about the *Kursk*—a collision with an American sub, a retaliatory torpedo strike—and he knew the truth would be his ticket out. Vesnen dialled the number he had memorised from the coded message in Kuznetsov's postcard — a CIA station number in Istanbul, Turkey. The line crackled to life, and a voice answered in English, thick with an American accent. "US Consulate, Consular Affairs, how may I help you?"

"This is Lieutenant Oleg Vesnen, Russian Northern Fleet, aboard the frigate *Smolensk* in the Barents Sea," Vesnen said, his voice in broken Russian-accented English. "I know the truth about the *Kursk*—an American submarine, a Los Angeles-class submarine, sank her. I want to defect. One million dollars and protection from the FSB—the Russian secret service. Now!"

The consular affairs officer, a 40-year-old diplomat named Michael Harper, blinked in disbelief, his coffee cup frozen halfway to his mouth. He had expected a routine call about a lost passport, not a Russian defector claiming to have intel on a naval disaster. "Sir, I… I need to confirm this," Harper stammered, his mind racing. "You are saying an American sub sank the *Kursk*? How do you know this?"

"I was on the bridge!" Vesnen yelled, his voice cracking with desperation. "I heard the sonar reports—a collision, then a torpedo launch. The Americans fired first! I have proof—logs, recordings, everything that proves that you Americans are to blame. My friend Sergei Kuznetsov came to you with important, valuable information, and now I come to you for help!"

Harper's heart pounded, his years of training kicking in despite his shock. Vesnen's urgency was convincing, and the *Kursk's* sinking was already creating waves in intelligence circles—seismic stations in Norway and Alaska had detected a 4.2-magnitude event, and rumours of US involvement were swirling. "I'll call you back," Smith said, his voice steady. "Give me a number and a time."

"Thirty minutes," Vesnen hissed, rattling off the secure satellite number. "Don't make me wait." He hung up, his hands trembling as he concealed the phone in a hidden compartment, his mind racing with the fear of discovery.

Harper immediately dialled the CIA station chief in Istanbul, a 50-year-old veteran named Elizabeth Carter. "Liz, it's Harper," he said, his voice urgent. "I just got a call from a Russian naval officer— Lieutenant Oleg Vesnen, aboard the *Smolensk*. He claims an American sub sank the *Kursk*, and he wants to defect. One million dollars and protection from the FSB."

Carter, a seasoned operative with a sharp mind and a no-nonsense demeanour, sat up in her chair, her coffee forgotten. "You're kidding," she said. "The *Kursk* is the Oscar-class sub that went down this morning. If he is telling the truth, this is a huge development. Get him back on the line as fast as you can—confirm his story. I will contact Langley. We need to move fast."

Vesnen's heart pounded as he slipped out of the storage compartment. His hands trembled as he adjusted his uniform, and his eyes darted around for any sign of eavesdroppers. He had been on the bridge when the *Kursk* went down, and had recorded the bridge transcripts, copied the sonar logs, and stored them on a USB drive hidden in a seam in his naval jacket. The truth was his ticket out—a chance to escape the navy, the FSB, and the life that had broken him. But if the FSB found him before he could escape, he'd be a dead man.

Udaloy-class destroyer Admiral Kharlamov, two nautical miles southeast of Memphis

Commander Nikolai Pyotrov gripped the railing on the bridge of the Udaloy-class destroyer *Admiral Kharlamov*. The air was thick with the acrid scent of spent munitions and the low rumble of the ship's engines.

The Silex depth charges—two salvos of eight SS-N-14 rockets

each—had detonated in a dispersed pattern at a depth of 300-500 feet, their shockwaves had rippled the surface. Yet, the American Los Angeles-class SSN, after its audacious emergency blow and breach, had dived and slipped away, its acoustic signature had dissolved into the biologics—shrimp clicks and whale calls were masking its retreat.

The failure appalled Pyotrov. The Silex, rocket-propelled with UMGT-1 torpedoes or depth bombs, was designed to saturate convergence zones and crush elusive foes. But the American submarine commander—had expected the pattern, using the blasts' own force to propel his sub skyward. "Such audacity," Pyotrov muttered, a grudging admiration creeping in. In his decade of service, from Black Sea exercises with Kolesnikov to Northern Fleet patrols, he had never guessed an enemy would turn a depth charge barrage into an ascent booster. The manoeuvre defied doctrine—risking hull stress and exposure—but it had worked. Sonar reported no debris, no oil slick; now the sub had vanished back below, silent as a grave.

"Battle stations!" Pyotrov barked, his voice echoing through the intercom. The crew of 300 snapped to, alarms blaring as the *Kharlamov's* Rastrub-B launchers were primed and the AK-130 guns swivelled. "Con, sonar—be on the lookout for retaliatory torpedoes directed at our ship. Mk 48s could be inbound; maintain active pings on all bearings."

Lieutenant Viktor Sokolov, the weapons officer, nodded from his station. "Aye, Captain. Torpedo decoys ready—UDT-1 systems online."

Pyotrov turned to Communications Officer Ensign Maria Petrova. "Coms, advise Admiral Chernov of our combat status and request orders. Further, advise the *Admiral Levchenko* to be on the lookout for counterattacks by torpedoes and to keep their Ka-27PLs well clear." The *Admiral Levchenko* was five nautical miles astern, her helicopters vulnerable after the mysterious downing of two Ka-27PLs—likely by some American subsurface-to-air weapon, a technology Pyotrov couldn't fathom.

Petrova keyed the encrypted radio: "*Admiral Kharlamov* to flagship *Pyotr Velikiy*. Silex barrage failed; American sub surfaced, evaded, and dived. No confirmed kill. Request orders. *Admiral Levchenko* advised: Torpedo threat imminent; hold helos at standoff."

The response came swiftly from Chernov on the Kirov-class battlecruiser *Pyotr Velikiy*: "Con, coms—Admiral Chernov orders you to stand by and wait for his commands. Maintain position; fleet converging," Petrova calmly responded.

Pyotrov exhaled, frustration knotting his brow. Standing by meant vulnerability—the Americans could counterstrike at any moment. He beckoned Senior Sonarman Petty Officer Alexei Kuznetsov to the bridge. "Sonar con," Pyotrov asked, his voice low, "did all the other ships in the Northern Fleet log the last known position of the surfaced American submarine?"

Kuznetsov, a wiry veteran with headphones slung around his neck, consulted his log. "Yes, Captain. The fleet's shared net—encrypted satellite link via Glonass broadcasts the coordinates instantly. *Pyotr Velikiy, Admiral Levchenko, Marshal Shaposhnikov, Admiral Tributs, Vice-Admiral Kulakov*—all Udaloy's confirmed receipt. Surface position: 69°40'N, 37°35'E, time 0925. We are all hunting; they have the fix."

Pyotrov nodded, feeling a flicker of relief amid the chaos. The Northern Fleet was a formidable force—over 80 submarines (49 nuclear, 31 diesel), including Oscar IIs like the *Kursk*, Akulas, and Typhoons; surface vessels like two Kirov battlecruisers (*Pyotr Velikiy* and *Admiral Nakhimov*), the *Kuznetsov* carrier, Slava cruisers, and a dozen Udaloy destroyers. Communication protocols enabled real-time sharing via radio, satellite, and fibre optics, where available. If Chernov activated all of them, the Americans—would be caught in a closing net. But Pyotrov's thoughts darkened. The Silex failure exposed gaps in Russian tactics— they were outdated compared to American ingenuity. He recalled his Black Sea talks with Kolesnikov about ASW patterns;

now; it felt prophetic. "Keep scanning," he ordered Kuznetsov. "If that sub resurfaces or launches, we end it."

As the *Admiral Kharlamov* held station, the sea mocked their vigilance—a vast, empty grey hiding predators below. Chernov's orders would come, but until then, Pyotrov admired the foe's boldness, even as he plotted their demise.

Pyotr Velikiy (Peter the Great), 20 nautical miles northeast of the Kursk wreck

Admiral Viktor Chernov paced the flag bridge of his Northern Fleet flagship. The air was heavy with the ozone tang of electronics and the distant boom of waves against its 28,000-ton hull. Chernov, at 52, his towering 6'4" frame clad in a crisp navy uniform adorned with the Order of Ushakov, slammed a meaty fist on the chart table.

"That fool Pyotrov!" he cursed, a gravelly roar that silenced the bridge crew. The failure of the Silex depth charges burned in his gut like bad vodka. Sixteen rockets, each carrying a 185-kilogram payload, had splashed down in a calculated pattern, yet the American submarine had evaded them with that insane emergency blow, using the blasts to catapult itself to the surface before vanishing below. Pyotrov's report from the *Admiral Kharlamov* confirmed the sub's brief surfacing at 69°40'N, 37°35'E, but its dive had erased it from sonar.

"If you want a job done properly, you have to do it yourself," Chernov growled, his eyes narrowing as he framed a plan.

He gathered his staff around the holographic plot; the screen glowed with fleet positions: the *Admiral Kharlamov* and *Admiral Levchenko*, his two closest assets, Udaloy's armed with Rastrub-B launchers capable of multiple Silex salvos. "We will herd the Yankee bastard," Chernov explained, tracing lines with a thick finger." *Admiral Kharlamov* from the northeast, *Admiral Levchenko* from the northwest—multiple salvos of nuclear depth charges in overlapping patterns. Drive it south into a kill zone, one square nautical mile. There, the *Pyotr Velikiy* finishes it with a nuclear 82R torpedo." The Kirov-class cruiser, with its massive armoured lower decks, stowed nuclear ordnance in the armoury—0.5-kiloton devices, relics of Soviet doctrine for decisive ASW strikes.

The order hung in the air like smoke from his unfiltered cigarette.

Captain Ristov coughed, "Admiral, the Russian Navy nuclear doctrine requires us to get Kremlin permission for atomics. Admiral, you put your proud naval career at risk by going ahead with this without explicit authority from Moscow."

Admiral Viktor Chernov paced like a caged bear, his massive frame casting long shadows under the red combat lights. "Yes, you are correct, Ristov, get me Moscow on the secure line," Chernov barked.

The Kirov-class battlecruiser's radio crackled with static, Chernov's encrypted request to Moscow's Naval High Command hanging in the ether: permission to deploy nuclear depth charges against the American Los Angeles-class submarines—that had evaded his fleet's salvos and mocked his command with their stealth. "We must end this insult," he had transmitted, his voice gravelly with rage. "Nuclear authorisation requested. Yankee blood for Russian honour."

...

In Moscow, the Naval High Command's bunker beneath the Admiralty Building erupted into controlled frenzy. Vice Admiral Sergei Ivanov, no relation to the frigate captain but a seasoned strategist with scars from the Afghan debacle, stared at the Teletype. "Chernov's gone mad," he muttered to his aides. "Nuclear in the Barents? That's Putin's call." The room, lined with glowing maps of fleet positions, hummed with urgency. Ivanov patched through to the Kremlin, the secure line buzzing to life.

"Comrade President, Foreign Minister, Admiral Chernov requests nuclear release. Situation critical."

Vladimir Putin, seated in the Kremlin's Situation Room, leaned forward, his ice-blue eyes unblinking. At 47, the former KGB officer had ascended to the presidency mere months ago, inheriting a Russia humbled by Yeltsin's chaos—economic collapse, Chechen insurgency, NATO expansion. Beside him, Foreign Minister Igor Lavrov, 50, with his diplomat's poise and scholar's mind, adjusted his glasses. The room's oak panels and crystal chandeliers belied the tension; screens flickered with satellite feeds of the Barents standoff, American carriers lurking in the North Atlantic, Chinese observers on the *Pyotr Velikiy* adding layers of intrigue.

Gather the seniors," Putin ordered, his voice calm but steel-edged. "Now." Within minutes, the room filled: Defence Minister Igor Sergeyev, weathered from Soviet Afghan campaigns; Chief of the General Staff Anatoly Kvashnin, a blunt tactician; and Admiral Vladimir Kuroyedov, Navy Commander-in-Chief, his uniform starched but face marked with worry over the fleet's post-Soviet decline.

Putin didn't beat around the bush. "Chernov wants to use nukes. He claims two American Los Angeles-class submarines are responsible for the *Kursk* disaster, the Northern Fleet has them cornered and they want to finish them off. Assess: Can we withstand American retaliation—non-nuclear or otherwise?"

The discussion ignited like a fuse. Sergeyev spoke first, his voice booming. "Comrade President, our conventional forces are strained. The Borei-class SSBNs—our next-generation ballistic missile subs—are still in design at Sevmash. Prototypes will not launch until 2007. We rely on the Typhoons—our aging giants from the '80s, vulnerable to the new Seawolf hunter-killers the Americans have. Their reactors are noisy; stealth is compromised against the Americans. They could find them and destroy them before we even knew about it, the new Seawolf-class submarines are that good."

Kuroyedov nodded gravely. "And the Yasen-class SSGNs—our new multi-purpose attack subs meant to rival the Americans—are years away. Anticipated commissioning 2010 at best. They will be quieter than the Seawolf, with Kalibr missiles and hypersonic Zircons, better armed for multi-domain strikes. But today? Our blue-water technology is currently inferior."

Lavrov interjected, his tone measured. "Escalation risks NATO invocation. Clinton's unpredictable—his Balkans strikes showed a willingness for precision air campaigns. Our air defences are patchy; Kaliningrad's S-300s won't stop B-2s."

Putin leaned in, fingers steepled. "Elaborate. How strong are we, truly?"

Kuroyedov cleared his throat and projected a classified slide: thermal wakes in the Pacific. "We tracked what could only be a Seawolf—SSN-21—transiting at 50 knots under the Pacific Ocean last month. Silent on our seabed sonar arrays off Kamchatka. Picked up via space assets—one of our new nuclear-powered LIDAR survey satellites detected the surface wake disturbance. Minimal, but unmistakable at that speed."

Sergeyev added, "We believe it was deliberate—an American demonstration to us and the Chinese. 'See our superiority,' they're saying. Their Virginia-class prototypes are already quieter and faster. Our Oscars and Akulas? Outdated. Nuclear exchange? We would strike hard, but their THAAD and Aegis would blunt our response. Non-nuclear: their carrier groups could blockade the Baltic in days."

The room fell silent, the weight of inferiority hanging like smoke. Putin absorbed it, his mind racing through geopolitical calculus—Chechnya draining resources, oligarchs scheming, the West's sanctions looming. Lavrov's earlier counsel echoed: stay calm, do not act impulsively.

"Thank you, comrades," Putin said finally, dismissing them with a nod. The officials filed out, leaving Putin and Lavrov alone amid the humming screens.

Lavrov spoke first. "Nuclear now? It is suicide. Chernov's grief blinds him—the *Kursk* was family to him."

Putin exhaled, rubbing his temples. "Agreed. Deny it. Order High Command: no nuclear release. Order Chernov into a hunting posture. We will think about our next move, Sergie. But mark this—the Borei and Yasen-class submarine programs speed up. Russia rises, or we fall."

Lavrov nodded, inputting the directive. As the order was sent, Putin gazed at the map, their billion-dollar submarine *Kursk* was lost along with its crew. The Americans had arrived; strong and technologically advanced, it was clear that the Russian Federation was vulnerable. But vengeance churned beneath the surface—cold, calculated, like the man steering the ship.

...

In the *Pyotr Velikiy*, Chernov received the denial, his fist crumpling the printout. "Cowards," he growled. The hunt continued, but the nuclear leash held—for now.

"Weapons, prepare the swap—conventional out, nuclear in," Chernov commanded, his tone brooking no dissent. The armoury was buried deep within the cruiser's layered armour, comprised of titanium and steel plates that were torpedo-proof. In it were the warheads, their plutonium cores shielded in lead casings.

Captain Ivan Ristov, the *Pyotr Velikiy's* commanding officer, exchanged alarmed glances with several officers on the watch. "Admiral, I must protest; this directly violates our orders," Ristov exclaimed.

"Noted, Captain Ristov. Put it in the ship's logs and carry out my orders, or I will have you shot for mutiny," Chernov practically spat at Ristov. Ristov, at 45, a pragmatic Sevastopol native with salt-and-pepper hair, had risen through the ranks on destroyers like the Udaloy, where nuclear escalation was theoretical, not tactical. He did what he was ordered and nodded to the senior officers on the deck.

Lieutenant Commander Elena Petrova, the navigation officer, paled. Ensign Dmitri Sokolov, communications, shifted uneasily, recalling Chernov's reputation for ruthlessness. Nuclear depth charges in the Barents—shallow shelf waters— the fallout risked contaminating Murmansk's fisheries, a NATO backlash, or even a global incident. The 1963 SSN *Thresher* loss had taught the world the perils of reactor breaches. Using a nuke might vaporise the American sub but it could irradiate the sea for years.

Ristov cleared his throat. "Admiral, the yield—0.5 kiloton at 300 feet—could create a tsunami effect, endangering our own fleet." Chernov whirled, his face reddening. "You question me, Captain? The Yankees killed the *Kursk*! Kolesnikov, Ivanov, all of them—vaporised by a Mk 48. This is retribution." Ristov backed down, but the glances persisted—whispers of madness in the admiral's eyes, driven by personal demons.

Chernov ignored them, barking into the radio: "*Admiral Levchenko*— begin herding salvos. Patterns alpha-three: dispersed grids, 150-300 feet depth. Drive south to kill zone 69°38'N, 37°30'E." Pyotrov, on the *Admiral Kharlamov*, acknowledged. The Udaloys began their salvos— their quad tubes belched smoke as Silex rockets arced skyward and splashed down in calculated barrages to funnel the prey.

Below decks, armoury crews in radiation suits swapped payloads, the nuclear charges—cylindrical, 500kg each— were hoisted into the launchers. Chernov paced, chain-smoking, his mind on the 1982 collision. "This time, we end it," he vowed. The fleet converged, sonar pings echoed like heartbeats. Ristov's alarm grew; a nuclear strike could escalate to war, but the Admiral's orders were absolute.

As the *Pyotr Velikiy* positioned for the kill, Chernov stared at the sonar plot, the American phantom's last fix a red dot. The herding salvos boomed in the distance, shockwaves trembling the hull. "Prepare nuclear launch," he ordered. The bridge fell silent; officers' glances a silent mutiny. In the armoury's glow, the warhead waited, a Pandora's box in the deep.

The crew held their breath, the nuclear threshold a razor edge. Chernov's plan, born of rage, teetered on the brink of apocalypse, the fleet's fate in his hands.

Rostov's further concern drifted to Lieutenant Commander Dmitry Sokolov in the weapons control centre. Sokolov's behaviour had been unusual all morning. He had seen Sokolov with Captain Li Jun, the PLAN officer; the timing seemed too coincidental. "Lieutenant Sokolov," Rostov called over the intercom, his voice calm but firm. "A word."

Sokolov's heart skipped a beat. "Yes, sir?" he said, his voice cracking slightly, once he arrived on the bridge.

"You've been on edge all morning," Rostov said, his eyes narrowing. "What's going on?"

Sokolov swallowed hard, his mind racing for an excuse. "It's… It's the *Kursk*, sir," he stammered. "I knew Captain Kolesnikov—we trained together. I am just… shaken."

Rostov's gaze lingered on Sokolov; his instincts told him that there was more to the story. "I understand," he said, his tone neutral. "But we need you focused. Focus on your post. You heard the admiral's orders. We are going to nuclear depth charge this American submarine."

Sokolov nodded and returned to the weapons control room. His hands were shaking. What did Rostov know? It was too late to turn back. He had given Li Jun the *Pyotr Velikiy's* ASW protocols—sonar frequencies, torpedo guidance algorithms, depth charge patterns—but it was not the complete *Shkval* data set. Li Jun would come for him again. The thought made him nauseous. As did the fact that the Chinese spy was, as far as he knew, still on the ship.

Sokolov was right. Captain Li Jun had hidden himself in a maintenance room near the *Pyotr Velikiy's* engineering section. He had retrieved the listening device from the comms room, capturing valuable intel—Russian ASW tactics, fleet movements, and even the K-335 *Gepard's* involvement. He had also downloaded the KN-3 reactor schematics, a prize that would advance China's naval ambitions even further. Li Jun's mission was clear: acquire as much intel as possible before getting off the ship in one piece and making his way to the safety of the waiting Type 091 Han-class submarine 60 nautical miles west. Getting the *Pyotr Velikiy's* ASW protocols and reactor schematics was a valuable consolation prize for losing the *Shkval*. Time to go. He slipped onto the starboard deck, his Russian naval officer's uniform blending in with the crew. The Russians were focused on hunting the Americans, and likely would not notice him—at least for the present. But he needed to move quickly. The Northern Fleet was on high alert. If they found out what he had been up to, he would face decades of rotting in a Siberian prison, or worse. A powered lifeboat was secured to a railing of the deck. He made his way towards it.

The Kremlin, Moscow, Russian Federation 12 August 2000

President Vladimir Putin sat behind the heavy oak desk in his Kremlin study; he was two months shy of his 48th birthday. His face was pale, but his piercing eyes were sharp with focus. He had been President of the Russian Federation for just five months, and now this—a crisis that could ignite a war.

The reports had come in swiftly: the *Kursk* had been sunk, with 118 crew members likely dead; a seismic event had been detected, meaning there was no hiding it; two Ka-27PL helicopters had also been shot down; and four more men were dead. And the Americans were to blame. And that lunatic Admiral Chernov wanted to use atomic weapons against the American submarines responsible.

Putin's hands were steepled in front of him as he processed the implications. My God, he thought, I didn't expect to be at war with the

Americans this fast. He glanced at the man seated across from him, Foreign Minister Sergei Lavrov, his most loyal confidant. His tailored suit was a stark contrast to Putin's military-style jacket. A 50-year-old diplomat with dark eyes and a receding hairline, he exuded a quiet confidence.

Putin, speaking softly, said the Admiral of the *Pyotr Velikiy* had cornered an American SSN submarine. His St Petersburg accent was clipped. "The *Kursk* is gone—118 men dead, an act of war, Sergey. It was a 4.2 magnitude seismic event. And now the Americans have shot down two of our helicopters with some wonder weapon."

Lavrov leaned back, his expression unreadable as he calculated the geopolitical fallout. "A seismic event that large—global powers will have already noticed," he said. "The Americans, the British, NATO—they will be watching. If Chernov sinks those subs, we are not just talking retaliation. We are talking war."

Putin clenched his hands into fists. "What do you suggest?"

Lavrov's dark eyes met Putin's. "Pick up the emergency phone, my friend. Call Clinton. We need to de-escalate before this spirals out of control. Chernov can hunt, but he cannot use atomics—not yet. We need to know what the Americans know."

Putin hesitated, rage clashing with pragmatism. He had come to power promising to restore Russia's greatness and to rebuild the navy that had crumbled after the Soviet collapse. The *Kursk* was a symbol of that resurgence, and its loss was a personal blow. But Lavrov was right— Russia was not ready for a full-scale war with the Americans, not yet.

Putin's mind raced as he thought of the consequences. The sinking of the *Kursk* was a disaster, not only for the Northern Fleet but also for Russia's international standing. The *Shkval* demonstration had been intended to showcase Russia's technological edge and secure Chinese investment in the Northern Fleet's modernisation.

Now, the *Kursk* lay in ruins. Putin thought of the men who had died— men like Captain Dmitri Kolesnikov, a rising star who had embodied

Russia's naval resurgence. A hero of the Motherland, Putin had pinned the Order of Nakhimov medal on him only last month. Putin felt the loss personally but knew he could not let emotion cloud his judgment. If this escalated into war, Russia would be at a disadvantage. The navy was still recovering from the post-Soviet decline and the disastrous 1990s.

Putin, sitting in the dimly lit Kremlin office, felt the weight of the *Kursk* disaster pressing on him like the Arctic depths that had claimed his submarine. He breathed out heavily, thinking about what Lavrov had said: stay calm, do not act, think. The foreign minister's words echoed in his mind, a restraint against the rage boiling within. The *Kursk* demanded justice, but hasty retaliation could unravel the fragile post-Soviet order he was rebuilding.

His thoughts drifted to Bill Clinton; the American president whose affable demeanour masked the West's unyielding grip. They had met in Moscow in June 2000, where Putin had floated the idea of Russia joining NATO, a bold overture to lay to rest the ghosts of the Cold War. The West had nothing to fear from the East, he had argued, the Russian Federation was an emerging democratic capitalist economy. Clinton had seemed intrigued at first, his Arkansas drawl warm as he called it "an interesting idea." But only 24 hours later, a polite decline arrived through diplomatic channels, deep state neocons in the Department of State no doubt pulling the strings. Their military-industrial complex was a profit-driven machine, enriching ex-presidents, vice presidents, and retired generals through endless arms contracts.

Putin sneered inwardly. The entire US economy revolved around it— senators lobbying for F-22s in Georgia or submarines in Connecticut, an obscene cycle of death for profit. Weaker nations, from Iraq to Yugoslavia, had paid the price in blood. It was totally foreign to the Russian mentality, where defence served the Motherland, not elites. His own Rostec, a government-owned entity, was being purged of corrupt holdovers from the Yeltsin era. The 1990s had been chaotic—oligarchs looting, the Ruble crashing, NATO expanding eastward despite Reagan's promises to Gorbachev. God had given him this presidency to restore Russia's might and make the West tremble once more.

But Lavrov was right: act in haste, repent at leisure. The Americans had denied involvement, blaming some accident on board the *Kursk*, but Chernov's reports painted a different picture: US subs shadowing, a collision, and torpedoes exchanged. Nuclear escalation loomed if Chernov deployed those depth charges. Putin exhaled again. Stay calm. Do not act. Think.

The *Kursk* survivors' faint taps haunted him; rescue efforts were impossible. But Russia would rise, not through a rash war, but through calculated strength. For now, observe—let the fleet hunt, but keep a tight hold on the nuclear leash. The Motherland's revenge would come cold, like the Barents' depths.

USS Memphis, 60 nautical miles north of the Kursk wreck

Commander John Rourke felt the first depth charge detonate—a low rumble that shook the *Memphis's* hull. The shockwave reverberated through the steel like a hammer attacking an anvil. The *Memphis* was at 200 feet, creeping at five knots to stay quiet, while the Russians closed in. The *Admiral Kharlamov* and *Admiral Levchenko* had launched the depth charges in a wide grid pattern designed to flush out or destroy a hiding sub. The explosions were getting closer.

"Conn, Sonar," said Lieutenant Dave Carter, his voice tight as he adjusted his headset. "Depth charges, bearing zero-one-zero, range three nautical miles. They are bracketing us."

Rourke scanned the tactical plot. At five knots, they could not outrun the destroyers; however, if they increased their speed, the screw cavitation turbulence would give them away. "Hold course," he said, despite the fear gnawing at his gut. "Trust in our ship to absorb these shocks. Stay quiet."

Another depth charge exploded, closer this time. The *Memphis* rocked violently. A pipe burst in the control room, spraying cold seawater across the deck and soaking Rourke's boots. Alarms blared as the crew scrambled to seal the leak with grim determination. Rourke clung to the chart table. He had promised to draw the Russians off the *Toledo*; the *Toledo* should be clear of the Russian Northern fleet by now.

"Gentlemen, it is time we got the hell out of Dodge. This will not end well if we stay here and OK Corral this." The *Memphis* was taking a beating, with *Admiral Kharlamov* and *Admiral Levchenko's* depth charges bracketing her position, and the *Peter the Great* bringing up the rear, closing the trap. It was time to save themselves.

"Conn, Sonar," said Lieutenant Mike Hensley, his lanky frame hunched over the console, his headset pressed tight against his ears. "Russian destroyers moving north, following our noisemakers. But the helos are still pinging—three Ka-27PLs, bearing zero-one-five, range five nautical miles."

Rourke's mind raced, his eyes narrowing as he weighed his options. The *Memphis* had already destroyed two helicopters, the Ka-27PL Orel and Ka-27PL Volk, using Sea Lance missiles, but the remaining three still posed a threat. The *Admiral Levchenko* was just 10 nautical miles away, her active sonar pinging relentlessly. "Weapons status on the Sea Lance?" Rourke asked, his voice steady.

"Tube three loaded, sir," replied Weapons Officer Ed Kline, his stocky frame moving with precision as he input the commands. "Solution locked on the lead helo—Ka-27PL."

"Hold fire for now," Rourke said, his voice steady. "We will use the noisemakers to draw them off. Launch tubes one and two—full spread."

Creeping north at five knots, the Memphis shuddered with the launch, mimicking a fleeing sub. The Ka-27PL helicopters—Ka-27PL Medved (Bear), Ka-27PL Tigr (Tiger), and Ka-27PL Bars (Leopard)— shifted their focus, their dipping sonars pinged after the decoys as they moved north. The *Admiral Levchenko* followed, its active sonar pings shifting away from the *Memphis's* position.

"Conn, Sonar," Hensley reported, his voice laced with relief. "*Admiral Levchenko* is moving north, following the decoys. *Memphis* has a window of opportunity to slip out of the Russian Northern fleet's net, sir."

Rourke exhaled, his body trembling with adrenaline, his eyes fixed on the plot. "Conn, Chief of the Boat, change course to bearing 270, 15 knots," he ordered, his voice steady. "As long as they are distracted, we will slip out, and I hope our luck holds, gentlemen."

Akula-class submarine K-335 Gepard, two nautical miles northeast of Toledo

Sonar contact! "We have him," reported the sonar operator, his eyes locked on the glowing trace hidden beneath the continental shelf. "Hiding in a deep valley within the continental shelf, Captain."

Volodin leaned forward in the command chair, the red lamps throwing shadows across his face. "Weapons, fire the 53-65 wake homing torpedoes."

Moments later, compressed air thundered through the launch tubes as the deadly 53-65s surged into the Barents Sea, their seekers hungry for their prey's wake.

"Clever," Volodin thought, a grim smile tugging at his scar. The Americans had exploited the valley's rugged acoustics—bottom bounces and thermal layers scattering pings—but the *Gepard's* MGK-540 Skat-3 sonar suite, with its flank arrays and towed hydrophone, had pierced the veil. Faint transients from the enemy's failing reactor pumps had given them away, a whisper in the noise of ice floes and biologics. The *Gepard*, commissioned in 1997 but drawing on late-Soviet design prowess, glided through the Barents Sea's continental shelf in silent mode, hunting the American submarine. Her aft-mounted OK-650 reactor hummed quietly, minimising noise in the cluttered underwater landscape.

The crew held their breaths as they monitored the two 53-65 wake-homing torpedoes Volodin had just fired from the forward tubes. 533mm calibre with 300kg warheads, they streaked through the water at 45 knots, their acoustic seekers sniffing for the signature of the target.

"Captain, sonar—torpedoes acquiring," reported Petty Officer Yuri Pavlov, his earphones pressed tight as he tracked the progress of the weapons. The 53-65s, oxygen-fuelled for high speed, homed in on the wake's cavitation bubbles, unfooled by decoys like the Nixie. At a depth of 500 feet, the American sub—likely the *Toledo*—was hiding, its damage from the *Kursk* collision limiting its ability to evade. Volodin visualised the lock: the torpedoes circling in a search pattern, then straightening for the kill.

But victory was no time for complacency. "All hands—ultra vigilance for counterattack," Volodin ordered, his voice crisp over the intercom. "This is a case of who sees whom first and strikes." The *Gepard's* control room tensed; the Akula was stealthy, her anechoic tiles and complex machinery quieter than older Victors, but an American Mk 48 ADCAP could turn the tables. At close range, in these shelf waters with no convergence zones, detection was mutual—ranges shortened to 10-15 nautical miles for passive sonar; at one nautical mile, however, they were practically on top of each other. The crew scanned for transients: pump whirs, screw beats, or the telltale hiss of a torpedo tube flooding.

Volodin, a stoic veteran, trusted his instincts, honed from years of cat-and-mouse games with the Americans deep under the surface. The *Gepard*, at 110 meters long and 8,600 tons submerged, carried eight torpedo tubes loaded with a mix: more 53-65s, TEST-71 wire-guided, and even VA-111 *Shkval's* for possible USN Carrier attack if so ordered. But against a wounded foe, the wake-homers sufficed.

Volodin watched the plot unfold, contemplating the Americans' next move with their submarine. The American sub's hiding spot was clever: the valley's 500-metre depth provided thermal camouflage, but the *Gepard's* flank arrays had detected the anomaly—a faint 15 Hz vibration from damaged pumps. "Found you," Volodin whispered, pride swelling for his sonar team. Pavlov's crew had sifted through the clutter—patchy ducts, rough seas scattering sound—to pinpoint the target at two nautical miles.

"Torpedoes locked—wake gained," Pavlov announced. The weapons sped up, homing with unrelenting precision. Volodin imagined the American captain—scrambling: decoys deployed, emergency manoeuvres executed. But crippled and silent, escape was unlikely.

"Ultra vigilance," Volodin repeated, scanning for countermeasures. The Mk 48 could launch quietly, guided by wire to strike from afar. "Sonar, full sweep—flanks and towed array." The *Gepard's* VSK towed array, streamed astern, listened for whispers in the deep.

As the seconds ticked, the control room held its breath. Impact was imminent—the torpedoes were closing at 45 knots relative. Volodin's mind flashed to Kolesnikov, lost on the *Kursk*. This strike was justice, but war underwater was unforgiving: see first, strike first, survive. The air was thick with tension, the crew's breaths shallow as they monitored the two 53-65 wake-homing torpedoes Volodin had just fired from the forward tubes. The weapons being 533mm calibre with 300kg warheads.

USS *Toledo*, *two nautical miles south of the Gepard*

Commander Tom Brennan stood in *Toledo's* control room, and the tension was palpable. The Los Angeles-class SSN crept into an undersea valley at 500 feet as she moved silently at five knots, her noise signature partially masked by the valley's rocky walls. The S6G reactor was at 20% power, with the noise level reduced to 30 decibels—a faint whisper, but still a risk in the shallow Barents Sea. Brennan's crew were tense—Lieutenant Dave Carter and XO Paul Reese quietly talked to the watch-keepers, reminding them to remember their training and focus on carrying out the commander's orders. They worked as a team, their focus unwavering despite the odds.

"Conn, Sonar," Carter reported, his voice tight as he adjusted his headset, his vision still blurry from the concussion. "Contact update Sierra One—bearing two-two-five, range two nautical miles! The Akula's closing in—she has slowed to five knots, likely refining her firing solution. I am picking up faint pings… she is preparing to attack, sir!"

Brennan's heart stopped, his eyes wide with dread. The Akula—likely the *Gepard*—had found them, even in the undersea valley. At two nautical miles, the *Gepard* was close enough to use wake-homing torpedoes, which would track the *Toledo's* turbulent wake with deadly precision. *Toledo* had less than three minutes to avoid or retaliate. The *Gepard* was undamaged, fully armed, and was moving in to kill its prey—a one-sided conflict in every way. The *Toledo* was crippled, her crew on edge, and her systems strained to the limit. This was a game of hunter and hunted, and failure meant death—not just for Brennan, but for every man aboard. Brennan decided on a course of action; it was do or die trying.

"Weapons, firing solution on Sierra One—four-shot spread!" Brennan ordered; his voice sharp as he devised a desperate plan. "Tubes one and two—wire-guided Mark 48s, direct approach to draw their attention. Tubes three and four flank the Akula, attacking from the rear. We need to hit them before they hit us."

Weapons Officer Lieutenant Blake Phillips worked swiftly at his station; his hands steady despite the dangerous adversary they faced. "Firing solution established, sir," he reported, his voice firm with determination. "Tubes one through four—Mark 48 torpedoes, wire-guided. Tubes one and two on direct approach, tubes three and four set to flank—bearing two-two-five plus ten degrees, then loop to one-three-five. Locked on target. Ready to fire on your command."

Brennan nodded, his eyes burning with focus as he glanced at his crew—Carter, Reese, Phillips, and the others, their faces etched with determination despite their injuries. They were a team, fighting for survival against a relentless enemy. "Fire all tubes—now!" Brennan ordered. Tubes one and two streaked directly toward the *Gepard* at 55 knots, their wire-guided systems feeding data back to the *Toledo*, while tubes three and four arced outward, flanking the Akula to attack from the rear.

"Conn, Sonar," Carter shouted, his voice panicked. "Torpedoes in the water—bearing two-two-five, range four nautical miles, speed 45 knots! Two 53-65Ks, wake-homing, have locked onto us!

Brennan's blood ran cold, his heart pounding as the *Gepard's* torpedoes closed in. The *Toledo* and the *Gepard* had fired on each other, their torpedoes searching for prey in the icy depths of the Barents Sea. This was a deadly duel—two subs, hunter and hunted, with only one likely to survive. The next few minutes would decide the outcome, and failure meant death for Brennan and his crew.

CHAPTER 5

SHADOWS IN THE DEEP

Moscow, the Kremlin, Putin's Office,
1415 — 1615 hours local time

Putin and Lavrov, having decided on their course of action, reached for the red phone on his desk. "Get me Clinton," he ordered, his voice cold. "Yes, I know it is 7.15am in Washington. I do not care if he is sleeping with his intern. Get him up and on the phone now or the nuclear missiles will fly."

Within five minutes, the line crackled to life. "President Putin, this is Bill Clinton. I understand we have a serious situation," he said, calm but tinged with concern.

"President Clinton, two of your Navy submarines have committed an act of war. They have sunk the Kursk, a billion-dollar vessel, and killed 118 Russian sailors. Along with two of our ASW helicopters, four flight crew members are dead. This is an attack on the Russian Federation. We demand answers—and justice," Putin stated calmly.

Lavrov leaned in, his tone diplomatic but firm. "Mr President, seismologists worldwide recorded the 4.2-magnitude blast. Your submarines were in our waters, shadowing the *Kursk*. We have evidence of their involvement. What do you say to this?"

White House, Washington, D.C., The Oval Office

President Bill Clinton hand tightened on the receiver, his Arkansas drawl steady despite the shock. "President Putin, Foreign Minister Lavrov, I am deeply sorry for the loss of your sailors. But I assure you, this must be some kind of mistake. The United States has had nothing to do with this terrible accident and does not want war with Russia—I most definitely do not want to go to war over this.

I need time to investigate. Let us take a step back—give me one hour, and I will call you back. Until then, there will be no escalation from either side. Can we agree on that?

Putin exchanged a glance with Lavrov, who nodded slightly. "One hour, Mr. President," Putin said, voice icy. "No escalation. But if we do not have answers, there will be consequences."

"Agreed," Lavrov added, his tone measured. "We will wait for your call."

Clinton hung up, his mind racing as he pressed the intercom for his chief of staff. "Get me Madeleine Albright, William Cohen, and General Shelton—now.

Within minutes, Secretary of State Madeleine Albright, Secretary of Defence William Cohen, and Chairman of the Joint Chiefs of Staff General Henry Shelton were on a secure conference call, their voices tense as Clinton briefed them.

"The Russians just called," Clinton said, his voice urgent. "Two of our submarines are being blamed for sinking the *Kursk*, with 118 sailors dead and a billion-dollar sub. They have also lost two ASW helicopters, four flight crew killed. They say that they have proof of our submarines being responsible and are calling it an act of war.

I understand that we have two Los Angeles-class subs out there—the USS *Toledo* and USS *Memphis*—at least 228 men at risk of being killed if this does not spiral into World War III. I need to know what the hell is going on, and I have less than one hour before Putin calls back.

Albright, a seasoned diplomat with a sharp mind, spoke first, her voice steady despite the gravity of the situation. "Mr President, if this is true, it is a disaster. A direct attack on a Russian sub—even accidental—could unravel everything we have built since the Cold War. We need to confirm what happened. I will reach out to our ambassador in Moscow, see if we can get more intel from their side."

Cohen, a pragmatic former senator, chimed in, his tone grim. "I will get USLANTFLT on the line—they oversee our subs in the Atlantic. If the USS *Toledo* and USS *Memphis* are involved, they will have logs, ULF transmissions, something. But if they fired on the *Kursk*, even in self-defence, we are in deep trouble."

General Shelton, a four-star general with a no-nonsense demeanour, spoke last, his voice clipped. "Mr President, I will contact the Pentagon's ops centre. We will pull satellite data, sonar records, anything we have on the Barents Sea at local time—that is when the seismic event hit. But we need to prepare for the worst. If the Russians escalate, the 228 men on the *Toledo* and *Memphis* are sitting ducks. And if this goes nuclear, we are looking at a global catastrophe."

Clinton frowned, the stakes sinking in. "Get me answers fast," he ordered. "We've got 50 minutes to figure this out—or we're looking at a war nobody wants."

USS Memphis, 100 nautical miles north of the Kursk wreck 1330 hours

Memphis glided through the sea; running ultraquiet at five knots, 200 feet down, her screw barely turning to minimise cavitation. The control room was thick with the scent of sweat and fear, red lights cast harsh shadows across the faces of the crew. Commander John Rourke stood within the control centre, his square jaw clenched as he watched the tactical plot, his eyes sharp with focus. The *Admiral Levchenko*, a Udaloy-class destroyer, was eight nautical miles north, searching after the decoys ran out of power, her active sonar pinging relentlessly. The three remaining Ka-27PL helicopters—Ka-27PL Medved (Bear), Ka-27PL Tigr (Tiger), and Ka-27PL Bars (Leopard)—continued their hunt, their dipping sonars forming a deadly net.

Suddenly, Rourke registered the *Admiral Kharlamov* switching tracks, boxing in the *Memphis*, and forcing them south.

"Conn, Sonar," said Lieutenant Mike Hensley, his lanky frame hunched over the console, his headset pressed tightly against his ears. "Multiple torpedoes in the water—bearing zero-one-zero, range six nautical miles, speed 45 knots. They are active and closing—ETA eight minutes."

Rourke's stomach churned as he processed the threat. The *Admiral Levchenko* had launched two 53-65K wake-homing torpedoes, their active sonars pinging as they hunted for a submerged target. The *Memphis* was at 200 feet, silently moving at five knots, but the incoming torpedoes were fast and closing, and the shallow Barents Sea continental shelf offered little room to manoeuvre.

"Weapons, status on the firing solution?" Rourke asked, his voice steady despite the ticking clock.

"Solution locked on the *Admiral Levchenko*, sir," replied Weapons Officer Ed Kline, his stocky frame moving with precision as he input the commands. "Tubes one through four loaded with Mark 48 war shots, ready to fire."

Rourke hesitated. Firing on a Russian destroyer would escalate the conflict beyond repair—an act of war, plain and simple. However, if he did not act, either these torpedoes or another Silex depth charge attack would destroy *Memphis*. He thought of Commander Tom Brennan, limping away in his crippled sub, counting on the *Memphis* to draw the heat. Rourke had no choice. "Fire tubes one and two," he ordered, his voice like steel. "Target the *Admiral Levchenko*. Launch noisemakers from tubes three and four—give those torpedoes something else to chase."

From the tubes, the *Memphis's* compressed air system launched Mark 48 torpedoes. The noisemakers followed, darting west, their acoustic signatures mimicking the sound of a fleeing submarine. The Russian 53-65K torpedoes wavered, two of them veered toward the decoys, but one remained locked on the *Memphis*, closing fast.

"Torpedo still tracking us," Hensley reported, his voice tight. "Range five and a half nautical miles, ETA five and a half minutes."

"Evasive manoeuvres," Rourke snapped. "Come left to two-seven-zero, increase to flank speed. Release countermeasures." The *Memphis* turned sharply, her screw cavitated wildly as the ship sped up to 35 knots. Vibrations ran through the deck plates under their boots. A cloud of bubbles and acoustic decoys erupted in her wake, a last-ditch effort to confuse the torpedo.

Rourke was calm under pressure. The *Memphis* was travelling at 35 knots, far slower than the torpedo's 45 knots. At flank speed, he had increased the time to torpedo hit to 36 minutes. The 53-65K was wake-homing, locking onto the turbulent wake left by the *Memphis's* wildly cavitating screw, and at this range, its active sonar would ensure a precise strike.

"XO, maintain flank speed—35 knots!" Rourke ordered. "All ahead full speed—let's make this harder for her!"

The *Memphis* surged forward. The steel creaked in protest as her noise level spiked to 120 decibels—a cacophony of cavitation and reactor noise that echoed through the shallow Barents Sea. The increased speed widened her wake, but it also made her a clearer target for the two remaining wake-homing torpedoes.

Rourke realised they had to break the lock; speed alone would not save them. Twenty minutes had passed, and the Russian 53-65 were coming on relentlessly. He had to break the deadlock and go silent again. They were making so much noise they could probably hear him in the Kremlin.

"Launch more countermeasures—AN/WLY-1, full spread!" Rourke barked. "Chief-of-the-Boat, create a knuckle—hard to starboard, 30-degree rudder and then hard to port! Emergency dive—take us to the seabed, 500 feet! Release a bubble cloud—now!"

The *Memphis* crew sprang into action. Weapons Officer Ed Kline deployed the AN/WLY-1 decoys, whose acoustic signatures, at 90 decibels, mimicked the *Memphis's* propeller cavitation and wake turbulence. "Decoys away, sir!" Kline reported, voice steady despite the tension.

"Making a knuckle, sir, aye, aye!" reported the helmsman, Chief Petty Officer Daniel Harris, gripping the wheel as the sub heeled violently.

The *Memphis* executed a sharp turn to starboard and then port, with alternating 30-degree rudder movements creating a "knuckle" in the water. This turbulent disturbance disrupted her wake and confused the torpedo's wake-homing sensors.

"Diving to 500 feet, aye, aye!" called the diving officer, Lieutenant James Carter, as the *Memphis* nosed down, its ballast tanks adjusting rapidly. The sub skimmed just above the rocky seabed and experienced a rapid depth change to 500 feet. A shallow depth left little room for error. The sudden descent further disrupted the *Memphis's* wake, causing the turbulent water to dissipate in the choppy currents and forcing the 53-65K to rely on its active sonar rather than wake-homing.

"Bubble cloud released!" Kline shouted, activating the compressed air system to eject a cloud of bubbles behind the *Memphis*. The bubble screen scattered the torpedo's sonar pings, creating a chaotic acoustic environment that masked the *Memphis's* signature. Confused by the knuckle, depth change, and bubble cloud, the 53-65K torpedoes struggled.

As the boat descended, the depth gauge steadied feet above the Barents Sea floor. Silt swirled outside the hull, a ghostly haze on the sonar tank's display. The control room was hushed, the usual background hum sharpened by tension.

"Captain, we're at five feet off the bottom," the diving officer reported, voice tight.

Rourke studied the chart table. The inertial plot showed their track vanishing into uncertainty. No GPS fix was possible this far under the surface, and the magnetic compass had long since given up. They were flying blind, with the seabed rising to meet them.

He made his decision.

"Sonar, energise active. One ping."

There was a beat of silence, then the petty officer's clipped reply: "Aye, sir. Active sonar — one ping."

The order rippled through the control room. A deep metallic thump reverberated through the hull as the bow transducer released its sound pulse into the black. Every man felt it in his chest, a reminder that the ocean itself had been struck like a giant bell.

Seconds dragged. Then the screen blossomed with hard white arcs — bottom contours, jagged ridges of high and low ridges on the Barents Sea floor, and the narrow channel through which they threaded.

"Contact reports… bottom at five feet, keel overhead at two-two-five. Egress is tight, but navigable, sir."

Rourke exhaled slowly. One problem solved, but the risk was now doubled. Every hydrophone from Murmansk to Novaya Zemlya had heard that ping.

"Very well. Helm, keep her steady. Sonar — back to passive. We have told the world where we are. Let us hope nobody's listening too closely."

"Conn, Sonar," Hensley reported, voice rising with hope. "Torpedoes are wavering—range 500 yards, it is searching… it is veering off! It is chasing the decoys, bearing two-six-zero, range 800 yards—it has lost us, sir!"

Rourke exhaled sharply, adrenaline rushing through him as he ordered the *Memphis* off the bottom and levelled out at 250 feet, silent battle stations. The 53-65K's had been thrown off by the combination of countermeasures, the knuckle, the bubble cloud, and the bottoming of the ship, an extremely dangerous high-risk manoeuvre, their sonar pings fading as it chased the AN/WLY-1 decoys westward.

"Maintain five knots, rig for ultraquiet and redeploy the towed array," Rourke ordered, his voice steady despite the sweat beading on his forehead. "Keep us on course two-seven-zero—let's put some distance between us and that destroyer."

The *Memphis* headed southwest, her crew breathing a collective sigh of relief, but the tension remained palpable. Rourke's had bought them time, but the Northern Fleet would not stop.

Udaloy-class destroyer Admiral Levchenko, eight nautical miles north of Memphis

"Captain, the *Pyotr Velikiy* has ordered the *Admiral Levchenko* to drive the American submarine southwest towards the *Pyotr Velikiy* with nuclear depth charges. Admiral Chernov wants to finish it with the *Pyotr Velikiy's* RPK-2 Vyuga atomic torpedoes. The order sent a chill down the spine of the ship's crew.

Commander Alexei Morozov stood on the bridge of the *Admiral Levchenko*, a hunter-killer ASW destroyer. He was not entirely sure that this was a good idea morally, but orders were orders, and he would carry them out to the letter. The sonar room was thick with tension. Operators, with headphones clamped tight, hunched over their consoles as the ocean's whispers turned into green lines across their scopes.

"Contact bearing zero-eight-six, range twenty thousand yards, depth two-fifty," the lead sonar man called, voice clipped. "Likely the

Los Angeles-class submarine, captain. Faint screw signature, but steady. Sir, our torpedoes have failed."

Captain Morozov leaned forward, eyes narrowing. The Americans were there, stalking, watching. They had incredibly avoided his 53-65 torpedoes. He would carry out his orders and drive it south using nuclear depth charges as ordered. In the CIC, Morozov's face was a hard coin of shadow and resolve as he stared at the tactical display. The contact—once a point on a scope—had become a calculus of risk and consequence. He raised his voice, not loud but absolute.

"Swap the SS-N-14 warheads. Replace conventional depth charges with tactical nuclear warheads. Execute now."

The weapons officer's face frowned. Around him, the crew moved with the staccato precision of men who had trained for a thousand contingencies but never for this terror. Lockers hissed open; mechanical arms strained as technicians unbolted plates and slid racks in a choreography practised in silence. Technicians stripped the SS-N-14 tubes, which usually bristled with their standard payload, to reveal the cold, guarded casings of the special munitions—sealed, serial'd, and stamped with the weight of treaties and the whispers of ministers.

In the sonar room, the steady pulse of pings became a pulsing drumbeat in every man's chest. The countermeasures sonar searched for a possible American torpedo counterattack. Morozov watched the tracks braid across the screen, then break away—an act of mercy, or of calculation. He felt the scale of the decision: not a tactical tweak, but a political fulcrum — a single command that could tilt the world.

"Authorisation?" the weapons officer asked, voice rough with what might be fear or discipline.

Morozov did not hesitate. He thought of the *Kursk* sailors' faces, of cold decks and the dull smell of ozone and burnt coffee. He thought of the captain he once was and the one the navy demands him to be. "Authorised," he ordered.

The launch crews secured the caps, the safety interlocks clicked into place, and the ship's weight seemed to shift with the knowledge it now bore. Outside, the Barents Sea continued—an indifferent expanse of slate—but inside the *Admiral Levchenko*, everyone measured every breath against the slow, inevitable tick of history. They readied the first rockets. There was no going back.

The weapons officer's hand hovered over the arming panel when suddenly another voice broke in, sharp and urgent.

"New contacts! Two fast inbound, bearing one-one-two, range six thousand yards and closing. Torpedoes! Wire-guided, heavy class—MK-48s!"

The compartment froze for a heartbeat. The Americans had struck back.

"Confirm!" Morozov snapped.

"Confirmed—double drive, cavitation spikes, speed fifty knots and rising!"

Alarms shrieked through the ship. The weapons officer slammed his hand on the klaxon, red lights flashing across the CIC. The image of the Los Angeles-class target vanished beneath the larger threat blooming across the sonar plot like a spreading stain.

"Deploy countermeasures! Launch decoys—both rails!" Morozov barked. "Hard turn to port, twenty-five knots. Bring the ship around now!"

Hydraulics shuddered as the destroyer heeled into her turn, the sea clawing at her hull. On the scopes, the twin American torpedoes split, homing, weaving through the depths.

The SS-N-14 Silex multiple launch nuclear depth charges sat primed in their launchers, forgotten in the chaos. Morozov realised grimly that his prey had become the predator. The fight was no longer about the hunt. It was about survival.

Morozov turned to his XO, a worried frown on his face. Using nuclear depth charges to defend his ship was one thing, but launching them at an American submarine was a different matter altogether. "Carry out the

Admiral's orders, XO," he growled. "Launch the nuclear depth charges."

The XO nodded, but his eyes flickered with concern. Chernov's obsession with vengeance risked escalating the conflict beyond control; nuclear depth charges designed to destroy submarines were a step too far without orders from the Kremlin. Alexey Bulavin, a 35-year-old weapons officer with a perpetual frown, launched the nuclear depth charges from the SS-N-14 Silex multiple rocket launchers with grim satisfaction, determined to avenge the *Kursk*.

However, his sonar officer's shout shattered his focus.

"Torpedoes inbound—bearing one-nine-zero, range 2000 yards, speed 55 knots!" the sonar officer, Lieutenant Ivan Kuznetsov, shouted, his hands trembling as he adjusted the MGK-345 sonar suite.

Morozov froze, his frown deepening as he processed the threat. "Hard to starboard!" he shouted, his voice sharp. "Launch countermeasures— deploy the RBU-6000 Smerch-2 multiple launch rockets with low-yield nuclear depth charges between us and those torpedoes immediately!"

The *Admiral Levchenko* turned sharply, its screws churning as the RBU-6000 rocket launchers on her deck roared to life. The system fired a salvo of low-yield nuclear depth charges—specialised 0.1-kiloton warheads designed to destroy submarines. Morozov's battle tactics aimed to detonate these incoming Mark 48 torpedoes at a safe distance, protecting his ship from collateral damage. The warheads splashed into the water, their sensors locking onto the incoming Mark 48s.

A muted flash and shockwave vaporised the first Mark 48 when the first nuclear depth charge detonated. The second detonated 300 yards astern, catching the second Mark 48 in its blast radius. The *Admiral Levchenko* rocked from the shockwaves, her hull rattled, but she held firm—her reinforced design weathering the low-yield blasts with only minor flooding in her lower compartments.

"Damage report!" Morozov barked, gripping the railing tightly as the ship steadied.

"Minor flooding in the engine room, sir," replied his XO, Lieutenant Commander Sergei Skrypka, a wiry man with a balding head. "Pumps are handling it. We are still in the fight."

"Signal the *Pyotr Velikiy*," Morozov ordered, his voice tense. "American sub fired on us—two torpedoes, neutralised by nuclear countermeasures. We are re-engaging with nuclear depth charges."

Morozov calculated their next move. The nuclear depth charges had saved them, but the Americans were fighting back. Morozov thought of the *Kursk's* crewmen he had known and trained with. The Americans would pay for this day.

USS Memphis, 100 nautical miles north of the Kursk wreck, 1330 hours

Commander John Rourke gripped the periscope stand in the USS *Memphis's* control room; his eyes narrowed at the sonar plot as the depths of the Barents Sea pressed in like a vice. The red battle lights cast long shadows, the air thick with the hum of the S6G reactor and the faint ozone scent of electronics pushed to their limits. Rourke's instincts screamed danger, the *Admiral Levchenko* had closed to ten thousand yards, her MGK-355 Polinom sonar was pinging aggressively, her Rastrub-B launchers likely primed. Chernov's fleet was a noose, and Rourke felt the rope tightening. "They're gearing for an attack," he muttered. "We struck in self-defence."

"Weapons, Kline—firing solution on *Admiral Levchenko*. Tubes one and two, Mk 48 ADCAPs, wire-guided," Rourke ordered, his voice steady as steel.

Lieutenant Commander Ed Kline, at the fire control console, tapped the plugin tablet, syncing with the BQQ-5 array. "Solution locked, Captain. Range 9,500 yards, bearing zero-three-zero. Wires ready."

The Mk 48s, 3,500-pound heavyweights with 650kg warheads, were optimised for anti-surface strikes, their propulsion system capable of pushing 55 knots.

"Fire one… fire two," Rourke commanded. There was a slight pressure drop within the *Memphis* as compressed air, wires spooling out for guidance, ejected the torpedoes. Kline and the sonar crew tracked them, the weapons diving to 200 feet before levelling, homing on the *Admiral Levchenko's* massive hull. "Torpedoes running hot, straight, and normal," Kline reported. "ETA to target: four minutes."

Rourke's gut twisted. This was self-defence—the *Admiral Levchenko's* active pings, previous torpedo attack, and helo deployments signalled imminent assault. But firing on a Russian warship crossed a line, escalating the shadow war to blood. The crew held breath, the sonar waterfall showing the Mk 48s closing: 5,000 yards… 3,000… 2,000.

At 1,000 yards, disaster struck. "Con, sonar—multiple transients! Massive explosions ahead!" Chief Petty Officer Dan Willis yelled, ripping off his headphones in pain. The crew followed suit, ears ringing from the acoustic assault. Several terminals flickered, switching to redundancy mode as overload protectors kicked in—the explosions so extreme they blew sonar circuits, feedback screeching like banshees.

Alarms blared, the *Memphis* vibrating from distant shockwaves. "Update—now!" Rourke barked, steadying himself against the conn.

"Con, sonar—nuclear depth charges, sir! The *Admiral Levchenko* deployed nukes to take out our Mk 48s," Willis gasped, massaging his ears. The 0.5-kiloton blasts had vaporised the torpedoes in a cataclysmic bubble, the yield designed for ASW but lethal at close range. Radiation warnings flickered amber—minimal exposure at this distance, but the acoustic hammer had stunned the sonar suite.

"New threat—multiple splashdowns in a 1,000-yard arc around our bow, covering northeast coordinates," Willis added, his voice hoarse. "Tonals match depth charges, sir—conventional pattern, sinking fast."

Rourke's mind raced—Chernov's herding tactic, funnelling them into a kill box. "Rig for depth charges! All hands, brace for impact! XO, all ahead flank—heading coordinates southwest of this position. Do it now!"

Lieutenant Commander Sarah Carter slammed the throttles; the *Memphis* surged to 35 knots. The crew braced—hands on rails, bodies tensed—as the first charges detonated at 300 feet. The sub bucked. Then hell erupted. A gigantic shock wave from a sub-sea nuclear blast threw the whole rear of the *Memphis* through the depths. Multiple nuclear detonations rippled in sequence, the 0.5-kt yields creating a wall of hydrostatic fury. Crewmen went flying—Petty Officer Richards slammed into a bulkhead; Ensign Lee tumbled across the deck. Alarms wailed: "Hull breach alert! Pressure anomaly!" Water pressure pipes burst, high-pressure sprays hissed like serpents, flooding compartments with icy seawater. Consoles sparked, emergency lights flickered as the boat pitched 20 degrees starboard.

Rourke clung to the conn, blood trickling from a gash on his forehead. "Engineering—status on the reactor?" he shouted over the chaos.

Chief Engineer Lieutenant Mike Hensley's voice crackled through the 1MC: "Lucky for us, sir—we were at full power and flank speed. Got the tail end of that series of blasts. Reactor did not scram; containment holding. Sustained minimum damage—auxiliary pumps offline, but primaries good. Sealing leaks now."

Relief washed over Rourke amid the pandemonium. The *Memphis's* speed had carried them to the blast's periphery, the nuclear fury dissipating in the water column. "Helm—get us out of here! Southwest, maximum depth, silent running once clear."

Carter adjusted course, the sub levelling as repair teams sealed pipes and reset systems. The nuclear detonations had lit the sea like underwater suns, but the *Memphis* had endured—a testament to her design. Rourke wiped blood from his eyes, his thoughts on Brennan and the *Toledo*. Chernov had crossed the nuclear threshold; the game had changed. "All hands, damage control—report in five. We're not done yet."

The *Memphis* fled southwest, her hull scarred but intact, the Barents' depths a graveyard of escalation.

Akula-class submarine K-335 Gepard (Cheetah), two nautical miles southeast of Toledo

Captain Yuri Volodin clung to the periscope control system in the *Gepard's* control room, his dark eyes wide with dread as the sonar plot lit up with new contacts. Moments ago, the Akula-class submarine had fired two Type 53-65 wake-homing torpedoes at the American submarine, but the Americans had counterattacked with terrifying precision. The *Gepard's* crew worked frantically, their hands flying over the controls as the reality of their situation set in.

"Conn, Sonar!" Lieutenant Ivan Kuznetsov shouted; his voice panicked as he adjusted the MGK-500 suite. "Four torpedoes in the water—bearing zero-four-five, range three nautical miles, speed 55 knots! They are Mark 48s, sir—wire-guided! Two on direct approach, two flanking from the rear!"

Volodin's heart slammed against his ribcage as the words sank in. Four Mark 48s—the Americans had fired a devastating spread, two to draw their attention and two to flank from the rear, a classic Los Angeles-class tactic. He had underestimated these Yankee cowboys, and now they were fighting back with lethal precision. "Countermeasures—full spread!" Volodin barked; his voice hoarse with desperation. "Emergency surface—35 knots, 25-degree bubble! Flank speed—now!"

The *Gepard* surged upward; its ballast tanks emptied with a roar as she climbed at a 25-degree angle, her screw pushing the Akula to 40 knots—beyond flank speed—in a desperate bid to escape. The sub's OK-650 reactor, 43,000 Hp strained under the load, every groan of the pressure hull further tightened the crew's jaws as she breached the surface, her titanium frame glistening in the pale Arctic sunlight.

Acoustic decoys launched from her tubes, their signatures blaring at 90 decibels to mimic the *Gepard's* noise, but the Mark 48s were wire-guided, with their active/passive seekers locking onto the Akula's hull despite the countermeasures.

"Torpedoes closing—400 yards… 200 yards!" Kuznetsov shouted, his voice cracking with fear as the Mark 48s homed in, the wire guidance feeding real-time data to the *Toledo*. The direct-approach torpedoes veered off, chasing a decoy, while the flanking pair looped around, striking the *Gepard's* rear. The twin 650-pound warheads detonated in a cataclysmic explosion, the shockwave ripping through the Akula's stern, blowing off her rear screw and shattering her propulsion shaft.

The conning tower swayed almost imperceptibly, reminding the crew how fragile the titanium tube was as the *Gepard* shuddered violently, floating disabled, her stern wrecked. Alarms blared, red lights flashing as the crew scrambled to assess the damage. "Propulsion lost, sir!" reported the damage control officer, his voice tight with panic. "Rear screw destroyed—flooding in compartments eight and nine! We are dead in the water!"

Volodin's face twisted with rage, his dark eyes burning with fury as he clung to the railing, the *Gepard* bobbing helplessly on the surface of the Barents Sea. The American submarine had outmanoeuvred him, its captain a genuine cowboy—fearless, aggressive, and wielding the best in Western technology. Volodin had failed Kolesnikov, failed his crew, and now they were at the mercy of the Americans—and the Northern Fleet's wrath.

"Comms, get me the *Petr Velikiy*—now!" Volodin ordered, his voice a low growl as he steadied himself. The control room was chaotic with alarms and shouting men. The comms officer, Lieutenant Alexey Bulavin, adjusted the encrypted satellite radio, his hands trembling as he established the connection.

"*Petr Velikiy*, this is *Gepard*," Volodin said, his voice steady despite the fury in his chest. "Two Mark 48 torpedoes have hit us from the

American submarine. We have sustained damage, but we are floating on the surface at 70 degrees north and 30 degrees east. All hands are safe; we need rescue and recovery—request immediate help."

USS *Toledo, eight nautical miles south of the Kursk wreck*

Commander Tom Brennan stood in the *Toledo's* control room. The *Toledo* remained in the undersea valley at 500 feet, its noise signature suppressed at 30 decibels, and its crew worked as a seamless unit despite their injuries. However, the *Gepard's* two Type 53-65 wake-homing torpedoes were closing fast, their sonar pings echoed through the shallow Barents Sea, a deadly threat at just four nautical miles.

"Conn, Sonar," Lieutenant Dave Carter reported, his voice was tight as he adjusted his headset, his concussion was making his vision blur, but his focus was unwavering. "Torpedoes closing—bearing two-two-five, range three thousand yards, speed 40 knots! They are wake-homing, sir—they are searching for our turbulence!"

Brennan assessed the threat. Wake-homing Type 53-65 torpedoes tracked a target's turbulent wake, but they might not be very effective against a submarine like the *Toledo*, moving slowly at five knots, in the shallow, choppy Barents Sea. At 500 feet deep, with a Sea State 4, the waves above and the rocky seabed below created a noisy environment, yet the *Toledo's* minimal wake still posed a risk. He needed to make her invisible—now.

Brennan ordered, "Countermeasures—full spread!" His voice was sharp. "Launch turbulence maker decoys—AN/WLY-1, maximum output! Emergency ballast change—flood tanks for a rapid dive! Shut down the screw and pumps—silent routine, now!"

The *Toledo* crew sprang into action, their hands flying over the controls with practised precision. Weapons Officer Lieutenant Blake

Phillips deployed the AN/WLY-1 decoys, whose acoustic signatures, at 90 decibels, mimicked the *Toledo's* propeller cavitation and wake turbulence. "Decoys away, sir!" Blake reported, his voice steady despite the tension in the control room. The decoys streaked outward, echoing through the shallow water, drawing the Type 53-65s toward false targets.

"Flood the ballast tanks—rapid dive!" XO Paul Reese barked, his cracked rib sent a jolt of pain through his chest as he relayed the order. The *Toledo's* ballast tanks filled with seawater, her nose dipped as she descended rapidly to 580 feet, just above the rocky seabed of the Barents Sea. The sudden depth changes disrupted *Toledo's* wake, with turbulent water dissipating in the choppy currents and further confusing the wake-homing torpedoes.

"Screw and pumps offline—silent routine engaged!" reported Lieutenant Mark Evans from the engineering compartment. The *Toledo's* screw stopped, her coolant pumps reduced to zero, dropping her noise level to near-ambient—30 decibels, a ghostly whisper in the noisy Barents Sea. The sub glided on momentum alone, its hull groaning as it settled into the undersea valley's rocky embrace, the seabed's clutter masking its residual signature.

"Conn, Sonar," Carter reported, his voice steady with relief. "Torpedoes evaded—decoys worked! The Type 53-65s are chasing the AN/WLY-1s, bearing zero-three-zero, range 500 yards—they have lost us, sir!

But the Akula—she is surfacing! Emergency ascent—40 knots, 25-degree up bubble… our Mark 48s are closing—impact!

Brennan's eyes burned with focus as the sonar plot confirmed the hits. The flanking Mark 48s had struck the *Gepard's* rear, the 650-pound warheads had detonating in a fiery explosion "Damage assessment?" Brennan asked, his voice sharp as he gripped the railing, his shoulder screaming with every movement.

"Direct hits, sir," Carter replied with relief. "Their propulsion shaft shattered, blowing off the Akula's rear screw. "The submarine is surfaced, bearing two-two-five, range two thousand yards. She is dead in the water, sir."

Brennan exhaled. He looked at his crew—Carter, Reese, Phillips, and the others—whose faces showed relief and exhaustion. They had avoided the *Gepard's* torpedoes with decoys, quick depth changes, and silent running—a testament to their skill and teamwork. Their counterattack had worked—the *Toledo* had forced the *Gepard* to surface, disabled, her rear screw a mangled wreck. The Akula was out of the fight, her crew at the mercy of the Northern Fleet's rescue efforts. "Maintain silence; at least we have prevented more deaths. "Set course two-seven-zero, depth 300 feet, all ahead five knots—let's get out of here before the surface fleet comes to the Akula's aid."

The *Toledo* crept west at five knots as she moved through the icy depths of the Barents Sea. They had survived the Akula's attack, but the Northern Fleet would not stop hunting. Brennan wondered how Rourke on the *Memphis* was doing; his focus was to make every second count to get his crew home.

Pyotr Velikiy (Peter the Great), 18 nautical miles northeast of the Kursk wreck

Admiral Viktor Chernov stood on the *Pyotr Velikiy's* bridge, his dark eyes burning with rage as *Admiral Levchenko* reported they had to use nuclear depth charges to avoid being sunk by two American Mark 48 torpedoes fired from one of the American Los Angeles submarines. The American sub was still out there, evading Morozov torpedoes with cunning and desperation, attacking at every opportunity. Chernov's hands clenched into fists, his cigarette forgotten as ash fell to the deck. The *Kursk* was gone and two helicopters had been lost to the Americans'

Sea Lance missile. He had to make them pay, or a court-martial would be his reward for failure.

"Signal the *Gepard*," Chernov ordered. "Find out whether they have engaged and sunk that Yankee submarine yet?"

"The *Gepard* reports two Mark 48 torpedoes have hit them, sir. They are on the surface, damaged, at coordinates 70 degrees north and 30 degrees east. All hands safe, requesting rescue," said Lieutenant Mikhail Orlov.

Chernov's face darkened, a snarl escaping his lips as he slammed his fist on the chart table, rattling the coffee mugs. "Pizdetz, those Yankee bastards!" he roared, his voice reverberating through the bridge. "They have crippled the *Gepard* now—they will pay for this! Signal the *Smolensk*—divert from the *Kursk* wreck and rescue the *Gepard* immediately. Full speed!"

Captain Ivan Rostov, the *Petr Velikiy's* CO, nodded and relayed the orders to Orlov. "*Smolensk*, this is *Petr Velikiy*," Orlov transmitted over the encrypted channel. "*Gepard* is on the surface, damaged, at 70 degrees north, 30 degrees east. All hands safe, requires immediate rescue. Divert and assist—full speed."

Chernov turned to Rostov, his rage barely contained. "The Americans think they can strike us and run," he growled. "Arm the RPK-6 Vodopad with nuclear depth charges and nuclear torpedoes. No more messing about. I want that submarine on the bottom of the Barents Sea. Make it happen now, Rostov."

Rostov nodded, but his eyes flickered with concern. The *Gepard's* survival was a small mercy, yet Chernov's obsession with vengeance risked escalating the conflict beyond anyone's control. What would the Kremlin think? They were all going to be court-martialled or worse. Rostov's mind drifted to Lieutenant Commander Dmitry Sokolov in the weapons control centre, pale and looking extremely concerned.

CIA Station, USA Consulate, Istanbul, Turkey

Elizabeth Carter, the CIA Station Chief in Istanbul, stood in her secure office at the US Consulate, her attention focused on the encrypted phone. At 50, Carter was a seasoned operative with a no-nonsense demeanour; her short grey hair and tailored suit testified to her professionalism.

She had spent 25 years at the Agency, running operations from Berlin to Beirut, but this call from Michael Harper, the consulate's affairs officer, had her on edge.

Harper, a 40-year-old state department official working for the CIA had a knack for handling crises, paced the room, his tie loosened, and his coffee cup forgotten on the desk. "Liz, I just spoke to him—Lieutenant Oleg Vesnen, Russian Northern Fleet, aboard the *Smolensk*," Harper said, his voice urgent.

The man is offering to defect, and he has proof of US involvement. He claims the *Toledo* collided with the *Kursk*, and the *Memphis* fired a Mark 48 in retaliation, sinking her and resulting in 118 sailors' deaths.

He also describes the destruction of two ASW helicopters. He is asking for a million dollars and asylum for his family.

Carter's jaw tightened, her mind racing as she processed the implications. The *Kursk* sinking was already a global crisis—seismic stations had detected a 4.2-magnitude event at 0638 hours Barents Sea time, and whispers of US involvement were circulating. If Vesnen's proof got out, it could confirm Russia's accusations of an act of war, derailing the delicate US-Russia talks that President Clinton was likely scrambling to manage.

"He's got the goods, Michael," Carter said, her eyes narrowing. "Those logs could blow this wide open—or give us the leverage to keep it quiet."

But he is on a Russian frigate in a war zone. The FSB will be onto him like sharks if they suspect he is talking.

Harper nodded, running a hand through his thinning hair. "He is terrified—he has a satellite phone, but he needs to get off the *Smolensk* now. The *Kursk* distracted the Russians and are hunting our subs, but that will not last. What do we do?"

Carter did not hesitate. "I'm calling Langley," she said, dialling the secure line to CIA headquarters. "We need to move fast; please wait outside my office, Michael."

The line connected, and Deputy Director for Operations Frank Bennett answered in a gruff voice. "Carter, what've you got?"

"Frank, it's Liz in Istanbul," Carter said, tone urgent. "We have a Russian defector—Lieutenant Oleg Vesnen, Northern Fleet, aboard the *Smolensk* in the Barents Sea. He is offering proof of US involvement in the sinking of the *Kursk*—collision with the *Toledo*, Mark 48 strike from the *Memphis*, 118 sailors dead. Also, details on the loss of two ASW helicopters—four flight crew killed by a US weapon. He wants a million dollars and asylum for his family. This is explosive—we need to act now."

Bennett's silence was brief, the weight of the intel sinking in. "Jesus, Liz," he said, voice low. "That is a geopolitical nuke. If the Russians capture him first, we are screwed. I am calling an emergency meeting—Director Tenet, DNI, the works. Stand by."

Within minutes, Bennett had convened an emergency video conference with CIA Director George Tenet, Director of National Intelligence John McLaughlin, and National Security Advisor Sandy Berger to brief them on Vesnen's offer. Tenet, a veteran spymaster with a sharp mind, spoke first. His tone was decisive: "We cannot let this intel fall into the wrong hands.

If Vesnen's proof confirms our involvement, we need to control it—either to manage the fallout with Russia or to bury it. A million dollars and asylum are a small price to pay. I say we green-light the extraction.

McLaughlin's analytical mind was already envisioning scenarios. "Agreed. But we need to move fast. The Russians are on a warpath—Clinton's on the phone with Putin right now, trying to de-escalate."

Berger, a pragmatic diplomat, weighed in. "We have 228 men on those subs—USS *Toledo* and USS *Memphis*. These men will be the first casualties if this escalates to World War III. Extract Vesnen, secure the intel, and give Clinton something to work with in the talks. I will brief the President."

Bennett turned to the screen, voice firm. "Extraction approved. Liz, coordinate with JSOC—we will deploy a SEAL fire team from the carrier USS *Theodore Roosevelt*, which is currently on patrol in the Norwegian Sea. A helicopter will transport the SEAL fire team to the modified fishing trawler we maintain in Kirkenes, Finland. It is right on the border with the Russian Federation, with direct access to the Barents Sea. Tell him to get off the *Smolensk* ASAP and maintain contact via his satellite phone."

Carter nodded, already getting up from her desk and opening her office door. "Michael, it's a go," she said, voice clipped. Langley approved Vesnen's terms: a million dollars and asylum for his family. Recover him and the intelligence before the FSB sniffs it out. I want that troubleshooter you maintain, Agent Smith, on the case. You have him in Oslo at present, don't you?" she added.

Harper, standing in the doorway with his tie slightly askew after a hectic morning, acknowledged. "Understood, Liz. Yes, Smith's there on that NATO leak to the FSB."

Carter leaned back, her fingers tapping steadily on the polished mahogany. "Precisely. Activate him immediately. He's our best troubleshooter in Europe, even though he's no spring chicken—get him moving."

Harper nodded, his mind already racing through the logistics like a well-rehearsed evasion drill. "Yes, Liz. Perfect timing. I will contact Smith at once. He has got the Agency G5 on standby—he can be wheels up in an hour, flight plan to Kirkenes in eastern Finland. The agency maintains a stealth trawler prepped there; he can handle the setup."

"Make it happen, Michael," Carter replied, her tone brooking no delay, as though she were dispatching a knight-errant on a quest for the

Grail. And the USS *Theodore Roosevelt*. That battle carrier strike group off the Norwegian coast—contact Rear Admiral William Fallon. Invoke Presidential Order 37578. Authorise the special operations forces for this urgent mission. Assign a SEAL fire team to support Smith.

Harper exhaled, feeling the adrenaline coil like a spring. "Got it, Liz. If the FSB gets wind, we are looking at Spetsnaz—or worse. Smith will need that backup."

Carter's gaze hardened, the room's fluorescent light catching the steel in her eyes. "Precisely. Now go—I will text you Fallon's secure line. You can handle Vesnen's end. Let's hope he can slip off that Russian destroyer without raising the alarm."

Harper turned on his heel, the door clicking shut behind him like the safety on a pistol. In his own office, he dialled the secure line, his fingers steady despite the pulse in his temples. The game was afoot, and in this world of shadows, one misstep could unravel the lot.

...

Meanwhile, on the waterfront in Oslo, Agent John Smith enjoyed the last puff of his cigar, the rich Cuban tobacco mixing with the fresh fjord air under a clear blue sky. At 51, he looked quite distinguished— salt-and-pepper hair brushed back, square jaw and wide cheekbones, a black Hugo Boss sports coat fitted to hide the faint bulge of his HK USP Kompakt 9mm, over a plain white shirt, designer jeans, and black rubber-soled Crocket & Jones dress shoes. He was discreetly watching the NATO officer suspected of selling military secrets to the FSB, who was having a coffee with his wife a few tables away. Meanwhile, he was talking to a pretty, aspiring Norwegian blonde model named Freja. It was an ideal cover for his position, and he thought to himself later, maybe dinner and a nice Chianti Classico with good company.

He had spent the morning at the Viking Ship Museum, with the ancient longships' oak hulls evoking a simpler era of conquest. The curator, a wiry Norwegian with a twinkle in his eye, had regaled him with a wartime yarn: Hitler's visit during the occupation, the Führer's sneer at the "primitive" vessels compared to the Kriegsmarine's might. The curator's retort—in flawless German—"But ja, my ancestors at least completed their English invasion in these, no?"—had sent Hitler storming off, an SS thug lingering to threaten execution. Smith chuckled inwardly; such insolence appealed to his sense of understated defiance.

His cellular phone vibrated in the top pocket of his coat—a discreet Nokia GSM 2G, untraceable and encrypted with a special agency patch. "Smith," he answered, his voice smooth as aged Scotch.

"Smith, it's Harper. Get moving to the airport—board the G5. Pilots are refuelling now; flight plan submitted to your destination in far eastern Finland. Secure fax aboard with the full mission brief."

Smith flicked ash from his cigar, his hazel eyes scanning the quay for tails out of habit, and glanced at his Rolex Submariner, checking the time out of habit. "And my mission here in Oslo?"

"This takes priority, Smith. You will understand once you read the brief. Use the secure sat-phone en route to discuss in depth during transit. You'll have company from the USS *Theodore Roosevelt*—a SEAL fire team once you get to Kirkenes."

Smith's lips curved in a faint smile, the thrill of the chase stirring despite his years. "Sounds serious. I'm leaving now."

He stubbed out the cigar, rose with a slight wince from his back, and apologised to Freja for his hurried departure. "Call me," she smiled demurely, discreetly adjusting her top to show a hint of young, firm breasts. Smith smiled and replied, "I most certainly will, young lady," and limped towards the waiting taxi, an old back injury after being hit by a car while on an assignment in Kazakhstan a few years ago, the cause of both the pain and limp. The fjord sparkled indifferently, but Smith's mind was already in the shadows—another game, another ghost to hunt.

...

Harper's eyes burned with determination as he hung up from Smith. Vesnen was their key to controlling the narrative in this crisis—but only if they could get him out alive.

Harper reflected on his best European-based field agent, Smith, an ex-US Secret Service agent. By the mid-1990s, his reputation within the Service as a "troubleshooter" had landed him in the Counterfeit Division, where he went undercover to dismantle global forgery rings. His pinnacle assignment: infiltrating a Southeast Asia USD counterfeiting operation linked to the North Korean regime under Supreme Leader Kim Jong-il. The "*super-dollars*"—near-perfect $100 bills produced in Pyongyang's Room 39—flooded markets from Bangkok to Manila, funding Kim's nuclear ambitions, and luxury imports.

Smith had posed as a shady currency broker in Kuala Lumpur, embedded with Triad syndicates, laundering the fakes. For 18 months, he built cases, wiretapped deals, and traced shipments back to DPRK diplomats. He had discussed the op's risks with his handler: North Korea's involvement meant state-backed assassins. The climax came in a sweltering warehouse in Johor Bahru, Malaysia, where Smith confronted a triad boss tied to Kim's network. After taking out five men firing indiscriminately at him, one lucky return fire shot put a 7.62mm round through his shoulder that shattered bone and nicked an artery. Smith was medevacked to a Kuala Lumpur hospital, where surgeons reconstructed his shoulder with plates and pins. After a brief recovery—three weeks of IV antibiotics and physio—he retired from the Secret Service at 49, citing "operational burnout." The agency awarded him the Valour Medal in a closed ceremony, but Smith craved anonymity, settling into a quiet life funded by a generous pension and covert bonuses.

Not long after, on a misty morning at his Lake Como villa in the Italian Alps—a sprawling exotic retreat with terraced gardens overlooking the azure waters—a nondescript black helicopter with no markings thundered over his villa and onto his rear lawn. Three men in black suits emerged; Harper was one of them.

Over espressos on the terrace overlooking the magnificent lake, Harper made him an offer he could not refuse: join the CIA as a "moment's notice" troubleshooting asset. "Your skills are too valuable to rust, and we have an unlimited budget," Harper said. Smith, intrigued by the autonomy and black-budget perks, signed on. By mid-2000, he was one of Langley's most deployable assets worldwide for deniable operations, ranging from asset extractions to counterintelligence.

Smith's life reflected his exclusive status. He had invested a modest half-million dollars in several dot-com stocks in early 1998, and this had reportedly made him over $50 million when he sold out in March 2000. Rumour has it he was in a taxi in NYC when the driver told him how much he was making from tech stocks. The moment he exited his ride, he called his broker downtown with the instruction, "Sell everything!".

Several weeks later, the dot-com bubble burst, vaporising countless paper fortunes almost overnight.

Smith maintained a Lake Como villa as a home base, a 19th-century estate with marble floors, frescoed ceilings, and a private dock. There, he housed his collection of exotic cars — a Ferrari F40, Lamborghini Diablo, and Porsche 911 Turbo. His personal favourite and daily driver: a black Bentley Brooklands, the 1998 model with a twin-turbocharged, six-and-three-quarter-litre V8 pushing 530 hp, blending British elegance with raw power. He called it his "gentleman's conveyance," cruising the winding lakeside roads often with a beautiful young companion, who he frequently thought was a better view than the stunning lake itself.

Unmarried, rumours circulated that Smith was dating five different beautiful women around the world—a supermodel in Milan, an actress in LA, a journalist in London, a diplomat's daughter in Beijing, and a tech heiress in Tokyo. Whispers in Agency circles painted him as a modern Bond, his charm disarming as his marksmanship. The most recent State Department scandal being rumoured is that he turned down the advances of the stunningly beautiful and intelligent daughter of the Chinese President. This lovely young Chinese woman had never been denied anything in her life.

But beneath the glamour, Smith's shoulder and his back ached in cold weather, and he sometimes found it hard to get out of bed—a reminder he was no longer a young man.

Now, as the *Kursk* crisis unfolded, Harper thrust him into the shadows once more, ready at a moment's notice to troubleshoot the unthinkable.

CHAPTER 6

A DASH TO FREEDOM

Smolensk Frigate, Barents Sea,
1615 — 1815 hours local time

Aboard the *Smolensk*, steaming towards the stricken *Gepard*, Lieutenant Oleg Vesnen stood in a storage compartment near the ship's stern, his gaunt face pale with fear as he clutched the concealed satellite phone. The ship was a hive of activity. Crew members rushed about, carrying out orders, which gave Vesnen a narrow window to act. Harper's words sent a wave of relief crashing over him, and his heart pounded with both terror and hope. "Yes, I can do it," Vesnen whispered, his voice trembling but resolute. "Four hours—I will be there. Thank you, Harper… thank you."

Vesnen hung up, a faint smile breaking through his fear as he pocketed the phone. His plan was secure—his future, along with that of his wife, Anna, and daughter, Maria, was within reach. But now he had to escape *Smolensk* without arousing suspicion, a task that could end in his death if he were caught. He slipped out of the storage compartment, adjusted his uniform, and blended in with the crew. He made his way to his cabin. Once inside, Vesnen moved quickly, stuffing his personal items—a photo of his family, a small notebook, and change of clothes into his crew duffel bag. He checked the data disc securely sewn into the sleeve of his naval jacket, making sure that the stitching was tight and undetectable. It contained the *Kursk* sinking intel—sonar logs and bridge transcripts proving US involvement—and was his ticket to freedom. He could not risk losing it. Slinging the duffel bag over his shoulder, he took a deep breath and steeled himself for the most dangerous part of his plan.

Several emergency lifeboats were located on the elevated launch platforms at the rear of the *Smolensk*. Vesnen made his way there. The deck was quieter here; most of the crew were focused on the forward sections. Vesnen climbed into the nearest lifeboat and strapped his duffel bag tightly to its bench with a cargo net. He glanced at the sea, rough and overcast. Waves were crashing against the *Smolensk's* hull and a heavy mist had significantly reduced visibility. Launching from the rear of the frigate might shield him from detection, but the risk was immense.

Securing himself in the pilot's seat with the safety harness, Vesnen scanned the deck one last time—no one in sight— but that could change instantly. The sea's roar and the ship's hum now masked his movements, but a single shout could end everything. He reached for the red emergency launch button, his finger hovered over it, his breath was shallow with fear. Now or never, he thought, and pressed the button.

The motorised lifeboat launched with a jolt out of its cradle and plummeting 10 meters to the sea below, a stomach-churning freefall. The boat hit the water with tremendous force; slamming Vesnen back into his seat. The seat belts dug into his chest but held him firm and uninjured. Water sprayed over the bow as the boat automatically righted itself and rocked violently in the rough waves, yet Vesnen did not hesitate. He activated the control station, and started the powerful inboard diesel engine, a defiant growl against the storm.

Pushing the throttle to full, Vesnen steered south away from the *Smolensk*, as the lifeboat surged to 15 knots, cutting through the choppy waves toward the rendezvous point 20 nautical miles north of Murmansk. Visibility was near zero; the overcast sky and mist cloaked him in a grey shroud, but Vesnen knew the Northern Fleet could still spot him if they were looking. He hoped the *Smolensk's* crew were too focused on making headway to the *Gepard* to have noticed his escape. He fixed his eyes on the horizon and felt his heart pound with the desperate hope of freedom.

USS *Theodore Roosevelt, Norwegian Sea, 1430 hours*

In the secure comms room of the USS *Theodore Roosevelt*, Rear Admiral William Fallon gripped the encrypted satellite phone, his weathered face set in grim determination. The Nimitz-class carrier steamed through the North Atlantic, her Carrier Strike Group (CSG)—destroyers, cruisers, and subs—arrayed in defensive formation. The Barents Sea crisis was unfolding like a powder keg.

"Admiral, this is Harper, CIA Istanbul station," the voice crackled, urgent but composed. "Authenticating: Echo-Foxtrot-37578."

Fallon verified the code. "Authenticated. Proceed."

"Presidential Order 37578, direct from POTUS via Langley. Authorise special operations forces for an urgent recovery mission. Target: defecting Russian naval officer, Lieutenant Oleg Vesnen, from the *Smolensk*, a Russian Northern Fleet frigate. He will head west in a motorised lifeboat toward Finland's coast in the Barents—coordinates 70°15'N, 31°10'E. Intel confirms he has got the *Kursk* sonar logs proving US innocence in the sinking. High-value asset; exfiltrate before Chernov's fleet intercepts."

Fallon nodded. He was used to covert ops for the State Department— from Balkan insertions to Gulf reconnaissance—he knew the stakes.

Vesnen's defection, signalled to Istanbul handlers, could avert war. "Understood. CSG assets in range?"

"Affirmative. Use your SEAL fire team on board. Helo insertion, transit by helicopter to Kirkenes in far eastern Finland. POTUS emphasises a minimal footprint—no escalation," Harper clarified.

"Roger. Fallon out." He hung up, turning to his aide. "Alert CSG SPECOPS Commander. Launch SEAL Team Six—fire team alpha. MH-60 helo prep for Barents infiltration. Mission: recover Vesnen, secure logs. Rules of engagement: defensive only."

Fallon watched from the bridge as the USS *Theodore Roosevelt's* 1,000-foot flight deck was a hive of activity. One man's defection could rewrite the crisis—or ignite it.

A piercing alarm sliced through the ship's steel corridors. In a dimly lit room, a four-man SEAL fire team from SEAL Team Six sprang into action. The team leader, Lieutenant Commander Jake "Hawk" Mitchell, stood at the head of the group, his piercing eyes scanning his men as he delivered the briefing.

"Immediate action orders from the CIA," Mitchell said, his voice steady but urgent. "We are extracting a high-value asset named Vesnen—a Russian naval officer with critical intel. He is on the move, and we have got a narrow window to get him out before the Russians lock him down."

Petty Officer First Class Carlos "Snake" Ramirez, the team's sniper, adjusted the strap of his M110 SASS rifle. "Where's the op taking us, sir?"

"Kirkenes, Finland," Mitchell replied, tapping a map pinned to the wall. "We are taking an MH-60 Seahawk from the Roosevelt. The flight time is 1.3 hours. Once we land, we will rendezvous with a CIA-modified trawler and agency field team to perform the extraction."

Chief Petty Officer Marcus "Doc" Johnson, the team's medic, zipped up his medical kit. "What's the opposition?"

"Potentially, the Russian Spetsnaz are in play," Mitchell said. "They could be after Vesnen, too; that is why we are here. We do not have the full picture yet. Speed and precision are our edge."

Petty Officer Second Class Tyler "Sparks" Lee, the communications specialist, tested his radio pack. "Comms are green, sir. We will stay linked with both the carrier and the CIA team."

"Move out," Mitchell ordered. The fire team grabbed their gear and double-timed it to the flight deck, where the rotors of a MH-60 Seahawk helicopter were already slicing the air. They boarded swiftly, strapping in as the aircraft lifted off and banked toward Finland. The four-man fire team, apart from Ramirez, armed with the fire team's sniper rifle, carried Colt M4 CQBR carbines and H&K USP SOCOM 45 sidearms.

Over the grey expanse of the Norwegian Sea, the Seahawk, propelled the team toward their mission goal at 170 knots. Inside, the SEALs sat in focused silence.

Mitchell reviewed the sparse intel on his tablet: Vesnen had signalled his intent to defect, offering proof of a geopolitical bombshell—details about the *Kursk* submarine sinking that could implicate foreign powers. The CIA had authorised the extraction less than an hour ago, and now, the clock was ticking.

Kirkenes, far eastern Finland, near the western border with the Russian Federation

After just over an hour, the coastline of Finland appeared through the helicopter's window, and Kirkenes was where the Seahawk landed. The flight had taken exactly 1.3 hours, as promised—a testament to the Roosevelt's proximity, the pilot's skill, and the mission's urgency. The team's boots struck the ground with practised efficiency, and they moved toward the fog-shrouded docks. It was bitterly cold, even during what passed for summer in the Arctic.

Lieutenant Commander Jake "Hawk" Mitchell stepped off the

Seahawk. The bitter Arctic wind whipped through his black tactical gear. The small port town, nestled near the Russian border, was a frozen outpost far from prying eyes —perfect for covert ops. SEAL Fire Team Six, four elite operators, including Hawk, moved like shadows. Presidential Order 37578 burned in Hawk's mind: extract Lieutenant Oleg Vesnen from the Barents Sea, secure the *Kursk* sonar logs proving U.S. innocence in the sinking. No footprints, no escalation.

Waiting on the pier was the CIA operative "Smith," a handsome middle-aged man with a square jaw, thick greying hair and stubble beard. He was wearing a black duffle coat; his breath fogged the air. Smith extended a gloved hand. "Mitchell? Smith, welcome to the edge of the world. Your bird will be fuelled and ready for your return; let's get you aboard."

The team boarded the *Nordstjernen*, a weathered Norwegian cod haulier that the CIA had converted. Below decks, Smith unveiled the internal layout: a reinforced hull for ice-breaking, an encrypted communications suite hidden in the wheelhouse, and sonar arrays disguised as fishing gear. "The galley's stocked, bunks for eight," Smith explained, tracing a blueprint on a tablet. "Engine's a quiet diesel-electric hybrid—runs silent at 10 knots. We've got RIBs for insertion, ECM jammers for radar evasion."

Hawk noticed Smith carried himself well—ex-military, probably Delta or Agency black ops. Under the duffle coat, a sidearm bulged in a shoulder holster, likely a HK USP Kompakt 9mm. More intriguing was an HK MP5K Kompakt submachine gun in a tactical shoulder holster on his right side with its suppressor peeking out. Ha ha, this guy was serious, Hawk laughed to himself. Smith's setup screamed "prepared for anything" he was a walking arsenal in civilian drag.

Smith led them to the armoury hold, flipping switches to reveal hidden compartments. "Onboard systems: .50 Cal machine gun mounts fore and aft, disguised as winches. Mini-RAM launcher for chaff and flares." He showed the Kompakt surface-to-air weapons system—a shoulder-fired Stinger variant integrated into a pop-up turret. "Handles Mi-8s or Ka-27s at 5,000 feet. Lock-on in seconds, infrared guidance. If Chernov sends helos, we swat 'em."

Hawk crossed his arms, his team scanning the gear with professional nods. "Impressive, Smith. But the POTUS's orders are explicit: avoid a fight at all costs. We are ghosts—extract Vesnen, grab the logs, exfiltrate. No heroics, no body count. Escalation could spark war."

Smith nodded, his eyes cold steel. "Understood, Commander." We are on a covert operation; however, in my world, if there is any doubt, there is no doubt. I will not hesitate to order you and your men and my two associates to go nuclear if we come under attack, understood? Hawk Mitchell nodded, this guy Smith meant business. "My job is to get Vesnen and to get you and your men, along with my associates, safely back to Kirkenes."

"Vesnen's signalling from the Barents Sea—he sounds panicked, and rightly so. He stole a motorised lifeboat right from under their noses. I can't imagine it will take too long for the crew of the *Smolensk* to notice that he is missing, along with the lifeboat. Your team dives in; we cover the exfiltration. But if the Northern Fleet crashes the party..."

Hawk cut him off. "We fade. Mission first." As the trawler cast off toward the Barents, Hawk felt the familiar adrenaline surge. See first, strike silent. Vesnen's defection could end the crisis; failure meant nuclear brinkmanship. The Aurora slipped into the night, a wolf in sheep's clothing.

Mitchell nodded. "Where is he now?"

"Last contact had him in a motorised lifeboat, 50 nautical miles west of the *Smolensk* in the Barents Sea," Smith said, pointing to a nautical chart. "He's running from the Russians, but we must assume the Russians are onto him and are closing in."

"How do we get to him?" Mitchell asked.

"We will take the trawler out under the cover of a fishing run," Smith explained. "Once we are close, you will launch our black ops Zodiac inflatable boat for the final approach. We have maybe a two-hour window to beat the Russians to him."

Mitchell turned to his team. "Snake, you are over-watch from the trawler. Doc, Sparks, you are with me on the Zodiac. We board the lifeboat, secure Vesnen, and exfiltrate. Questions?"

The team shook their heads, already moving to prep their gear. The *Nordstjernen's* engines rumbled to life, and the trawler slipped out of Kirkenes harbour into the cold, choppy waters of the Barents Sea.

An hour into the journey, the Nordstjernen's radar pinged—a small blip, they hoped marked Vesnen's lifeboat. Smith dialled Harper, who dialled Vesnen on the satellite phone.

Vesnen answered on the second ring. "Hello? Where are you, Harper? I am afraid they are coming for me. They must have realised my absence, and the missing emergency lifeboat is gone."

"Do not worry, Oleg, we have your back. I have sent our best man to rescue you; his name is Smith, and he and his team are on a fishing trawler. They have you on their radar and are closing in fast," Harper told him. Once they are close, they will launch a small Zodiac inflatable to come alongside and pick you up. Do not worry; you are safe and in excellent hands.

"Thank you, Harper, thank you. You are saving my life," Vesnen answered, relief sweeping over him. Safe at last, he thought.

FSB Headquarters, Lubyanka Building, Moscow

In the dimly lit operations room of the FSB's headquarters in Moscow's Lubyanka Building, Colonel Dmitry Voronov sat at a secure terminal scanning the latest intercept from a mole within the CIA's Istanbul station. Voronov, a 45-year-old FSB veteran with a shaved head and a permanent scowl, had spent decades rooting out traitors to the Motherland. The encrypted message from the mole was a bombshell:

Lieutenant Oleg Vesnen, a navigation officer aboard the *Smolensk*, had offered to defect to the Americans, providing top-secret *Kursk* sinking information—sonar logs and bridge transcripts proving US involvement in the *Kursk's* sinking and the destruction of two Ka-27PL helicopters, which had killed four flight crew.

Voronov's scowl deepened as he processed the betrayal. Vesnen's intel could help the Americans take control of the narrative, putting the Motherland further at a disadvantage in the ongoing crisis—but only they, the Americans, could secure it. "Traitor," Voronov muttered, slamming his fist on the desk.

"We will shoot him before he can talk." He grabbed the secure phone and dialled *Smolensk's* encrypted channel. "*Smolensk*, this is FSB Colonel Voronov," he barked, voice cold as ice. "Lieutenant Oleg Vesnen is a traitor—he is defecting to the Americans with classified *Kursk* sinking information. Arrest him immediately and secure all evidence—sonar logs, transcripts, everything."

Captain Sergei Ivanov, the *Smolensk's* CO, answered. "Colonel Voronov, this is Captain Ivanov," he replied. "I… I will order Vesnen's arrest immediately. Stand by."

Ivanov relayed the order to his executive officer, Lieutenant Commander Alexei Petrov, who led a security team to Vesnen's quarters. However, when they arrived, the cabin was empty—no Vesnen, no clothes or personal items, nothing.

Petrov's heart sank as he checked the ship's logs, confirming his worst fears. "Captain, Vesnen's gone," Petrov reported over the intercom, his voice tight. "He has taken one of the motorised lifeboats— it launched two hours ago, heading southwest toward Finland."

Ivanov's face paled. He returned to the phone, his voice grim. "Colonel, Vesnen has escaped with a motorised lifeboat. He is heading southwest—likely toward a US extraction point. What are your orders?"

Voronov's eyes burned with fury. Vesnen and his intel must not reach the Americans.

"I'll handle it, Captain," he growled. He hung up and picked up the phone again.

"Get me Major Alexei Gromov, the Spetsnaz commander—now."

The line connected, "Colonel Voronov, this is Major Gromov. What is the situation?"

"Major, we have a traitor—Lieutenant Oleg Vesnen, navigation officer on the *Smolensk*," Voronov said. "He is attempting to defect to the Americans with top-secret information about the *Kursk*—proof of their involvement in its sinking.

He has escaped in a motorised lifeboat, heading west toward Finland, likely for a US extraction. You must intercept him before the Americans get him—use a Kamov Ka-50 Black Shark to search for and capture him. Take a team of six men armed to the teeth. Bring Vesnen back alive, if possible, dead if necessary. The intel cannot reach the Americans. Move now.

Gromov's scarred face hardened, his dark eyes burning with determination. "Understood, Colonel," he replied, voice steady. "We will launch immediately. Vesnen will not make it to the Americans—I will see to it personally." Gromov, who had proved his brutal loyalty to Mother Russia time and time again, not least when presiding over the capture and live organ removal of Chechen rebels. Standing at 6'3" with a broad, muscular frame, Gromov was a powerfully built warrior for Russia. His bald head, a trait inherited from his father, and his full, black Cossack beard gave him a formidable presence.

In September 1999, the Beslan school siege, where Chechen terrorists took over 1,100 hostages, including 777 children, and killed 334 people, 186 of them children, cemented Gromov's hatred of the Motherland's enemies.

The Kremlin's response was merciless: Gromov had orders to eradicate the separatists by any means necessary, including targeting their leadership and dismantling their networks through extreme measures.

Earlier in the year, the military had deployed Gromov's unit to the mountains of southern Chechnya. It tasked it with hunting down a group of separatist fighters responsible for a series of bombings in Grozny. On a frigid February morning, Ivanov led his team through a snow-covered ravine near the village of Shatoi, tracking a cell of 12 Chechen fighters.

His bald head glistened with sweat despite the cold, his full Cossack black beard streaked with frost as he moved silently through the terrain, his AN-94 rifle ready. Intelligence had pinpointed the separatists in a cave network, and Gromov's team cornered them after a gruelling three-hour stalk, cutting off their escape routes with precision.

The firefight was swift and brutal. Gromov's Spetsnaz operatives, trained for close-quarters combat, killed six separatists within minutes, their silenced weapons cutting through the enemy with ruthless efficiency. The remaining six, low on ammunition and trapped, threw down their weapons, raising their hands in surrender.

Gromov stepped forward, his imposing figure casting a shadow over the cave entrance, his dark eyes cold with fury as he surveyed the defeated fighters. "You thought you could bomb our schools and walk away?" he growled, his voice low and menacing. "You'll pay for every child you murdered."

As Gromov signalled his men to secure the prisoners, a flicker of movement caught his eye—a seventh separatist, hidden behind a boulder, had evaded detection. The fighter, a wiry Chechen in his early 20s with a wild look in his eyes, lunged at Ivanov from behind, a combat knife flashing in the dim light.

The blade sliced across the right side of Gromov's face, from his temple to his jaw, opening a deep, jagged gash that sprayed blood across the snow. Pain seared through Gromov's skull, but his training kicked in, adrenaline dulling the agony as he reacted on instinct.

Gromov drove his elbow back into the fighter's stomach; the impact doubled him over with a grunt. Spinning around, Gromov drew his Makarov pistol in a fluid motion, pressing the barrel to the Chechen's forehead. The fighter's eyes widened in terror, but Gromov's face was a mask of fury, blood streaming down his cheek, staining his black beard crimson. "For Beslan," Gromov hissed, pulling the trigger. The gunshot echoed through the cave, the fighter's head snapping back as he crumpled to the ground, a single bullet hole between his eyes.

Gromov staggered, clutching his face as blood poured through his fingers, but his dark eyes burned with a savage satisfaction as he turned to the remaining prisoners. "Bind them," he ordered, voice hoarse with pain. His men zip-tied the separatists' hands, their faces pale with fear as they realised surrender would not save them.

Gromov's unit hauled the prisoners back to a Russian forward operating base near Grozny, where a medical tent awaited under the direction of Kremlin orders. The Beslan massacre had shifted Russia's policy—POWs were no longer just interrogated; they were to be used in a gruesome retaliation. Inside the tent, a team of military surgeons operated under FSB oversight, harvesting the organs of captured separatists for Russian citizens who urgently needed organ transplants, a brutal response to the Chechen bombing that had killed hundreds of innocent schoolchildren. The Kremlin authorised the operation to send a message: terror would be met with terror.

Gromov watched as they dragged the prisoners into the tent, and their pleas for mercy fell on deaf ears. He took grim pleasure in their fate, the pain of his fresh scar fuelling his hatred. "You wanted war," he muttered, wiping blood from his beard. "Now you'll pay the price."

Methodically, the surgeons worked, their faces expressionless while carrying out the Kremlin's orders, the prisoners' screams muffled by the tent's walls.

Gromov had a permanent scar, a jagged line from temple to jaw, on the right side of his face after the incident, which became a badge of honour. The wound healed over the months, but the scar remained, a constant reminder of the Chechen fighter's blade and the brutality of the war.

Gromov's beard grew fuller, hiding part of the scar, but his bald head and the visible portion of the mark gave him a menacing aura that struck fear into subordinates and enemies alike.

By 2000, Major Gromov was a legend in the Spetsnaz, known for his ruthlessness and unyielding loyalty to Russia. When the FSB Colonel called on him to hunt down Lieutenant Oleg Vesnen, a traitor fleeing with *Kursk* intel, Ivanov saw it as another chance to serve the Motherland—and to exact the vengeance that had become his life's purpose.

Gromov hung up and turned to his team—six Spetsnaz operatives armed with AN-94 assault rifles and silenced Makarov pistols, already gearing up on the tarmac at Severomorsk Naval Base. The Kamov Ka-50 Black Shark, a single-seat attack helicopter modified to carry the team in its cramped internal compartment, stood ready, its coaxial rotors gleaming in the pale Arctic light. Gromov climbed aboard and checked his weapon as the helicopter's engines roared to life. The Ka-50 lifted off from the naval base at Arkhangelsk, its rotors clawing at the air as it headed south over the Barents Sea, a predator hunting for a fleeing traitor. Two hours flight time, Gromov calculated, and they would intercept the traitor Vesnen.

CIA Extraction Team, north of Murmansk in the Barents Sea

Smith, the middle-aged CIA operative with a thick mop of greying hair and a neatly trimmed beard, stood in the pilothouse of a Norwegian fishing trawler, monitoring the radar 30 nautical miles off the Russian coast at coordinates 70 degrees north, 25 degrees east.

Smith's hazel eyes scanned the horizon, his hands gripping the railing, as he spoke into the encrypted radio. "Harper, this is Smith," he said, his voice steady. "We have Vesnen on our radar and are in a position. The SEAL fire team is on board. Any update on Vesnen?"

Harper's voice crackled through the radio, sharp and urgent. "He is on the move in the lifeboat from the *Smolensk*, heading west toward your position. But our intel confirms the FSB is onto him—they have a Spetsnaz team in a Ka-50 Black Shark, closing fast from the White Sea. You have maybe an hour before they catch him."

Smith frowned. "Understood," he said.

"I spoke with him an hour ago." Harper said, "He is panicked."

"We will move to intercept. Any intel on his proof?" Smith added.

"He claims to have logs, sonar recordings, and bridge transcripts," Carter replied. "If true, it will allow us to control the narrative with the Russians. An American submarine may have sunk the *Kursk*, and Vesnen can prove it, but we want the truth to hold over the Russians. The entire Russian Northern Fleet is hunting our two Los Angeles-class submarines, and they might not make it out with their intel. Get him out, Smith. We need that intelligence."

"Copy that," Smith said, turning to his team. "Let us move—full speed east. We have got a defector to save." Smith was looking at a small "blip" on the radar screen; got you, he thought, the adrenaline building as it did in every field operation he was tasked to carry out. There was always a risk, and he did not want to encounter a Russian Spetsnaz special operations group. Those guys were more hardcore than the SEAL fire team with him.

The *Nordstjernen* surged forward, her hybrid diesel engine a muted powerhouse as she sliced through the icy waves, heading east to intercept Vesnen's lifeboat. Smith checked his weapon—a HK MP5K submachine gun with a suppressor hanging from the tactical sling in front of him, his HK UMP Kompakt 9mm sidearm slung under his black duffle coat in a shoulder holster. He focused his mind on the Spetsnaz team closing in. This would be a race against time, and the stakes could not be higher. The FSB closing in, Smith knew they would stop at nothing to silence Vesnen. He thought of his team—six operatives, two CIA field agents, former special forces soldiers, trained by the Agency for high-stakes extractions, and a four-man SEAL fire team. They would get Vesnen out, or they would die trying. He was glad to have the four-man SEAL fire team on board.

Petr Velikiy, 30 nautical miles west of the Kursk wreck

Captain Li Jun moved through the corridors of the *Petr Velikiy*. His Russian Naval officer's uniform blended in with the Russian crew, his heart pounded as he clutched a small encrypted device in his pocket. The Chinese intelligence operative had spent hours gathering intel—partial *Shkval* schematics, ASW protocols, and KN-3 reactor data—stolen with the help of Lieutenant Commander Dmitry Sokolov, a disillusioned Russian officer whom he had bribed with $500,000.

But the *Gepard's* disabling and the FSB's focus on a traitor named Vesnen had turned the ship into a hornet's nest. Li Jun knew this was his opportunity to escape—before the Russians turned their attention to him.

He slipped into a maintenance room near the starboard deck, where he had hidden a small duffel bag containing the stolen data and a concealed knife. The *Pyotr Velikiy* was on high alert, with crew members rushing to their stations as Chernov ordered a full ASW sweep, but the chaos was working in Li Jun's favour. He checked his watch. His extraction team, a Chinese intelligence unit posing as fishermen out of Gromov, would wait north of Murmansk on a fishing trawler, 50 nautical miles away. The extraction team would then deliver him to a new Type 093 Shang-class Chinese navy nuclear submarine, the SSN *Angen*, lying in wait in the Barents Sea north of Murmansk.

His best chance was a motorised lifeboat on the starboard deck, but he needed to move quickly.

Li Jun adjusted his uniform, pulled his cap low over his Chinese features, and stepped onto the deck. The wind bit at his face. Someone had secured the lifeboat near the railing, and the maintenance check earlier that day had primed its motor. Two Russian sailors stood nearby, smoking cigarettes. Their attention was focused on the horizon where the *Gepard's* smoke plume was faintly visible. Li Jun's pulse raced as he approached, feigning a casual inspection of the deck equipment. One sailor glanced at him, eyes narrowing, but Li Jun nodded curtly, gesturing to the lifeboat as if he were engaged in official business.

The sailor shrugged and returned to his companion. Seizing the moment, Li Jun unhooked the lifeboat's straps, his movements were swift and silent, adrenaline surged as he climbed aboard. He pushed the side-mounted derrick control to lower the powered lifeboat into the water 15 meters below. Once in the water, he turned the key to start the small craft. With a low hum, the engine roared to life. He cast off. The sailors shouted, but Li Jun waved casually at them and gunned the throttle, and the lifeboat surged to 20 knots, bobbing in the swell, heading southwest toward Murmansk.

...

Admiral Viktor Chernov stood on the bridge of the *Petr Velikiy*, his dark eyes burned with rage at the crippling of the *Gepard* by American torpedoes. A cigarette was firmly lodged in his mouth, when the secure phone on the chart table buzzed—an encrypted line from FSB headquarters in Moscow.

Chernov snatched the receiver, his voice a growl. "This is Chernov. What now?"

"Admiral, this is Colonel Dmitry Voronov, FSB," came the unfriendly reply. "You have a traitor in your fleet—Lieutenant Oleg Vesnen, navigation officer on the *Smolensk*. He is attempting to defect to the Americans, offering top-secret *Kursk* sinking information—sonar logs, bridge transcripts proving their involvement in the *Kursk's* sinking and the destruction of two Ka-27PL helicopters, four flight crew dead. He escaped in a stolen motorised lifeboat from the *Smolensk*, heading southwest toward a likely US extraction point. I have dispatched a fast-attack special forces helicopter and Spetsnaz team to retrieve him."

Chernov's face darkened, a snarl escaping his lips as he slammed his fist on the table, rattling the charts. "Pizdetz!" he roared, voice reverberating through the bridge. "Another traitor? First the *Kursk*, then the *Gepard*, and now this?

Captain Ivan Rostov, standing nearby, nodded as he relayed the orders to the comms officer, Lieutenant Mikhail Orlov. "Signal all units," Rostov said, voice tense. "Lieutenant Oleg Vesnen, *Smolensk* navigation officer, has defected. Last known heading west in a motorised lifeboat. Capture or kill—priority one."

As Orlov transmitted the order, Rostov's mind shifted to Lieutenant Commander Dmitry Sokolov in the weapons control centre below decks, his strange actions suggested a similar kind of guilt. Rostov had suspected Sokolov's disloyalty for hours; his meetings with Captain Li Jun, the Chinese operative, had been too frequent, too secretive. With Vesnen's betrayal fresh, Rostov's asked two armed ensigns to follow him. They made their way to the weapons control room where he seized Sokolov by the collar, slamming him against the bulkhead.

"You've been lying to me, Sokolov," Rostov growled, voice low and menacing, drawing the attention of the combat station's crew. "I saw you with the Chinese—Li Jun. You have sold them technical information, haven't you? You betrayed us—just like Vesnen."

Sokolov's face drained of colour. "Captain, I—I had no choice! The navy's falling apart, my family's starving—I needed the money! They offered $500,000—I only gave them partial schematics, I swear!"

Chernov arrived, Rostov's sudden disappearance from the bridge raising concern, his rage flaring anew as he overheard the confession. "Traitor!" he bellowed, storming over, his meaty hand grabbing Sokolov by the throat. "You sold our secrets to the Chinese while the Americans were destroying us? You will hang for this!" He shoved Sokolov toward the security officer, Lieutenant Nikolai Petrov. "Arrest him—lock him in the brig. I will deal with him later."

Petrov dragged Sokolov away as the weapons control centre crew watched in stunned silence. Chernov's was furious. Two traitors in one day—Vesnen and Sokolov—while the Americans continued their rampage. Rostov thought about the situation. If Sokolov had betrayed them to the Chinese, Li Jun was likely a Chinese intelligence officer and if he hadn't left with the official party then he had been on the ships for hours, his actions unaccounted for.

"Petrov, wait," Rostov ordered, his voice low and urgent. "Before you take Sokolov, assemble the security team. Search for Captain Li Jun, the Chinese Navy attaché. Show his picture to members of the crew to see if they have seen him. If he is on board, I want him arrested immediately. Bring him to the bridge in cuffs!"

Petrov nodded, signalling his team—six armed sailors in tactical gear—who fanned out across the *Petr Velikiy*, and began searching every corridor, maintenance room, and deck. They checked Li Jun's assigned quarters, the comms room where he had planted a listening device, and the engineering section from where he had stolen reactor schematics but found no sign of him.

Tension mounted as Petrov led the team to the starboard deck, where a maintenance officer had reported a missing motorised lifeboat.

When Petrov showed Li Jun's picture to two sailors smoking near the railing, their faces went pale with guilt. "We saw him, sir," one stammered, a young ensign named Ivan Kuznetsov. "We just saluted him, sir—he took the lifeboat about an hour ago. He said it was official business, but then he just… took off, heading southwest."

Petrov's jaw tightened as the implications sank in. He radioed the bridge, his voice grim. "Captain Rostov, Admiral Chernov, this is Petrov. A motorised lifeboat is missing from the starboard deck. Two sailors confirm they saw Li Jin dressed in one of our uniforms and taking it heading southwest toward Murmansk an hour ago. He has escaped, sir."

Chernov's face turned crimson, a roar escaping his lips as he slammed both fists on the chart table, sending a mug crashing to the deck. "Pizdetz!" he bellowed, his voice echoing through the bridge. "Another traitor slips through our fingers? First Vesnen, now the Chinese spy? Signal all units—find that lifeboat! I want Li Jun in custody, or I will have every officer on this ship court-martialled!"

Rostov's eyes darkened. Li Jun had likely stolen critical intel—possibly the *Shkval* schematics Sokolov had sold him—and was now heading for Murmansk, 50 nautical miles away, where there was likely a Chinese extraction team waiting. The *Petr Velikiy* was too far to pursue directly, but the Northern Fleet's helicopters and smaller vessels could intercept him—if they moved fast. "Orlov, signal the *Admiral Levchenko*," Rostov ordered, his voice steady despite the chaos. "Launch their Ka-27PL Sokol—find Li Jun's lifeboat, southwest toward Murmansk. Capture or destroy him."

Orlov nodded, transmitting the order, but Rostov's gaze lingered on Chernov, whose rage threatened to escalate the crisis further out of control. The bridge was a powder keg, and Rostov feared they were running out of time to contain it.

Powered Lifeboat, 20 nautical miles north of Murmansk

Captain Li Jun clung to the wheel of the stolen lifeboat as it powered at nearly full throttle, making 20 knots, south toward Murmansk. A Chinese extraction team would wait there to pick him up in a small coastal vessel and deliver him to a new Type 093 Shang-class Chinese navy nuclear submarine, the SSN *Angen*. He clutched the encrypted device in his pocket, containing *Pyotr Velikiy's* ASW protocols and KN-3 reactor schematics—valuable intel that would advance China's naval ambitions. He had relayed the positions of the two American submarines to Admiral Zhang Wei before departing, ensuring China's advantage in the unfolding crisis.

A Ka-27PL Bars (Leopard) helicopter patrolled the sky in the distance, its coaxial rotors clawing the air in search of American subs. Li Jun's heart pounded, his sharp features set in a mask of determination as he steered the lifeboat closer to the coast. He hoped they would not be sending one out to find him. Being 20 nautical miles from Murmansk, he was close. Li Jun's mind raced as he calculated his chances. Li Jun figured that the Russians were too focused on the Americans to notice his actions, at least for now. However, he needed to move quickly. The Northern Fleet was on high alert, and if Chernov or Rostov discovered his espionage, he would be a dead man.

CIA trawler *Nordstjernen*, *Barents Sea north of Murmansk*

The 60-foot *Nordstjernen* sliced through the choppy waves of the Barents Sea, her weathered hull belying the advanced tech hidden below deck. John Smith directed the crew on the CIA-modified trawler. Lieutenant Commander Jake "Hawk" Mitchell and his four-man SEAL fire team from SEAL Team Six stood ready, their gear prepped for a high-stakes extraction.

"Contact—bearing two-eight-zero, range five nautical miles," Smith announced, eyes locked on the screen. "It is a motorised lifeboat, matching Vesnen's last known trajectory. That is our guy."

Mitchell's felt a surge of adrenaline. "Sparks, you're with me on the Zodiac," he ordered. "Snake, over-watch from the trawler. Doc, standby for medical. We are intercepting now—move!"

Petty Officer First Class Carlos "Snake" Ramirez set up his M110 SASS sniper rifle on the trawler's deck, while Chief Petty Officer Marcus "Doc" Johnson prepped his medical kit below. Mitchell and

Sparks launched the Zodiac inflatable boat, its silenced 70 hp Mercury outboard hummed softly as they surged toward the target at 20 knots, nearby the Russian ASW forces were patrolling and a Spetsnaz team was rumoured to be hunting Vesnen.

The lifeboat came into view, cutting through the waves at 20 knots, its occupant a shadowy figure at the wheel. Mitchell signalled Sparks to cut the engine 50 yards out, the Zodiac glided in silently on its momentum. "On my mark," Mitchell whispered, gripping his suppressed Colt M4 CQBR carbine. "Three… two… one—go!"

The Zodiac surged forward, and Mitchell leapt aboard the lifeboat, Sparks was right behind him after securing the Zodiac, "Hands up—now!" Mitchell barked; their silenced weapons were trained on the figure. His voice was low but potentially lethal. The man spun around. His sharp features were illuminated by the pale Arctic light—He was Chinese not Russian. Mitchell's heart skipped a beat; shock flashed across his face. "What the hell?" Sparks muttered, lowering his weapon slightly, equally stunned.

Li Jun's eyes widened, his own surprise mirroring that of the SEALs. He had expected a Chinese extraction team, not American commandos. His hand darted to his belt and pulled out a concealed knife. He lunged at Mitchell with a snarl. "Die, American!" he hissed, aiming for Mitchell's throat.

Mitchell instinctively sidestepped the blade, grabbed Li Jun's wrist, and twisted it until the knife clattered to the deck. Sparks moved in, slamming the metal butt of his M4 CQBR carbine into Li Jun's temple, dazing him. Mitchell forced Li Jun to his knees, pulled his arms behind his back and secured them with zip-ties so the plastic bit into his wrists. "Stay down," Mitchell growled, pressing a knee into Li Jun's back, who cursed in Mandarin.

Sparks searched Li Jun, and discovered the waterproof bag inside his jacket. Inside were an encrypted device and a USB drive. He pulled out his tactical tablet and plugged in the USB drive. Li Jun hadn't seen the need to encrypt it. Mitchell knew enough Russian to know that what they had was potentially more significant than what they had come for.

"Let's get back to the trawler," he said, hauling the operative to his feet. The Zodiac sped back to the Northern Star, with Li Jun glaring daggers but remaining silent, his plans shattered.

Aboard the trawler, Smith's eyes widened as he saw Li Jun in zip-tie cuffs, with the USB drive in Sparks' hand. "Holy hell," he muttered, a rare smile breaking through his stoic demeanour. He plugged the USB in. He was fluent in Russian and what he saw impressed him. Windfall-classified Russian Northern Fleet data, including *Shkval* schematics, ASW protocols, and KN-3 reactor schematics, streamed onto his screen. "Jackpot," he said. "This is not Vesnen, but we just hit the motherlode."

"Russian data stolen by the Chinese? Langley's going to lose it."

The team gathered on deck. Ramirez clapped Sparks on the shoulder, grinning. "Nice work, man." Doc checked Li Jun's vitals, noting a bruised temple but no serious injuries. Mitchell secured the prisoner below deck.

Smith grabbed the encrypted sat phone and Harper. "Harper, it's Smith," he said, voice urgent but triumphant. "Mission update—we did not get Vesnen. The Russians must have beaten us to him and taken him out before we arrived. However, we intercepted a Chinese operative instead—Captain Li Jun, a PLAN intelligence officer. He was in a motorised lifeboat, thinking we were his extraction team. We have got him in custody. Even better, he was carrying a whole bunch of stolen Russian Northern Fleet data—*Shkval* schematics, ASW protocols, reactor specs. It is a gold mine.

Harper's voice crackled through the line, sharp with focus. "Smith, that's an incredible break. Vesnen's capture complicates things—we will pivot to a rescue op for him if possible. But Li Jun and that data is priority one; head straight back to Kirkenes. The crew has refuelled the MH-60 Seahawk, and it is waiting. Take Li Jun to the USS *Theodore Roosevelt* for interrogation—they will want to debrief him immediately. I want you on that bird with the SEALs to oversee the handoff."

"Understood," Smith replied, hanging up as he turned to Mitchell. "You heard him—back to Kirkenes, full speed. We are taking our friend to the Roosevelt."

Mitchell nodded, his eyes hard with resolve. "Let's move," he said. The *Nordstjernen's* engines roared to life as the trawler turned southwest, racing toward Kirkenes with its unexpected prize.

Powered Lifeboat, 40 nautical miles west of Smolensk

Lieutenant Oleg Vesnen clung to the wheel of the stolen lifeboat from the frigate *Smolensk*. The satellite call from Harper had been a relief; he was safe and would soon enjoy the Americans' hospitality and money. He imagined himself drinking warm American coffee as they took him away to safety and a life of American comfort with his one million dollars. His hands trembled as he gripped the steering wheel of the small vessel, cutting through the icy waves of the Barents Sea. The 20-foot craft, powered by an inboard diesel engine, was making 15 knots, heading west toward Finland—coordinates 70 degrees north, 25 degrees east—where the CIA had promised an extraction team. But the sound of rotor blades in the distance coming from the east put the terror back into his soul. It was not from his ship. And the Americans had not said anything about a helicopter, which meant that he had likely been discovered, and the FSB were coming after him. They would stop at nothing to apprehend him—or kill him. He just hoped his family were already out. He pushed the throttle to full, and the small engine roared as the lifeboat surged forward. Finland was only 40 nautical miles away—a long shot, but it was his only hope. The information on the USB was his ticket out—a chance to escape the navy, the FSB, and the life that had broken him. But if the FSB caught him, he was a dead man.

Kamov Ka-50 Black Shark, 30 nautical miles west of Smolensk, 1700 hours

Major Alexei Gromov scanned the grey expanse of the Barents Sea through the Kamov Ka-50 Black Shark's canopy. He gripped his AN-94 rifle, as the helicopter's sensors picked up a faint blip on the horizon—45 nautical miles west of *Smolensk*. The Ka-50 flew low towards it at 170 knots.

"There," Gromov barked, as the target came into view—a motorised lifeboat cutting through the choppy waves at 15 knots, heading west toward Finland. "That's Vesnen—the traitor. Take us in, low and fast!"

The pilot, Captain Mikhail Volodin, nodded as he pushed the Ka-50 into a steep descent, skimming just 20 feet above the waves.

As the helicopter approached, Vesnen gripped the wheel in the lifeboat, his gaunt face pale with fear, his eyes darting toward the horizon. The CIA had promised extraction, but the roar of rotors overhead sent a chill down his spine.

Vesnen pushed the throttle to full; the lifeboat's engine roared as it surged to 18 knots, but the Ka-50 was almost ten times as fast and closed the gap in seconds.

"No, no, no!" Vesnen shouted as he swerved the boat in a desperate zigzag, trying to evade the helicopter hovering just 30 feet above him, its downdraft whipping the sea into a frenzy.

"Rope down—now!" Gromov ordered. The Ka-50's side door opened, and Gromov's team—four Spetsnaz operatives in black tactical gear— fast-roped down, their boots pounding onto the lifeboat's deck. Vesnen lunged for the satellite phone to send a final message to the CIA, but a gloved hand seized his wrist and twisted it until he dropped the device.

"You're done, traitor!" barked Sergeant Viktor Kuznetsov, a wiry Spetsnaz operative with a cruel sneer. He slammed Vesnen against the wheelhouse and pinned him with a knee to his back. Another operative,

Corporal Alexei Morozov, snapped metal handcuffs onto Vesnen's wrists. The metal froze onto his skin.

"Please don't kill me!" Vesnen pleaded, his eyes wide with terror and guilt. "I did it for my family—my wife, my daughter—they will die if I don't get out!"

Kuznetsov backhanded Vesnen across the face, splitting his lip. Blood streamed down his chin "Traitor!" He grabbed Vesnen by the hair and slammed his head against the wheelhouse wall. "You sold out the Motherland—118 sailors dead because of the Americans, and you are helping them? You will die for this! We will rape your wife and daughter and then kill them too."

Morozov joined in, delivering a brutal punch to Vesnen's temple. He slumped to the deck, his vision blurred. "Please… I am begging you…" Vesnen gasped. The Spetsnaz operatives ignored his pleas and dragged him to the centre of the deck.

"Extract him—now!" Gromov ordered from the Ka-50's open door. The winch cable descended, and the team hooked Vesnen's handcuffs to the harness, his body went limp as they secured him. The winch whirred, hoisting Vesnen into the air, until he was hauled into the helicopter's external compartment by his handcuffed wrists. Gromov's team followed, roping up one by one, their movements swift and precise. Once everyone was aboard, Gromov leaned out, dark eyes cold as he surveyed the lifeboat below. "Pilot, destroy the evidence," he ordered/ "Use the 30mm auto-cannon—leave nothing for the Americans to find."

Captain Volodin nodded, angling the Ka-50's nose downward as the 30mm auto-cannon roared to life. A burst of high-explosive rounds tore into the lifeboat, shredding its hull in a fiery explosion. Debris scattered across the waves as the fuel tank ignited, sending a plume of black smoke into the sky. The lifeboat sank rapidly, its wreckage swallowed by the sea, erasing any trace of Vesnen's escape.

Gromov watched the destruction with grim satisfaction, then turned to Vesnen, slumped in the compartment, blood dripping from his face.

"You'll talk, traitor," he growled, voice low and menacing. "You will tell us everything—or I will make sure your family pays for your betrayal."

Vesnen's eyes flickered with fear, and his body trembled as the Ka-50 banked east, heading back to *Smolensk* with its prize.

CHAPTER 7

THE FINAL RECKONING

Barents Sea,
August 12, 2000, 1815 — 2015 hours local time

K-335 *Gepard* lay crippled on the surface of the Barents Sea, her titanium hull glistened in the pale twilight, her single screw and rudder shredded by *Toledo's* Mark 48 torpedo. At 1530 hours, the Akula-class hunter-killer sub, named for its speed and agility, was a wounded predator. Captain Yuri Volodin stood in the control room burning with rage. A low metallic shudder rippled through the *Gepard's* hull. The American submarine had evaded his torpedoes with cunning and desperation; and now, she had struck back, leaving the *Gepard* a sitting duck. Were they going to finish them, he thought?

"Damage report!" Volodin barked, his voice steady despite the chaos. His shaved head glistened with sweat, and a scar across his right cheek stood out starkly against his pale skin.

"Engine room flooding, sir!" replied the damage control officer, Lieutenant Sergei Ivanov. "Propulsion disabled—screw and rudder gone. We are on the surface, but life support is holding. Pumps are at 80% capacity—we cannot take another hit."

Volodin exhaled, his hands trembling as he grabbed the radio, his mind racing. "*Petr Velikiy*, this is *Gepard*," he said, his voice steady despite the turmoil in his chest. "We are dead in the water, Admiral—propulsion disabled, on the surface. Respectfully asking, Admiral, when our help will arrive?"

The radio crackled, and Admiral Viktor Chernov's voice came through, a low growl that made Volodin flinch. "*Gepard*, this is *Petr Velikiy*. Hold position—I have ordered the *Smolensk* to assist. We will finish the Americans. Out."

USS Toledo, 20 nautical miles west of the stricken Gepard

Commander Tom Brennan stood in the *Toledo's* control room, his shoulder throbbing. The gash above his left eyebrow that had bloodied the collar of his navy-blue jumpsuit had stopped. More importantly, the *Toledo* had evaded the *Gepard's* second torpedo with a desperate move within the submarine valley. His wire-guided Mark 48s, launched earlier, had crippled the *Gepard*, disabling her propulsion and forcing her to the surface. But the *Toledo* was still in danger, her hull battered and her crew pushed to the breaking point.

"Conn, Sonar," said Lieutenant Dave Carter, his voice a mix of relief and urgency as he adjusted his headset. "Sierra Two is on the surface—propulsion is disabled, and the engine room is flooding. She is out of the fight, sir."

Brennan exhaled, his body trembling with adrenaline, his blue eyes fixed on the sonar plot. "Good," he said, his voice steady despite the exhaustion on his face. "But we are not out of this yet. The Russian fleet is still out there—let us put some distance between us and the *Gepard*."

"Maintain 5 knots, bearing two-seven-zero, strict electronic emission control," Brennan ordered, his voice steady. "We stay quiet, stay deep. Let's quietly creep the hell out of here."

In the engineering compartment, Lieutenant Mark Evans adjusted the S6G reactor's coolant flow. He had been at the nuclear control panels for twelve hours straight and was exhausted. The reactor was at 25% power, with the pumps set low to minimise noise, but *Toledo's* systems were strained. "Reactor holding, sir," Evans reported via intercom. "Noise levels at 45 decibels—we're as quiet as we can get."

Brennan nodded, a flicker of gratitude in his blue eyes. "Good," he said, his mind already on the long journey to Norway. He grabbed the ship's intercom, "Ship, this is your captain speaking," he said in a measured tone. "We are out of danger for now. I want to congratulate you all on the outstanding job you did under extreme conditions today. You make me proud to be your commanding officer. You make one hell of a team."

A wave of relief washed over the crew, their hands paused as they listened to Brennan's words. In the engineering compartment, Evans leaned against the console, his sandy hair matted with sweat and a faint smile on his lips. In the torpedo room, Petty Officer First Class Emily Chen, her black hair tied back and her jumpsuit stained with grease, closed her eyes momentarily. Spontaneous, quiet applause erupted throughout the compartments, a testament to their resilience and camaraderie.

"Listen up," Brennan continued, his voice firm. "We have a broken sub to nurse back to the nearest friendly port. It is a long way, and the Russian forces are still out there, very pissed off about what happened today. Remain focused and I will endeavour to get you all home safe."

The applause faded, giving way to a renewed sense of determination. Brennan set the intercom down and fixed his eyes on the chart table, his mind now on the 300-mile journey to Tromsø, Norway. The *Toledo* was a mess—leaks in three compartments, a damaged pump, her sail gone—but her crew remained unbroken. He would do everything in his power to get them home.

The Kremlin, Moscow, President Putin's Office

President Vladimir Putin sat behind his oak desk in the Kremlin, his face a mask of controlled fury, his piercing blue eyes locked on the red phone that connected him to the White House. Beside him, Foreign Minister Sergei Lavrov adjusted his glasses, ready to navigate the diplomatic minefield ahead. Putin's earlier call with President Bill Clinton had bought time, but now, with the crisis spiralling, a resolution was imperative.

The line crackled to life, and Clinton's Arkansas drawl came through, steady but strained. "President Putin, Foreign Minister Lavrov, this is President Clinton. I have Secretary of State Madeleine Albright, Secretary of Defence William Cohen, and National Security Advisor Sandy Berger here. We are ready to talk."

"President Clinton, your submarines sank the *Kursk*, a $1 billion vessel, with 118 sailors dead. You shot down two of our helicopters, killing four flight crew. This is an act of war. Russia demands compensation, or we will respond in kind."

Lavrov leaned in, his tone measured but firm. "We have evidence—sonar logs, seismic data, eyewitness reports from the *Smolensk*. The USS *Toledo* collided with the *Kursk*, and the USS *Memphis* fired a Mark 48 torpedo. A US weapon downed the helicopters—likely a new type of sub-surface-to-air missile, which is remarkable. We estimate the total loss, including the *Kursk's* value and the lives lost, to be over $5 billion. We expect a comprehensive settlement."

Clinton exhaled, the weight of the crisis pressing down on him. "President Putin, Foreign Minister Lavrov, I deeply regret the loss of your sailors and pilots. We are still investigating, but I assure you, we are innocent of your accusation, and this was not an act of war.

Our subs were in international waters, responding to a perceived threat. We want to de-escalate—let us find a way forward."

Albright, her voice sharp with diplomatic precision, took the lead. "We are prepared to offer a compensation package to resolve this peacefully. The US proposes $3 billion in direct financial aid to Russia for the loss of the *Kursk*, paid over three years. Additionally, we will provide private payments to the families of the 118 *Kursk* crew members and the four Ka-27PL flight-crew—$50,000 per family, totalling $6.1 million, routed through a neutral Swiss bank to ensure privacy."

Putin's eyes narrowed. The $3 billion was substantial, but he saw an opportunity to leverage the crisis for long-term gains. "That's a start," he said, voice cold. "But it is not enough. Russia's economy has suffered since the Soviet collapse—Western sanctions, NATO expansion, you have crippled us."

"We seek economic concessions: a preferential deal on Siberian oil—100 million barrels annually for the next ten years at a 15% markup to market rates—and approval for a new gas pipeline into Europe."

"Europe's power demands are growing, and Russia can meet them, but we need US support to bypass opposition from Poland and the Baltic states."

Clinton exchanged a glance with Albright. The stakes were clear. The oil deal would cost the US billions in trade adjustments, and the pipeline would strengthen Russia's energy dominance in Europe—a geopolitical win for Putin.

However, war was the alternative, and with 228 American sailors on the USS *Toledo* and USS *Memphis*, Clinton could not risk escalation.

Cohen chimed in, his tone pragmatic. "Mr President, the oil deal is workable—we can redirect energy contracts to accommodate it. The pipeline… It's a tougher sell, but we can pressure NATO allies to approve it under the guise of energy security."

Berger nodded, added, "We will frame it as a stabilising measure—Russia gets economic support, Europe gets energy, and we avoid a conflict. However, we require assurances—no further military escalation—and Russia agrees to a joint investigation into the *Kursk* incident to prevent future misunderstandings. But we control the narrative, and no one must know what really happened. Agree?"

Lavrov adjusted his glasses, sensing the Americans' willingness to compromise. "We can accept a joint investigation if a neutral third party, like Switzerland, conducts it."

And we will issue a public statement from the Kremlin acknowledging the incident as a tragic accident, not as an act of aggression. Mr President, perhaps you could follow up with a statement of condolence from the United States and an offer to assist in a rescue mission?"

President Clinton agreed, "We will issue a statement expressing regret and committing to assisting the Russian Federation in a rescue mission and all humanitarian assistance required. That is our final position."

Putin exchanged a glance with Lavrov, who gave a slight nod. The deal was a victory—$3 billion, family payments, oil, and the pipeline would strengthen Russia's economy and global standing, while the joint investigation would buy time to manage the domestic fallout.

"Agreed," Putin said. "But we must jointly strive to maintain the narrative of a tragic accident and ensure the independent investigation comes to the same conclusion."

Clinton exhaled; relief tempered by unease. "Understood," he said. "We will complete the details through diplomatic channels. Let us end this crisis here, Mr President."

The call ended, both sides had stepped back from the brink, though the undercurrent of mistrust lingered. Putin leaned back. The compensation package was a win, but Russia would not forget the loss of the *Kursk* and would rebuild, stronger than ever.

USS Memphis, 25 nautical miles southwest of the Pyotr Velikiy

The control room of the USS *Memphis* buzzed with a low, electric hum, and the S6G reactor's steady pulse was a heartbeat in the steel confines of the Los Angeles-class SSN. At 250 feet, the sub crept south-westward at eight knots; her screw turning just enough to maintain headway in the shallow, treacherous Barents Sea. Commander John Rourke stood at the centre of the chaos, his eyes bloodshot from twelve hours of unrelenting stress. He was leaning against the chart table as he scanned the tactical plot. The Russian Northern Fleet had resorted to using nuclear weapons; things were getting way out of control.

Sweat beaded on his forehead, dripping onto the illuminated flat-tactical screen, the air was thick with the acrid tang of fear and exhaustion. His crew was on edge—pale, trembling, their uniforms stained with sweat and grease, the weight of survival pressing down like the crushing depths outside.

"Conn, Sonar," Lieutenant Mike Hensley called from the sonar suite in the forward sonar room, his voice a strained whisper. "*Admiral Kharlamov* and *Admiral Levchenko* are moving to flank our last known sonar position. They are moving to deploy their RPK-2 Vyuga systems— likely nuclear depth charges, sir."

Rourke's jaw clenched as his mind raced to process the threat. The 28,000-ton *Pyotr Velikiy* Kirov-class battlecruiser sat 25 nautical miles to the northeast, its gigantic size powering a lethal arsenal.

The Udaloy-class destroyers were located 10 nautical miles northwest, their combined firepower forming a deadly net. Rourke was aware of the RPK-2 Vyuga—designed for submarine and surface deployment, carrying 82R or 83R torpedoes with 86R nuclear depth charges, or standalone 90R charges.

A single 5-kiloton detonation could obliterate *Memphis,* vaporising steel, and flesh alike.

"They are trying to box us in," Rourke said, voice low and steady despite the storm in his gut. He turned to XO Paul Reese; his wiry frame hunched over the fire control station with a cracked rib that made every breath a grimace.

"Admiral Chernov is playing hardball—flanking us with nuclear depth charges, to drive us south into his kill zone."

Reese nodded, his face pale but resolute, hands steady on the tactical console. "RPK-2 Vyuga means they are not messing around, sir. If they corner us, the *Petr Velikiy* will finish the job—likely with RPK-6 Vodopad or RPK-7 Veter. Both are dual-role, rocket-propelled, carrying 400mm torpedoes or nuclear depth charges. We are looking at a 55-knot killer."

"Conn, Sonar," Lieutenant Mike Hensley interjected. His lanky frame hunched over the AN/BQQ-5 suite, his headset pressed tight against his ears, as his voice trembled; the strain of hours under pressure was cracking his composure.

Kharlamov and *Levchenko* are speeding up—35 knots, bearing zero-one-zero, range nine nautical miles. They are moving at flank speed, sir. A crescent pattern is forming northwest of our position.

Rourke's eyes narrowed as the sonar plot painted a grim picture. The *Memphis* was a ghost in the water, her noise signature at 40 decibels, but the Barents Sea—averaging 150–300 feet in this region—offered little cover. The Russian fleet was closing in, its active sonar pings a relentless drumbeat, each pulse bringing them a step closer to annihilation.

Rourke knew they could not outrun the destroyers, and a nuclear depth charge did not require a direct hit—a near miss would crush the *Memphis* like a tin can.

"Rig for ultra-quiet," Rourke ordered, his voice a steel thread cutting through the tension. "Coolant pumps to 5%, screws to four knots. Let us buy some time."

The crew moved with practised precision, their hands steady in the face of extreme danger, flying over the controls as the *Memphis's* noise fell to a whisper. At depth, even silence carried weight. But Rourke knew time was a luxury they did not have—Chernov was coming for blood. The destruction of the *Kursk*, along with the two Ka-27PLs, must have pushed him over the edge.

Admiral Kharlamov, 28 nautical miles north of Memphis

Commander Nikolai Petrov stood on the bridge of the *Admiral Kharlamov*; his face twitched with every sonar ping on the tactical display. The 7,900-ton destroyer surged at 35 knots, flanked by the *Admiral Levchenko* two nautical miles to port. Petrov's uniform remained crisp despite the chaos, his voice a whip-crack as he relayed orders.

Petrov ordered. "Weapons, prepare the RPK-2 Vyuga—swap conventional warheads for 86R nuclear depth charges," he barked, hands clasped behind his back. "Target the Yankee submarines' last known position—form a crescent west, drive them into the *Petr Velikiy's* range."

Lieutenant Alexei Popov, *Admiral Kharlamov's* weapons officer, stood at the fire control station, his wiry frame tense as he input the coordinates. "Tubes one through four loaded, RPK-2 Vyuga, 86R warheads, aye, sir," Popov reported, voice steady despite the gravity of the order. "Firing solution locked—range 28 nautical miles, bearing two-seven-zero. Ready to launch."

"Fire," Petrov ordered, his scar pulled tight as he watched the launch sequence. The RPK-2 Vyuga systems fired and the *Admiral Kharlamov* shuddered as the 82R rockets streaking skyward.

In tandem, the *Admiral Levchenko* launched tubes three and four. The combined salvo was a deadly arc descending west of *Memphis*.

Sinking to 300 feet, the depth charges detonated in a crescent. Each explosion created a cataclysmic shockwave that rippled through the sea.

The damage to the Barent Sea floor and marine life was cataclysmic.

USS *Memphis*, 28 nautical miles south of the Admiral Kharlamov

The *Memphis* jolted violently as the first nuclear depth charge detonated five nautical miles to the west; the shockwave slammed into her hull with a force that rattled every bulkhead. Alarms blared, red lights flashed, pipes howled and a valve in the control room hissed as it sprayed steam across the deck.

"Conn, Sonar!" Hensley shouted, voice cracking as he clutched his headset. "Nuclear depth charge detonation—bearing two-seven-five, range five nautical miles! Second detonation—bearing two-six-five, range six nautical miles! They are forming a crescent, sir—pushing us east!"

Rourke steadied himself against the periscope stand, his crew's faces were ashen with terror as the second shockwave hit and the hull creaked under the strain. Petty Officer James Carter, a sonar tech with a boyish face, winced as he adjusted the dials. Ensign Laura Hayes gripped her station, her headset slipping as she fought to maintain focus. "They're… they're trying to kill us all."

"Steady, Hayes," Rourke snapped "They are herding us—east into the *Petr Velikiy's* kill box. Chernov's playing for keeps."

Reese's cracked rib screamed, but his wiry frame held firm, hands steady on the fire control console. "RPK-2 Vyuga's just the start, sir. The *Petr Velikiy* will hit us with RPK-6 Vodopad or RPK-7 Veter—533mm or 650mm anti-sub missiles, rocket-propelled, dual-role. They will carry a nuclear depth charge—5-kiloton yield, 55 knots. We cannot outrun that."

A third nuclear depth charge detonated four nautical miles west, the shockwave was closer, the *Memphis* howled as a panel in the overhead sparked, showering the deck with embers. The crew flinched, some muttered prayers, others gripped their stations as the reality of nuclear warfare sank in.

Rourke calculated the odds—slim to none, but he would be damned if he let his crew die without a fight.

Petr Velikiy, 25 nautical miles northeast of Memphis

Admiral Viktor Chernov stood on the bridge of *Petr Velikiy*, his dark eyes glinted with predatory focus as he watched the sonar plot update. His crumpled uniform had cigarette ash on his chest and his rage was a living thing after *Memphis's* earlier escape from the RPK-6 Vodopad torpedoes. The American sub had defied him, slipping through his net like a ghost, but not this time.

"The *Admiral Kharlamov* and *Admiral Levchenko* have the American submarine on the run," Chernov growled, turning to Captain Ivan Rostov, whose dark eyes flickered with unease at the nuclear escalation.

"They are driving her east—into our range. Weapons, prepare RPK-7 Veter—650mm, 90R nuclear depth charge. I want that Yankee submarine obliterated."

Lieutenant Mikhail Orlov, *Petr Velikiy's* weapons officer, stood at the fire control station, inputting the commands. "RPK-7 Veter loaded, 90R nuclear depth charge, aye, sir," Orlov reported, voice clipped. "Firing solution locked—range 25 nautical miles, bearing two-eight-zero. The missile will splash 10 nautical miles ahead of the American submarine's projected path."

"Launch," Chernov ordered, his voice a snarl, cigarette dangling from his lips as he watched the launch sequence. The RPK-7 Veter missile roared from its tube, its solid-fuel rocket igniting with a fiery plume, arcing high into the sky before splashing down 10 nautical miles west of *Memphis*.

The parachute released and dropped the 82R nuclear-armed torpedo into the sea, its active sonar pinging went active shortly after as it searched to acquire the *Memphis*, turning to intercept at 55 knots, a 200-kiloton harbinger of annihilation.

Admiral Kharlamov, 20 nautical miles northwest of Memphis

Petrov watched the sonar plot on the *Admiral Kharlamov's* bridge, his face drawn tight as the RPK-2 Vyuga detonations formed a deadly crescent, forcing the American submarine east. "*Admiral Levchenko,* confirm your charges," he ordered over the encrypted channel.

Commander Alexei Morozov on the *Admiral Levchenko* responded, his tone equally tense. "Charges deployed, bearing two-six-zero, range 15 nautical miles from target. Crescent pattern holding—the American submarine has nowhere to run."

Petrov's dark eyes narrowed, a grim satisfaction settling in his chest. "Good," he said, gripping the railing as another nuclear depth charge detonated, the shockwave rippling through the sea. "Chernov will finish her. Keep the net tight—no mistakes."

USS Memphis, 25 nautical miles southwest of the Pyotr Velikiy

The *Memphis* rocked violently as a fourth RPK-2 Vyuga charge detonated four nautical miles west. The shockwave was closer now, and the hull protested loudly as a seam in the engineering compartment sprang a leak, spraying seawater across the deck.

"Flooding in engineering!" Lieutenant Mark Evans shouted over the intercom; his boyish face was streaked with grease as he wrestled with the valves. "Sealing now, but we can't take much more of this, sir!"

"Conn, Sonar!" Hensley called, voice hoarse with panic, hands trembling as he adjusted the hydrophones, the deafening blasts leaving his ears ringing. "New contact—bearing two-eight-zero, range 10 nautical miles, speed 55 knots! It is an RPK-7 Veter, 82R torpedo, likely nuclear, from the *Petr Velikiy*! It has acquired us, sir—closing at 65 knots relative!"

Rourke's blood ran cold; the reality hit like a sledgehammer. The *Admiral Kharlamov* and *Admiral Levchenko* had driven them east with nuclear depth charges, their detonations a relentless assault that had left his sonar team on the verge of collapse, with Carter and Hayes clutching their headsets as if they could block out the trauma.

Now, the *Petr Velikiy* had launched a nuclear torpedo, closing at 55—65 knots relative to the *Memphis's* 10 knots eastward. At 10 nautical miles, they had less than six minutes before impact, a 200-kiloton detonation would obliterate them, even at a distance.

"We're under nuclear attack," Rourke said, his voice a steel blade cutting through the panic, his eyes burning with resolve. "Hayes, send an emergency beacon to COMLANTFLT—now!"

Hayes encoded the message, her fingers shaking, voice barely a whisper. COMLANTFLT, THIS IS *MEMPHIS*. UNDER NUCLEAR ATTACK—RPK-2 VYUGA AND RPK-7 VETER. LIKELY TO BE DESTROYED. LAST POSITION 69N, 28E. The beacon launched, a desperate signal as Rourke's mind raced for a last gambit to save his ship and crew.

"XO, Sonar, Fire Control—get over here!" Rourke barked, seizing the wire-guided control joystick, a desperate plan forming. "Weapons, load tubes one and two with Mark 48 ANCAP torpedoes—snapshot, wire-guided, target that incoming 82R!"

Weapons Officer Ed Kline moved precisely, tubes one and two humming as the Mark 48 torpedoes spun up, their guidance systems locking on. "Tubes one and two loaded, Mark 48 ANCAP, wire-guided, locked on target, sir!" Kline reported. His stocky frame was tense, and his voice was steady despite the extreme danger.

"Fire tubes one and two—now!" Rourke ordered, the *Memphis* whispered as the compressed air launch systems pushed the Mark 48 torpedoes out the tubes, wire-guided, streaking toward the incoming nuclear depth charge torpedo at 55 knots. "Kline, give me the joystick control now," Rourke ordered. The two torpedoes closed at a combined speed of 110 knots, the 10-mile distance shrinking rapidly, with less than six minutes to impact.

Rourke gripped the joystick, his eyes, locked onto the fire control screen, guided the Mark 48s with precision. Sweat poured down his face as the *Memphis* rocked from another nuclear depth charge detonation 10 nautical miles west, that cracked a gauge in the control room and shattered glass across the deck.

"Sonar, XO—give me 30 seconds' notice of terminal crossing!" Rourke shouted. His voice cutting through the cacophony of alarms and the crew's murmured prayers, some were clutching rosaries while others stared at their stations with hollow eyes.

Reese and Hensley worked in sync, tracking the converging paths. Hensley's hands shook as he called out the distances, his voice a ragged whisper.

"Eight nautical miles… seven nautical miles…" A fifth nuclear depth charge detonated, eight nautical miles west, a pipe in the overhead bursting, spraying coolant across Rourke's back, soaking his uniform as he held firm.

"Six nautical miles… five nautical miles… four nautical miles… three nautical miles… two nautical miles… 30 seconds to terminal!"

"30 seconds to terminal!" Reese echoed, his cracked rib a searing agony, hands clenched on the console as he watched the sonar plot, the crew's prayers growing louder, a desperate plea for salvation.

Rourke's finger hovered over the self-destruct button, his heart pounding as he waited for the precise moment, the *Memphis* trembling under the strain of the nuclear assault. "Now!" he roared, pressing the button. The two Mark 48 torpedoes detonated instantly, their 650-pound warheads exploding 1.5 nautical miles from the *Memphis*, a twin fireball of pressure and heat erupting in the water, the shockwave rippled outward with ferocious force—a blinding pulse of energy that lit up the sonar screens like a supernova.

The crew braced, their prayers intensified as they waited for the incoming 82R nuclear torpedo to strike, its 200-kiloton yield a death sentence.

Chief Petty Officer Daniel Harris, the helmsman, clutched the wheel, whispering a prayer for his daughter back in Norfolk. Petty Officer James Carter stared at his sonar screen, tears streaming down his boyish face as he braced for the end.

Seconds ticked by—five, ten, fifteen—agonising, endless seconds—nothing happened. The control room remained silent, the only sounds the hum of the reactor and the drip of coolant, as the crew held their breath as if the silence itself might shatter.

"Conn, Sonar," Hensley called, his voice trembling with disbelief and his hands shaking as he adjusted the hydrophones, marvelled at the absence of the nuclear detonation. "The 82R—it has gone silent, sir! The Mark 48 detonations damaged it, disabling its warhead and drive system; it has fallen harmlessly to the bottom. Range 1.2 nautical miles—it did not detonate!"

Rourke exhaled. The adrenaline surged as the crew gasped with relief. Some crossed themselves; others collapsed against their stations; tears of disbelief streamed down their faces. Reese burst into the control room, his wiry frame trembling with emotion, his cracked rib forgotten as he threw his arms around Rourke, his voice breaking with awe.

"You did it!" he exclaimed. "You used the Mark 48s as a self-defence system—knocked out that nuclear torpedo! You saved the ship, the crew—everything!"

Rourke disentangled himself from Reese. "The Mark 48s' explosion disrupted the 82R's guidance and drive system," he said. "The shockwave must have damaged its warhead mechanism—sent it inert. We got lucky, Paul. Damn lucky."

The crew gazed at Rourke in awe, their commander's desperate gamble had defied the odds, and transformed two conventional torpedoes into a shield against nuclear annihilation.

Chief Harris wiped his eyes and whispered, "Thank you, sir." Carter and Hayes exchanged a look, their trauma giving way to a flicker of hope as they returned to their stations. The *Memphis* turned and tracked west, her hull battered but unbroken, her crew clinging to survival through sheer ingenuity and defiance.

Petr Velikiy, 25 nautical miles northeast of Memphis

Admiral Viktor Chernov stood on the *Petr Velikiy's* bridge, his dark eyes wide with disbelief as the sonar plot updated, the 82R nuclear torpedo's signature fading as it sank to the seabed, 1.2 nautical miles short of the *Memphis*. The American submarine had survived, its sonar ping was faint but unmistakable, moving west at eight knots, a ghost that refused to die.

Chernov's cigarette fell from his lips and ash scattered across the deck as his rage erupting like a volcano. "Pizdetz!" Chernov roared, slamming both fists on the chart table, sending a coffee mug flying. The black liquid pooled around his boots. "How did they do that? The Yankee submarine—it should be a smoking hole in the seabed! They stopped a nuclear torpedo—impossible!"

Captain Ivan Rostov stood uneasily nearby. Nuclear escalation was a line he had hoped never to cross. "Sir, the American sub must've used countermeasures—likely detonated its own torpedoes to disrupt the 82R."

Rostov said, voice low but steady, hands clasped behind his back. "Their commander—he is formidable. We underestimated him."

Chernov whirled on Rostov, his face crimson, veins bulging in his neck as he jabbed a finger at the sonar plot. "Underestimated?" he snarled, voice dripping with venom. "They have humiliated us! The *Kursk*—gone, 118 men dead! Two helicopters, four flight crew—gone! And now this? I will bury that sub myself!" He turned to Lieutenant Mikhail Orlov, his voice a feral growl. "Prepare two nuclear depth charges—RPK-6

Vodopad, 90R warheads set to maximum yield! Launch immediately once the nuclear codes are clear. I am inserting my authorisation key—I want that American sub vaporised now!"

In the depths of the giant battlecruiser, the armoury smelled like gun oil and old thunder. Fluorescent strips hummed above a row of locked vaults; each vault's painted number read like a verdict. Lieutenant Petrov kept his palms flat on the workbench as if pressing them down might slow the sea.

"Codes confirmed," the messenger on the bridge said over the intercom — the voice small, impossible to argue with. Someone stamped the paper on the bench in red. Ink meant business, and everything shifted.

They did not speak of the warhead itself. In the armoury, its name was whispered in drills and nightmares: Vodopad. Out in the world, it meant headlines and rumours. Here, it was a sealed thing that made men look at each other differently.

The armoury chief—Mikhailov—moved with slow, ceremonial economy. He did not rush; speed felt disrespectful. The deputy handed him a maintenance log; they read the pages for more than dates. Outside, the cruiser's catlike silhouette rode the heave of a black ocean. The ship seemed to inhale.

Petrov watched fingers slide across metal like a priest tracing a cross. There were checks and marks, signatures scratched in the margins. Ritual more than recipe. Each motion threaded them tighter to the decision on the bridge.

Then came the terse order through the speaker: "Command authorised." The words landed like a hammer on the deck. No one cheered. The weapons crew attended to the minor tasks at hand: logging this, sealing that, and signing there. They were doing ordinary paperwork for an extraordinary thing.

Petrov felt the world narrow to a hinge—one signature, one sealed locker, one man's breath. He thought of his father's hands, scarred from winter work; he thought of his daughter's last letter asking when he would come home. He slid a pen across the page and wrote his name in a hand that would carry blame or absolution, neither of which he could predict.

When he stepped back, the vault's latch clicked shut. Outside, the ocean kept its indifferent rhythm. Inside, they had changed the axis of a small, terrible world.

In the weapons control centre, Orlov's hands flew over the controls of the *Petr Velikiy's* missile systems, priming the next salvo for launch. "Tubes five and six loaded, RPK-6 Vodopad, 90R nuclear depth charges, aye, sir," Orlov reported over the intercom to the bridge, his voice steady, but his eyes flickered with the weight of the order.

Admiral Kharlamov, 18 nautical miles north of Memphis

Commander Nikolai Petrov gripped the railing on *Admiral Kharlamov's* bridge; his focus was on the tactical plot as the sonar plot updated. The *Memphis's* faint signature was still moving west despite the nuclear assault. "They're still alive," Petrov growled, his voice thick with frustration, as he turned to Lieutenant Alexei Popov.

"*Petr Velikiy's* 82R failed—how?" Popov shook his head with disbelief. "Unknown, sir. They must have disrupted the warhead with countermeasures, maybe a torpedo detonation. The Americans… they are tougher than we thought."

Petrov's dark eyes burned with fury; his face burned red as he turned to the comms officer. "Signal the *Admiral Levchenko*—tighten the crescent," he ordered, voice a whip-crack. "Launch another salvo— RPK-2 Vyuga, 90R charges."

We will drive them into Chernov's next strike."

The *Admiral Kharlamov* and *Admiral Levchenko* launched again, their RPK-2 Vyuga systems fired in unison, with the nuclear depth charges descending in a tighter crescent, five nautical miles west of *Memphis*. Their detonations formed a relentless barrage that shook the sea, each blast a promise of destruction. The entire crew was determined to see the *Memphis* crushed.

USS Memphis, 25 Nautical miles Southwest of the Pyotr Velikiy

A new wave of RPK-2 Vyuga charges detonated and the *Memphis* shuddered. Five nautical miles to the west, the shockwaves grew closer, the hull pitched as a seam in the torpedo room sprang a leak, "Flooding in the torpedo room!" Kline shouted, his stocky frame moving to assist the damage control team, voice tight with urgency. "Sealing now, sir!"

Rourke stood at the fire control station; eyes locked on the tactical plot of *Admiral Kharlamov* and *Admiral Levchenko's* second salvo—RPK-2 Vyuga nuclear depth charges. Rourke's heart pounded as the *Memphis's* crew looked to him for salvation again.

The *Admiral Kharlamov* and *Admiral Levchenko's* nuclear depth charges hammered from the west, driving them further into the *Petr Velikiy's* kill zone. The last thing the *Memphis* needed was another RPK-6 Vodopad atomic attack.

The Oval Office, Washington, D.C.

President Bill Clinton was pacing the Oval Office, his face pale with worry. They had agreed upon the $3 billion compensation deal with Putin, but the situation in the Barents Sea was spiralling out of control. The phone rang. Secretary of Defence William Cohen and Secretary of State Madeleine Albright sat nearby; their expressions grim as Pentagon officials relayed the latest updates.

"Mr President," said General John Abrams, Chairman of the Joint

Chiefs, his voice urgent over the secure line, "our submarine, the USS *Memphis*, is under nuclear attack. We just received an emergency communication from *Memphis*, and they do not expect to survive. Seismic stations in Alaska and Norway confirm a 3.8-magnitude event in the Barents Sea, consistent with low-yield nuclear detonations."

Clinton's face turned ashen, he gripped the edge of the Resolute Desk. "Get me the Russian President—immediately," he snapped.

The red phone rang, and Putin's voice came through, cold but uncertain, his St. Petersburg accent clipped. "Mr President, what is this about?"

"President Putin, are you out of your goddamn mind?" Clinton shouted, his voice trembling with rage. "We have confirmation of the use of nuclear depth charges against our submarines. This is an act of war, sir!"

Putin hesitated, surprised. "You must be mistaken, Mr President," he said, his voice cold but uncertain. "I commanded the *Pyotr Velikiy* to stand down immediately. The Russian Federation would never dream of using nuclear weapons. We are a peaceful nation of civilised, God-fearing people."

Foreign Minister Sergei Lavrov, quickly stepped away to a side room and grabbed a secure line to Russian Naval Command. His voice was low and urgent. "Stand down, Admiral Chernov, on the *Petr Velikiy* immediately," he ordered. "Use lethal force if you have to."

Clinton's mind raced as he waited for Putin's response. The sinking of the *Kursk* was a tragedy, but the use of nuclear depth weapons was a clear escalation, a violation of every international norm. He thought of the *Memphis*'s crewmen like Commander John Rourke, a veteran officer he had met at a naval review two years ago. Rourke had a family, including a wife and children, waiting back home. Now, they might never see him again.

Pyotr Velikiy (Peter the Great), 25 nautical miles northeast of the USS Memphis

Admiral Viktor Chernov stood on the *Pyotr Velikiy's* bridge. The next salvo would finish the job, avenging the *Kursk* and the *Gepard's* crippling blow. "Prepare to launch the nuclear depth charges," he ordered, his voice a growl. "We end this now."

Captain Ivan Rostov, the *Petr Velikiy's* CO, approached calmly, flanked by several armed MPs, their AK-74 rifles at the ready. "Admiral, we've just received orders from the Kremlin to stand down," Rostov said, his voice steady but firm. "You are to be relieved of your command immediately. I am sorry, sir." He nodded to the MPs. "Please escort the Admiral to his quarters."

Chernov's face twisted with rage, his hands clenched into fists. As he turned to face Rostov, his cigarette fell to the deck. "You dare?" he roared, his voice a snarl. "I'll have you court-martialled for this!"

The MPs moved swiftly, their weapons were drawn and their faces set in grim determination. Chernov's loyalists—two junior officers on the bridge—reached for their sidearms, but the MPs were faster and disarmed them with practiced efficiency. Chernov had no choice but to comply. Rostov took command, his voice steady as he addressed the crew. "Signal the fleet—stand down," he ordered, his tone firm. "Cease all ASW operations immediately. We are turning back."

The *Petr Velikiy's* communications officer, Lieutenant Mikhail Orlov, relayed the orders. The *Admiral Levchenko*, *Admiral Kharlamov*, and the remaining Ka-27PL helicopters—Medved (Bear), Tigr (Tiger), and Bars (Leopard)—turned away, their active sonar pings fading as they broke off the hunt. Rostov's mind raced. The Kremlin's orders were explicit— stand down, de-escalate, avoid a full-scale war with the Americans. But Rostov knew the cost. The failure to exact vengeance and the arrest of the Admiral would shatter the Northern Fleet's morale. He thought of Chernov, a man he had served under for years, a man whose rage had driven him to the brink of madness. Rostov had had no choice but to relieve him, but the decision weighed heavily on his conscience.

USS Memphis, 14 nautical miles southwest of the Pyotr Velikiy

"Conn, Sonar," said Lieutenant Mike Hensley, his voice laced with disbelief as he adjusted his headset. "The *Pyotr Velikiy* and the fleet are turning away, sir."

Commander John Rourke blinked, unable to process the words. He had been silently praying, his heart heavy with guilt and sorrow, resigned to never seeing his wife, Rachel, and their children, Sarah and Michael, again. He had condemned his crew to a watery grave—or so he had thought. "Say that again, Sonar," he whispered, his voice hoarse.

"They're turning away, sir," Hensley repeated, his voice steady. "Bearing shifting to zero-three-zero—range increasing. They are breaking off the hunt."

Rourke trembled with relief; his hands gripped the chart table as the weight of their survival sank in. "Maintain 250 feet, ahead two-thirds," he ordered, his voice hoarse with emotion. "Let's get the hell out of here before they change their minds."

The control room crew exchanged looks of palpable relief. Ensign Laura Hayes, at the comms station, wiped a tear from her eye, as she adjusted her headset. Weapons Officer Ed Kline, his stocky frame slumped against the fire control system, let out a shaky breath.

Rourke leaned against the tactical plot table; images of his family flashed through his mind; but the guilt of the *Kursk's* sinking was a heavy burden he would carry for the rest of his life. He set a course west to rendezvous with the *Toledo* at Tromsø Naval Base in Norway. Unbroken, the *Memphis's* S6G reactor ran at 40% power, the screw driving the ship at 15 knots as it dived to 500 feet in a deeper section of the Barents Sea. The Russian fleet had turned away, but he did not know why or whether they would be back. The sinking of the *Kursk* was an effective declaration of war, and the Northern Fleet would not rest until the Americans had paid for their actions. Rourke thought of Commander Tom Brennan, limping ahead in the *Toledo*, his wounded sub had barely survived the day.

Rourke was mentally and physically exhausted; the trauma of the constant nuclear depth charges and narrowly avoiding being vaporised by an atomic torpedo had taken its toll on him. Despite how bad he felt, what he saw in the control room shocked him. His crew were traumatised; some were still crying; and one young ensign was curled up in his station chair and rocking in a fetal position.

He picked up the ship's intercom handset. "Well, good afternoon, ladies and gentlemen, this is your captain speaking. If you look to the right, you will see the entire Russian Fleet leaving; I hope you all enjoyed the fight."

Nervous laughter swept through the ship, many of the crew hugged each other as they realised, they had been to hell and back and survived.

"Crew of the *Memphis*, you have made me extremely proud to be your Commanding Officer today," Rourke formally addressed the crew through the ship's intercom. "You worked as a team, trusted in your ship, and most of all, put your trust in me. Hooyah!"

"Hooyah!" shouted the general chorus of the entire ship's company.

CBG USS *Theodore Roosevelt*, August 13, 2000

Captain Li Jun stepped off the MH-60 Seahawk in handcuffs; his sharp features were concealed beneath a wool cap. Smith flanked him, with Mitchell maintaining a firm grip on Li Jun's cuffs.

The SEAL fire team extraction unit followed, their operation a success, despite failing to intercept Vesnen as planned. Li Jun's Chinese intelligence coup had turned into a nightmare for him but was a godsend for the CIA.

Agent Smith stood on the windswept flight deck of the USS *Theodore Roosevelt*, the massive Nimitz-class carrier pitching gently in the North Atlantic swell. With the encrypted satellite phone pressed to his ear, he relayed the update to Langley with his trademark clipped efficiency. "Jun's stonewalling. Claims diplomatic immunity, spouting PLA loyalty. No actionable intel yet except the encryption devices we found on him."

The line crackled with the brief pause of consultation—senior department heads at CIA headquarters conferring, then looping in the State Department. Secretary Madeleine Albright's office green-lit the escalation: "Proceed with persuasion. National security imperative." Langley got back within minutes. "Smith, use your powers. We are dispatching the *Sunflower*, a Panama-flagged freighter with a black ops' configuration. You'll helicopter over with Jun Li and rendezvous off Finland then set sail to international waters. Begin the debrief en route."

"Roger that," Smith replied, pocketing the phone. At 51, ex-Secret Service agent Smith was the agency's go-to troubleshooter—deployable at a moment's notice for wet work or extractions. His Kuala Lumpur scar throbbed in the cold, a reminder of a North Korea counterfeit op where he had held off a small army. Now aboard the *Roosevelt* for the Vesnen defection support, he had pivoted to handle Li Jun, the Chinese captain caught spying during the *Kursk* mess.

Below decks, Smith approached the holding cell where Jun sat cuffed, his sharp features defiant under the harsh fluorescents. "Time to move, Captain. Your cooperation's lacking."

Jun sneered. "You have no jurisdiction. Beijing will protest."

Smith smiled thinly. "Beijing doesn't know where you are. We're past protests."

Hours later, a Seahawk helo lifted them from the carrier, rotors thumping against the Arctic dusk. The *Sunflower* loomed on the horizon—a nondescript 200-foot freighter, but her holds had been retrofitted with interrogation suites, armouries, and ECM gear. Disguised as a grain haulier, she was a floating black site, crewed by ex-Special Ops ghosts like Smith.

The helicopter touched down on the aft deck. Two burly assistants—former Delta operators—hauled Jun below and strapped him to a chair in a soundproof cell. Smith shed his duffle coat to reveal the HK MP5K and HK USP Kompakt 9mm. "Gentle debriefing time, Jun. You have got stories—Japanese sonar theft, *Shkval* blueprints. Let's chat."

Jun spat. "Torture? Your American—Geneva Conventions."

Smith chuckled darkly, his past "gentle" sessions with foreign dignitaries flashed by: a Saudi prince waterboarded in a Riyadh safe house, yielding Al-Qaeda financiers; a Venezuelan general broken in a Caracas basement, spilling coup plans. "Conventions are for wars we declare. This is off the books."

A horrendous stench seeped in from the adjacent hold. "Be thankful you're not Muslim," Smith said, leaning close. "We keep a herd of pigs next door. For my Islamic guests, I bunk them with the swine—shared cell, slop, water trough. After 48 hours, they're singing like canaries, begging to confess."

Jun paled but held firm. "I won't talk, psycho."

Smith sighed theatrically. "International rules, you say? We're in open waters now—I make the rules." He nodded to the assistants. "Get him on the gurney."

The men hauled Jun off the chair, one landed a gut punch that doubled him over They slammed him onto the gurney—a tilted board with restraints—strapped his head, arms, and legs, so he was immobile. "You like water, my friend?" Smith asked with ironic politeness.

"Qu ni de!" Jun shouted.

"Oh, we're going to get along famously." One assistant draped a thick white towel over Jun's face; the other poured water steadily, simulating drowning. Jun thrashed and choked; the panic of asphyxiation broke his resolve in waves. Hours blurred—starts and stops, Smith's voice remained a calm tormentor: "It pains me to see you suffer. Just cooperate. Tell me about your ops—the full setup in Chinese intel, PLA connections."

Jun resisted at first, invoking Party loyalty, but the relentless "persuasion" eroded him. Water filled his sinuses; terror clawed at his mind. By dawn, he had broken and spilled everything: his operational history, from the 1994 Sea Serpent mission that had stolen the Japanese OQR-3 sonar, to the *Shkval* acquisitions via Sokolov. He detailed the Chinese intelligence hierarchies—MSS agents embedded in PLAN, links to cyber units in Beijing, even ops beyond infiltrating US tech firms in Silicon Valley, honey traps on diplomats in Geneva. Smith realised they had caught "the Ghost"—a legendary operative who had evaded identification and capture for years.

Smith rang Langley on the encrypted line. "Debrief complete. Jun's a goldmine—fills gaps in counterintelligence that go back years. MSS-PLA nexus confirmed, plus bonus ops."

"Good work," the controller replied. "POTUS says dispose. He's cost us millions; no dime for Gitmo."

Smith sighed. "Understood." He entered the cell where Jun slumped, exhausted. "Well, my friend, it's time to meet your ancestors."

"But I told you everything!" Jun pleaded, eyes wide.

"You did—and America's grateful." The assistants hauled him to the railing, the Arctic Ocean black and churning below. "Face me or look away?"

"You can't—you're civilised Westerners!"

Smith drew his HK USP 9mm pistol and shot Jun between the eyes. The body crumpled; the men heaved it overboard; it floated for a moment then vanished into the depths.

Smith lit a cigarette and stared at the waves. Another ghost dispatched, another gap filled. The *Sunflower* steamed on, a shadow in international waters.

Back at Langley, the CIA schemed how they could use the intel to pressure Beijing, leveraging the threat of exposure to the Russians to secure concessions in trade negotiations.

Krivak-class frigate Smolensk, one mile north of the Kursk wreck

Lieutenant Oleg Vesnen sat in the *Smolensk's* brig, his hands cuffed behind his back, his gaunt face was pale with terror as Major Alexei Gromov continued the interrogation. The FSB Spetsnaz team had apprehended the 32-year-old navigation officer, with haunted eyes and a wiry frame, after stealing a lifeboat, his attempt to defect to the CIA had been thwarted by the Ka-50 Black Shark's swift intervention. Gromov, the Spetsnaz commander, stood over him, his shaved head gleamed with sweat, a scar across his left cheek starkly contrasted with his dark eyes and full black beard.

"You'll tell us everything," Gromov growled, his voice a low snarl as he leaned in close, his breath hot on Vesnen's face. "The USB drive—where exactly is it?"

Vesnen's eyes darted to the floor, his hands trembling in the cuffs, his mind racing with fear. "I… I told you, "He stammered, his voice cracking. "Storage compartment near the stern—under the floor panel, starboard side. It is hidden in a waterproof bag."

Gromov's lips curled into a grim smile, his scar twisted with the motion. "Liar, my men have checked everywhere and found nothing."

One of the Spetsnaz team moved with lethal efficiency and smashed the bridge of Vesnen's nose with the butt of his AN-94. "If he doesn't tell us immediately where he has hidden the data, shoot him in the head," Gromov ordered.

"Ok, ok," screamed Vesnen. Blood poured out of his nose, urine stained his pants. "It's sewn into the seam in my uniform jacket, please don't hurt me further."

Gromov ripped off Vesnen's uniform jacket and sliced open the seam with his razor-sharp combat knife. "This is the only smart thing you have done today, traitor," Ivanov said, looking at the data drive. He pulled his satellite phone from his combat fatigues and dialled the FSB's headquarters in Moscow's Lubyanka Building. Colonel Dmitry Voronov sat at a secure terminal and answered, "Da? Comrade Gromov?"

"Sir, we captured Vesnen, destroyed the motorised lifeboat, and I have the data drive he intended to sell to the Americans in my hand," Gromov said with satisfaction in his voice.

"Excellent, Major Gromov, you have done well as always, my trust in you and your team is well placed," Voronov said, "Load the traitor onto the Kamov Ka-50 Black Shark and fly to Murmansk as soon as possible." I will send a military jet to pick you up and bring you to Moscow. Once again, well done, Major."

"Consider it done, sir," Gromov replied. He instructed his men to secure Vesnen and get the Kamov Ka-50 Black Shark pilot underway back to the Murmansk naval base.

Captain Sergei Ivanov, the CO of the *Smolensk*, watched as the Kamov Ka-50 Black Shark took off from his rear deck, rose sharply and banked south. Vesnen—a man he had trusted, a man he had served with for years—was a traitor. He thought about Vesnen's fate and shivered in relief at seeing the last Spetsnaz commandos leave his ship. The order from the *Petr Velikiy* to divert to the *Gepard's* position, rescue its crew and tow the crippled Akula to Murmansk was a blessing, allowing him to focus on his duty to the living, and the *Gepard* needed him now.

"Helm, maintain course for the *Gepard*." He ordered. "Full speed—we've got a sub to save."

ECHOES IN THE DEEP

Setting: Various locations,
August 14 — December 15, 2000

Norwegian naval base at Tromsø

Through the Arctic mist, the Norwegian naval base at Tromsø loomed like a sanctuary. The USS *Toledo* limped into the harbour, her once-sleek Los Angeles-class hull a mangled testament to the hell she had endured in the Barents Sea. Commander Tom Brennan, his uniform salt-crusted and bloodstained from the gash on his forehead, felt the submarine's final groan as she eased alongside the pier. Norwegian tugs nudged her gently, their crews in awe at the wreck that was once a Los Angeles nuclear attack submarine. Brennan's eyes, hollow from 48 hours without sleep, moved to exit his ship and survey the damage. The conning tower was out of the question—a crumpled ruin, its periscopes mangled like broken spines. He opted for the rear vertical access hatch, a narrow emergency egress amidships. "XO, secure the ship. I am going topside," he radioed Carter.

The hatch clanged open under his grip, and Brennan hauled himself onto the hull, the cold wind whipped his face like a slap from the deep. He staggered; the deck was slick with oil and seawater, and he gazed at the fjord's granite cliffs. Relief flooded him—his crew was safe; the *Toledo's* reactor had cooled with no radiation leaks despite the *Kursk* collision that had thrown them like a rag-doll. But the weight of 118 Russians lost on the *Kursk*, from a shadow game's poor orders and fatal misstep, haunted him. Brennan knew the ghosts would linger.

As medics swarmed the pier, Norwegian officers approached, their faces etched with concern. "Commander Brennan? Welcome to Tromsø. Your embassy is en route." Brennan nodded. His mind replayed the chaos: the 53-65 torpedoes dodged by desperate surfacing; the Akula's wake-homers foiled by Evans' jury-rigged silence. The *Gepard* had come closest; a deadly duel of death was played out at 500 feet beneath the angry Barents Sea. The *Gepard* and the *Toledo* exchanged deadly torpedo fire, and the *Toledo* emerged victorious.

Brennan turned to see his crew emerging—Hensley with a bandaged head, Carter barking orders, Evans limping but grinning. Relief swelled, a counter to the guilt. They had survived the unthinkable: collision, pursuit, torpedoes. But whispers of escalation had reached him— Chinese spies extracted, defectors spilling secrets, Putin raging in the Kremlin. The *Kursk's* logs, if recovered, might prove aggression against an accident, but Brennan doubted peace—the deep-held grudge.

As the sun pierced the mist, Brennan saluted his ship. "Well done, *Toledo*."

•••

Twelve hours later, the *Memphis* arrived, her hull intact yet showing obvious signs of battle damage from her various encounters with nuclear depth charges and torpedoes, her crew no less haunted. Commander John Rourke stepped onto the pier, his square jaw set and his eyes shadowed with guilt. Commander Tom Brennan met him on the dock. The two commanders embraced, silently acknowledging the nightmare they had survived together. But the men of the *Kursk* had not. Brennan had been too close; his orders to shadow the *Kursk* had led to the collision that had triggered the disaster. Rourke had fired the fatal Mark 48, sinking the Russian sub in retaliation. They had saved their crews, but at a cost neither could fully reconcile.

NATO officials swarmed the subs, debriefing the crews and assessing damage. The *Toledo* would need months in drydock—her sail was gone, her reactor had been strained, and her hull still leaked in three compartments. The nuclear depth charge's shockwave still haunted the *Memphis's* crew, who were shaken but had fared better. Technicians scanned its hull for dangerous levels of radioactivity from the Russian Northern Fleet's atomic attacks.

Rourke thought of his family—Rachel, Sarah, and Michael—waiting for him in Groton, Connecticut. He had promised to be home for Sarah's birthday, and now, against all odds, he would keep that promise. But the faces of the *Kursk's* crewmen, who he had never met, but who he had killed, kept swimming into his head.

U.S Navy Atlantic Submarine Fleet Base – Groton, Connecticut, October 10, 2000

Commander Brennan's debrief with USLANTFLT was brutal. The sinking of the *Kursk* caused a geopolitical firestorm, with Moscow accusing the US of aggression and NATO scrambling to manage the fallout. The $3 billion compensation deal, the oil offtake agreement, and the gas pipelines into Western Europe—brokered between Clinton and Putin—had maintained a fragile peace. Yet, the truth behind the incident remained concealed—officially, a torpedo malfunction. Brennan knew the real story, and carrying that knowledge was a heavy burden. He had been too close, and his orders led to the collision that ignited the crisis. He would probably face a court-martial, but he was now instructed to stay silent, as the truth was too dangerous to reveal.

...

Commander John Rourke stood at attention in the briefing room of the US Naval Base at Groton; his dress whites were crisp despite the exhaustion etched into his face. His eyes, bloodshot from days of relentless tension, scanned the panel of senior Navy officers seated before him, their stern expressions a display of experience and authority.

The air was thick with the weight of judgment, and the hum of fluorescent lights starkly contrasted with the cacophony of the Barents Sea battles he had survived. The USS *Memphis* and USS *Toledo* had limped into port weeks ago, their crews battered but alive, and now Rourke faced the reckoning of his decisions.

At the head of the panel sat Admiral Robert Natter, Commander of US Submarine Forces Atlantic (COMSUBLANT), his silver hair, and steely blue eyes commanded the room. Natter, a Vietnam-era veteran known for his unyielding standards, had chaired the debriefing personally, a rare move that underscored the gravity of the *Kursk* incident.

Flanking him was a cadre of senior admirals, their insignia gleamed under the lights—Rear Admiral John Padgett III, Deputy Commander of Submarine Forces; Vice Admiral Edmund Giambastiani, Commander of Submarine Group Two; and Rear Admiral Malcolm Fages, Director of Submarine Warfare. Among them was Rear Admiral Charles Griffiths, a grizzled submariner under whom Rourke had served as a junior ensign on the USS *Boston* (SSN-703) in 1989, his first tour on a nuclear attack sub.

Griffiths' weathered face, lined from years beneath the waves, gave a flicker of acknowledgment as he met Rourke's gaze. The panel had read Rourke's written submission—a detailed 50-page report chronicling the USS *Memphis's* actions from shadowing the *Kursk* to the climactic nuclear assault in the Barents Sea.

Now, Rourke delivered his personal account, voice steady but raw, recounting the *Kursk's* collision with the *Toledo*, its sinking, the Sea Lance missile engagements against Russian helicopters, and the final battle where he detonated Mark 48 torpedoes to disable a nuclear depth charge.

The admirals listened intently, their expressions unreadable, pens scratched notes as Rourke described the *Toledo's* crippled state—sail gone, reactor scrammed—and his decision to draw the Russian fleet away, risking his own ship to protect Brennan's crew.

"I knew the odds were against us, sir," Rourke said, his hazel eyes locking with Natter's. "The *Admiral Kharlamov* and *Admiral Levchenko* were closing with RPK-2 Vyuga nuclear depth charges, driving us west into the *Pyotr Velikiy's* kill box.

I had less than six minutes to act when the RPK-7 Veter launched—a 90R nuclear depth charge torpedo, 200-kiloton yield. Detonating the Mark 48s to disrupt the 82R was a gamble, but it was the only way to save my ship and crew."

The room was silent as Rourke finished, the weight of his words hung heavy. Natter leaned forward, his steely blue eyes piercing, hands clasped on the table. The other admirals exchanged glances, Griffiths giving a slight nod, his weathered face a mask of pride for the ensign he had once mentored.

Natter cleared his throat, his voice resonant with authority as he addressed Rourke and the panel.

"Well, Commander Rourke," Natter began, his tone measured but carrying the weight of finality. "I think I speak for all of us when I say:

Outstanding leadership in the face of a deadly conflict. You overcame overwhelming odds and knowingly risked your ship, crew, and person in an extraordinary act of courage to protect the *Toledo* and its crew, which were severely damaged. Your actions—engaging the Russian fleet to draw their fire, deploying the Sea Lance against their helicopters, and using Mark 48 torpedoes to disable a nuclear depth charge— demonstrate a level of bravery and ingenuity that is the hallmark of the US Navy's submarine service."

Natter paused, his gaze sweeping the panel, each admiral nodding in agreement. "We are unanimous in our decision to recommend you to the President for the Congressional Medal of Honour," he continued, his voice firm.

"Thank you, Commander Rourke. The US Navy needs more men like you."

Rourke stood straighter, a flicker of relief passing through his eyes, though the weight of the past days lingered. "Thank you, sir," he said, his voice steady, saluting sharply. "It was an honour to serve."

The admirals stood and returned the salute, Griffiths offering a rare smile, his gruff voice breaking the silence. "You have come a long way since the *Boston*, John. I knew you would make a hell of a commander."

Natter dismissed Rourke as the panel rose when he exited the room. The echoes of their praise served as a bittersweet counterpoint to the memories of the *Kursk's* 118 fallen sailors, a burden he would carry for the rest of his days.

…

Lubyanka Prison, Moscow, September 1, 2000

Lieutenant Oleg Vesnen sat in a cold, windowless cell in Lubyanka Prison, his gaunt face bruised and hollow, his eyes dull with despair.

The contents of the USB drive hidden in the sleeve of his naval uniform confirmed the *Kursk* had collided with the *Toledo* and had subsequently been struck by a Mark 48 from the *Memphis*.

Vesnen's proof—sonar logs, bridge transcripts, recordings—had been destroyed; the data erased to protect the Russian Federation's cover story of a torpedo malfunction.

Vesnen's interrogation had been brutal. The FSB had extracted every detail of his contact with the CIA in Istanbul, including his demand for $1 million and protection and his plan to defect to Norway. Major Alexei Ivanov oversaw the process, his dark eyes burning with rage as he ensured Vesnen's silence. The court sentenced the navigation officer to life in a Siberian gulag, disgraced his family in Severomorsk, and erased his name from naval records. Vesnen thought of his wife, Anna, and their daughter, Maria, as they led him away in chains. He had failed them, and his dream of freedom was a cruel illusion.

...

Moscow, and then Penal Colony IK-17, 13 December 2000

In the shadowed halls of Russian justice, where the weight of the Motherland's secrets pressed heavier than Siberian snow, Lieutenant Sokolov's court martial unfolded with the grim inevitability of a firing squad's volley. The court martial took place in a fortified chamber beneath the Kremlin, away from the world's prying eyes, during the last days of 2025. The panel—comprising grizzled admirals and FSB generals, their faces etched with the scars of Cold War betrayals—wasted no time on theatrics. Sokolov's guilt was as undeniable as the classified schematics he had funnelled to foreign hands.

The betrayal had begun innocuously, or so Sokolov had convinced himself. As the ship's weapons officer, he had access to the crown jewels: hypersonic missile guidance systems, stealth countermeasures, and nuclear propulsion blueprints that could tip the scales in any global conflict. But his desire to escape the poverty of the post-collapse of the USSR, and a shadowy Chinese operative named Li Jun had appeared like a ghost in the fog, offering salvation for whispers of state secrets.

Sokolov had complied, smuggling data via an encrypted drive. The Chinese, eager for an edge in the South China Sea tensions, had offered to pay handsomely. But hubris bred sloppiness. Li Jun's exfiltration from the *Pyotr Velikiy* went disastrously awry—the Americans had captured him. Captured with Sokolov's data cache, Li Jun had cracked under interrogation, spilling not just the intel but much more. Worse still, the Americans—ever the opportunistic vultures—had capitalised on the fallout, arming the Pentagon with Russia's most guarded naval innovations. The *Kursk* disaster of old paled in comparison; this was a haemorrhage of power that could embolden NATO fleets from the Baltic to the Black Sea.

The court martial lasted mere hours. Evidence piled like indictments: encrypted messages, bank transfers traced to offshore accounts, and Sokolov's own confession, extracted in the Lubyanka's cold cells. "I did it for my family," he muttered, but the panel saw only treason. Admiral Kuznetsov, presiding with the stoic fury of a man who had lost comrades in submarine depths, delivered the verdict: death, as per Article 275 of the Criminal Code. They shackled Sokolov, stripped of rank and uniform, and sent him to the frozen abyss of Penal Colony IK-17 in Siberia, a maximum-security fortress where the wind howled accusations through barbed wire.

Months blurred into a monotonous hell of isolation. Sokolov, once a decorated officer with dreams of commanding his own vessel, now scrubbed floors and endured the stares of fellow inmates—thieves, murderers, and political dissidents who whispered of his infamy. He clung to a sliver of hope: appeals, perhaps a presidential pardon if the geopolitical winds shifted. But in the Kremlin, mercy was a relic of weaker eras.

One bitter dawn, as auroras danced mockingly overhead, a guard rapped on his cell bars. "Sokolov, gather your belongings. You're being transferred." His meagre possessions—a frayed photo of his wife, a dog-eared Tolstoy novel, and a few crumpled letters—fit into a small sack. Flanked by a single uniformed escort, he shuffled down the dim stone corridor, the echo of boots amplifying his dread. The air grew colder, laced with the metallic tang of impending doom.

They arrived at a nondescript door, heavier than the others, guarded by a silent sentinel who swung it open without a word. Sokolov stepped inside, his eyes adjusting to the gloom. The cell was barren: no bunk, no toilet, just a coiled water hose dangling from the wall and a rusted drain plug embedded in the concrete floor, stained with years of unspoken horrors. It was a room designed for endings, not incarceration.

"Please don't turn around," the escorting guard intoned, his voice flat as the tundra. Sokolov froze, heart pounding like depth charges in his chest. He felt the chill kiss of steel—a Makarov pistol's muzzle—pressed firmly against the base of his skull. Time stretched, a final mercy or cruelty. In that instant, fragments of life flashed: the *Pyotr Velikiy's* bridge under starlit skies, Li Jun's sly grin in a smoke-filled bar, the Kremlin's unyielding gaze.

Then, a muffled crack. Sokolov crumpled forward, blood pooling toward the drain, efficient as the system that had condemned him. No fanfare, no witnesses beyond the guards who would file a report of "natural causes" or "escape attempt." In the annals of Russian history, he became a footnote, a cautionary tale whispered in naval academies: betray the Federation, and oblivion awaits.

Yet, in the wider world, ripples persisted. The leaked secrets fuelled an arms race, with American carriers retrofitted and Chinese submarines silenced. Diplomats in Geneva postured, but the damage was done. Silence sealed Sokolov's fate, making him a ghost in the machine of empire, where loyalty was the only currency that mattered. As snow blanketed IK-17, the guard holstered his weapon, stepping back into the corridor. Another transfer complete.

The Kremlin, Moscow, October 10, 2000

President Vladimir Putin stood before a sea of cameras; his eyes were cold as he addressed the nation. The *Kursk's* sinking had been a national tragedy, a blow to Russia's naval pride, but Putin's narrative was unwavering: a torpedo malfunction, a tragic accident, no foreign involvement.

The $3 billion compensation from the US had bought silence, and the Kremlin's stand-down order had averted a full-scale war, but the truth lingered in the shadows, a whispered rumour among naval officers and intelligence operatives.

Putin's speech was a call for unity, a promise to rebuild the Northern Fleet, to honour the 118 men who had died aboard the *Kursk*.

But behind closed doors, his rage was palpable. The Americans had escaped, their submarines had slipped through the Northern Fleet's net, and the FSB had failed to silence Vesnen before he had contacted the CIA.

Putin ordered a purge of the Northern Fleet's command structure—Admiral Viktor Chernov was court-martialled, his career destroyed, and Captain Ivan Rostov was demoted, his loyalty questioned despite his role in averting disaster.

The *Shkval* technology remained out of Chinese hands thanks to the CIA's capture of Li Jun. Still, the *Shkval's* partial schematics-propulsion and guidance systems—along with the entire Northern Fleet's ASW protocols were now in American possession, because of the Chinese agent being captured at sea by the CIA, marking a bitter loss for Russia's naval strategy. Putin vowed to strengthen the FSB and root out traitors like Vesnen, to ensure the Northern Fleet's resurgence. They would avenge the *Kursk*—not today, but in time.

...

Naval Station Norfolk, Virginia, December 15, 2000

Commander Tom Brennan stood on the pier at Naval Station Norfolk; his navy-blue submariner's uniform was crisp despite the weight on his shoulders. They had towed the *Toledo* for repairs at the Electric Boat Company on the Thames River in Groton, Connecticut. The court had deferred Brennan's court-martial because they deemed his actions in the Barents Sea reckless but not criminal, and saw his survival as a testament to his leadership. The order given to shadow the *Kursk* in an unsafe manner was not explored. USLANTFLT assigned him to a desk job, which marked a quiet end to a career defined by the sea. The *Memphis* had returned to Groton, too. Her crew were hailed as heroes, even if Rourke's decision to fire on the *Kursk* had triggered a classified inquiry. He had faced a board of review, but he was sworn to secrecy. Now he was on leave, providing moral support to his friend Brennan, and eager to return to Emily and their children.

Brennan and Rourke shared a last nod; a silent acknowledgment of the bond forged in the crucible of war. They had survived, but the *Kursk's* 118 souls would forever weigh on their consciences. The Barents Sea had claimed its due, and the echoes of that day would reverberate for years to come.